When Silence Kills

Mark Griffin

PIATKUS

PIATKUS

First published in Great Britain in 2021 by Piatkus

1 3 5 7 9 10 8 6 4 2

A CIP catalogue record for this book is available from the British Library.

ISBN 978-0-349-42896-3

Typeset in New Baskerville by M Rules
Printed and bound in Great Britain by
Clays Ltd, Elcograf S.p.A.

Papers used by Piatkus are from well-managed forests
and other responsible sources.

Piatkus
An imprint of
Little, Brown Book Group
Carmelite House
50 Victoria Embankment
London EC4Y 0DZ

An Hachette UK Company
www.hachette.co.uk

www.littlebrown.co.uk

An amazing English teacher is hard to find and impossible to forget.
To Father Jeff Risbridger
who once read a short story of mine out loud in English class
and inspired and encouraged me to write more

One

At thirty-nine years old, Vee still believed in fairy tales.

She still believed that a person must be loved before they are lovable, that the goodness of the soul will always triumph over evil and that the princess is as likely to be the hero of the story as the prince. But most importantly, the fairy tales helped her escape and imagine a world outside her own.

Her Lycra skirt had rolled up to her hips with her last john, and she pushed it down to her knees when they had finished. She watched him pull his trousers up and buckle his belt then scurry away until he disappeared into the car park.

'Good night, Prince Charming,' she whispered. Vee had been a sex worker for over twenty-five years and had kissed a million frogs.

The coastal town of Brighton in the south of England had a small red-light district. A few other girls were smoking and chatting, arms linked, extra protection in the early hours. At her lamp post Vee brushed her teeth and lit up a cigarette. She was watching a car that had been circling all night. A dark-coloured Volvo that would pace and slow and then lower a window and move off.

'All right, Vee?'

Vee turned. She hadn't heard the girl come up behind her. Thin legs and thin arms, a platinum wig and a smear of red lipstick.

'Got any smokes?' the girl said.

'Two – and they're mine for the walk home.'

'You're fucking useless, aren't you?'

Vee stared at the girl. That's all she was – a girl. Fourteen, maybe fifteen. She wanted to give her a stick of gum but instead she gave her a pack of condoms and baby-wipes.

'Don't say I never give you anything,' Vee said.

Ulyana was Ukrainian with a shoulder-length blonde wig that she changed every other day. Her accent was thick in places, soft in others, the Cyrllic *R* religiously rolled.

'He's back again,' Vee said.

'The Volvo?'

Vee nodded and said:

'What protection do you have?'

Ulyana pulled a small switchblade from her handbag.

'It won't kill 'em, but it will make 'em stop and think twice.'

The Volvo slowed to a halt by the kerb. One of the girls leaned through the window, a few seconds of conversation, then she ducked back and walked away, gave the driver a finger and told him to fuck off.

'Who was it, Ally?' Vee shouted across the street.

The other girl shrugged, went back to her friend and pulled another smoke.

'I'm gonna go home,' Vee said.

'Stay, keep me company.'

'Can't be arsed. You want to do something tomorrow?'

'Sure.'

'How about I cook for you? Sunday roast.'

'It's Friday.'

'Don't care,' Vee said. 'I bought a chicken yesterday from Aldi, fat little bugger he is. I'll get him out of the freezer tonight and put him in the oven. What time do you want to come over?'

'Late afternoon – then we can walk here together for the night shift.'

'Perfect.'

The girl smiled at her. Vee tried to smile back, but her jaw hurt.

'If you look good, you feel good, right?' Vee said.

The girl nodded and gave Vee a hug before she turned and walked away.

It had been a hot day, but the nights by the sea were always chill and as Vee walked along Marine Parade, she listened to the waves breaking on the beach. The first cigarette took her to Rottingdean, and by Telscombe Cliffs she had finished the second. She lived in a one-bedroom bungalow on Wellington Road. It was white painted with an entrance porch and a large square window to the right. The curtains had been pulled shut but sagged apart in the middle. The front gate creaked as she pushed it, but everyone else in the street was asleep.

She put the keys in her front door and opened it and switched on the hall light. Her sobriety diary was on the hall-stand and she wrote *Day 278* and put an *x* by it and said: 'All it takes is faith and trust in myself.'

In the bedroom, she unstrapped her heels, pulled off her top and kicked her skirt onto the bed. She showered and when she got out, the bathroom mirror was misty. She wiped it down and gave her reflection a cursory glance, played with her dishevelled red hair, then brushed her teeth.

She took the chicken out of the freezer and checked the vegetable cupboard. Carrots, parsnips, potatoes, and she could go out and get some frozen peas tomorrow morning. She made a cup of coffee, didn't mind the chipped mug, and leaned back on the charity shop sofa in her pink-walled living room. She used to get lonely when she came home. She used to think she needed someone to survive, a partner, but that was because she always thought she was never enough by herself. Now she knew she was enough. She had changed, she was getting her life together and this time she was getting out of this business for good.

She stared at the TV with one elbow on the arm of the sofa, a cigarette scissored in her fingers. After an hour she realised she was falling asleep. She should go to bed, her hands were starting to get cold.

In the hall she heard a knock at the front door. It was three thirty in the morning and she hesitated before she whispered:

'It's late, who is it?'

A voice. Unfamiliar.

'Who?'

The same voice, but muffled, so she opened the door.

Vee pulled a smile from somewhere and said:

'Do I know you?'

And suddenly there was a memory. A memory of a burning princess dress.

And Vee's smile vanished and she couldn't breathe and felt herself falling towards the floor.

Two

Holly Wakefield stared at the small bungalow with its bright yellow police tape.

It was at the end of a cul-de-sac on a slightly upward-sloping road. Either side were more bungalows and, beyond, a housing estate with an acre or so of grasslands.

Her phone rang. It was DI Bishop and he was running late:

'I had to get something from the police archives,' he said. 'Traffic is bad, I'll be there in twenty minutes. Go in – don't wait for me.' A pause. 'Get a feel for it by yourself.'

The phone went dead.

Holly didn't carry a handbag, everything she needed was in her pockets, including a pair of forensic latex gloves which she snapped on without breaking stride. She lifted the police tape around the front gate and showed her ID to the officer stationed at the door.

'Holly Wakefield,' she said.

'Right, DI Bishop said you would be coming. Do you need anything?'

'Just privacy. Thank you.'

He nodded as if he had been expecting as much, opened the door and moved out of the way as she stepped inside. Holly heard the door click shut behind her. She had no idea what to expect in the house. Bishop had been cagey about giving her more information, which was strange. She stayed very still and took a deep breath.

The coppery smell of blood mixed with stale perfume.

There was a diary on the hallstand. She opened it up – a sobriety book for Alcoholics and Narcotics Anonymous, and the last entry had been Thursday, with a 278 and an x next to it. There were telephone numbers and people's initials scattered throughout with appointment dates and meetings with sponsors.

The small bathroom on the left was neat and painted blue – the living room and kitchen on the right were painted pink. There was a retro radio on the mantelpiece that was pink like the walls and there were beach shells, an empty vase and books on shelves: *Lark Rise to Candleford*, Shakespeare and a book about ballet by Darcey Bussell. There were no photos anywhere, not a single one.

Laundry was scattered across the radiator and in the kitchen plates and cutlery had been left in the sink. A few flies buzzed and it was beginning to smell.

Get a feel for it, Bishop had said.

The victim's name had been Vee and profiling the victim was just as important as profiling a killer, sometimes more so. If you wanted to get to know your victim, you had to tread in their shoes.

Vee had been a sex worker in Brighton for the past eleven years and was known to the police.

Holly turned the radio on to the last station that was

listened to. It was Heart FM – talking heads and then Johnny Cash started singing 'Hurt'. She sat on the side of the sofa that was worn and sagged and stared around the room. This was what Vee would come home to: cheap prints on the walls, a few shells from the beach and lipstick-kissed cigarettes in ash mugs on the coffee table.

How did you end up here, Vee?

Holly had been brought up in the foster system after her parents had been murdered and knew how easy it was for girls to get sucked into prostitution, having seen it first-hand, and knew the torture of wanting intimacy and closeness but never knowing where to find it. She had heard many versions of the story over the years and it made her sad: a mix of poverty and desperation, abuse and no one to talk to. Maybe Vee had dreamed of becoming a ballerina when she was a child? Classes after school, auditions and rehearsals, but then somehow ended up mixing with the wrong crowd. Hash had turned to coke, coke to heroin and by then all morals and principles had left the room. Holly wondered how often Vee sat on this sofa and thought about everything that had happened in her life.

She got up and made her way along the hall. There had been no signs of a struggle, so it appeared the killer had been invited inside. A regular client perhaps? Or at least someone Vee recognised or knew at a distance. There was no blood anywhere in the house apart from the bedroom, so that was where she had to go. She pushed open the door. The curtains were drawn so it was dark and she flipped on the light.

Dozens of bright yellow evidence tags littered the room. The bed had been stripped by the SOCO team. There was a bloodstained mattress and an empty brass frame entwined by fairy lights and fluffy animals: multicoloured bears, dolphins and a unicorn. Not the bed of a jaded sex worker, but the bed of a woman who liked to pretend she was still thirteen years old and living at home. Different men, different sheets, and Holly wondered how often Vee slept alone, crossing off the days in her diary and drying her eyes.

Blood spatter on the walls, the carpet and the ceiling above the bed that had gone brown. There was a partial red hand-print on the wall behind the bed. Vee had been alive when the stabbing had started.

Holly took a moment, then climbed onto the middle of the bed and stared down at where Vee's head would have been. This is how the killer would have done it, and from her position Holly could be right there with the murderer, witnessing events. She had a sudden sense of him and what had happened in that room. She could hear the music from the radio and she could feel the anger, the fear and the smell. The smell of the blood.

The fluffy animals watched her with their plastic eyes and she eased herself off the bed and took the rest of the room in. No photos, but things that sparkled – clothes with sequins that would reflect the glow of the streetlights. The chest of drawers was full of skirts, bras, underwear and denim. She sat in the wooden chair at Vee's dressing table. In one of the drawers were sex toys, handcuffs, condoms, and Tic Tacs. The lipstick and eye make-up were metallics, sparkles and glue-sticks. In the other drawer was the first photo Holly found and it had been tagged by forensics. It showed a teenage Vee with copper-coloured hair and her arms around a boy of about the same age. They were both smiling at the camera and wearing cos-tumes from a drama of some kind or fancy-dress party. There was nothing written on the back.

She became quiet and still as she tried to piece together what she was seeing and how it made her feel.

Lonely. Sad.

The thought made her look up in the dressing table mirror and glance at the reflection of the bed. Her imagination gave her a glimpse of a heavily built man leaning over Vee. Hand repeatedly dropping and raising the knife. Deep throaty breaths with every strike and the creak of the mattress as he killed her.

She blinked away the vision and stood up.

After the kill he would have wanted to see what he had done. Breathe in that feeling of power until it slipped away like a shadow. He hadn't rushed. He had been calm and very much in control, and then he had placed his calling card beneath some stockings on top of the chest of drawers. The police had left it for her – a single piece of A4 paper with a drawing of two childlike stick figures in frenzied streaks of coloured crayon.

She picked it up. The figure on the left had a grinning balloon head and held a knife in one hand. The figure on the right was the victim and she had been drawn with long red hair and eyelashes and was wearing a green dress made up of three straight lines that formed a triangle. Spreadeagled on the bed, her face was a mess of reds, and where her eyes should have been were scratched black holes.

Holly ran her fingers over the waxy surface. She had never seen anything like it before. There was a realness about the figures which was disturbing on so many levels. Childlike, infantile, but the violence . . .

She frowned and her eyes were drawn away as she heard a noise that startled her. She hadn't heard the front door open and now footsteps scuffed on the carpet. A hulking shadow appeared in the doorway.

'Holly?'

It was Bishop. Six foot two, ex-military and she could smell the polish on his shoes.

'Hello, Bishop,' she said.

He met her at the dressing table and removed two plastic evidence sleeves from his jacket. In each one was a childlike crayon drawing of two stick figures. The grinning killer on the left, the bloody body on the right. Holly stared at them for some time, trying to elicit an answer.

'Where did you get these?' she said. 'Bishop?'

Bishop was very still. It was as if he had shut down.

'He's back,' he said.

'Who's back, Bishop? Who?'

But he couldn't answer.

He was just staring at the drawings as if he were somehow lost in time.

Three

'Who is he?' Holly said.

Holly and Bishop had ordered a fry-up brunch at Fat Jack's Burger Bar on the promenade. Sitting at the window, they both had a view of the beach and the pier. Families braved the pebbles carrying hampers and deckchairs and the sea was a briny green.

'We never even got close,' Bishop said. 'I was still a sergeant, only four years in with the Met when the first body turned up in May 2013. The victim's name was Stephen Freer. He was a sixty-five-year-old retired GP who left behind a wife and two children. His body was found in the bedroom of his house in Croydon. He'd been drugged with chloroform and GHB and stabbed ten times in the face, mainly in the eyes. He had also been castrated and the missing body part was never recovered.'

'Jesus.

'No CCTV, no DNA or forensic evidence and the killer left a stickman drawing. This was body number one and the task force conjured up all sorts of ideas as to who could have done it, but as we checked into his past and patient files, we found nothing. He was well-liked by work colleagues, friends and family members alike, who were all questioned and eliminated. We brought in every ex-con or recent release we could find and then after four weeks the press and television lost interest and we had no new clues or suspects so the investigation ground to a halt. After eight months the task force was reduced to a skeleton crew and I was one of them. I'd never felt so helpless. I'd go into work thinking today's the day we get our break, but it never was. It was as if we were waiting for him to kill again to see if he tripped up next time. Two years went by with no new leads, and the murder was classified as a cold case. I got assigned to a gangland killing, but I never forgot about it, I don't think anybody did. We all accepted it was probably a one-off, so everybody moved on until the summer of 2016, when the second body turned up.'

'Same MO?'

He nodded.

'The victim's name was Mike Thomas and he ran an art gallery in Sunbury. He was killed in his bedroom, a thirty-minute walk from the gallery, drugged with GHB and chloroform. Thirty-five years old, stabbed twenty times in each eye and castrated and the killer left a second stickman drawing. Again, there were no witnesses, no forensics and no CCTV. The task force was re-established, the cold case reopened and we tried to find a link between the two victims, but everything was a dead end.'

'There was nothing?'

'We had fifty officers working on it, organising major press coverage, and we brought in analysts, psychologists, even school teachers to talk to us about children's drawings. We had one shrink tell us the castration had all the hallmarks of a sexual sadist.'

'It does. The men were degraded and humiliated after death,' she said. 'The killer wanted to punish them beyond killing them.'

'Yes, but it was the desecration of the eyes that stumped everyone,' he said. '*See no evil* – that was what the press ran with.'

Holly was remembering some of the details of the cases now. She knew she probably had copies of the original newspaper articles back home in one of her files. She had an extensive home-made library on serial killers throughout history.

'We had anybody who ever displayed a warped phobia about eyes brought in,' Bishop said. 'People do that, you know? Make-up and stuff to give them teddy bear eyes, dolls' eyes, cartoon eyes, clowns' eyes – there's a scary interview if I ever did one. Never realised there were so many people who still dressed up as clowns for kids' parties. We even had an optometrist come in and talk to us about ommetaphobia – you know what that is?'

'Fear of the eyes.'

'Not just the fear of the eyes, but the fear of eye contact. Social situations, when you have to look at someone, touching your eyes or getting something in your eye. Makes people feel queasy, and we wondered if that could be something to do with it. Windows to the soul and all that crap. The need to destroy that fear.'

'Did you ever have any suspects?' Holly said.

'A guy called Ralph McQuarrie was a person of interest for a while. He was a homosexual rapist who had been in Broadmoor for seven years on attempted murder charges.'

'Were either of the victims gay?'

'No. We had circumstantial evidence against McQuarrie – he was seen on CCTV near Sunbury train station an hour before the murder and then again walking around Hampton Court an hour after, with no account of where he went. CPS said it wasn't enough. It probably wasn't, but it was the fact he was a handyman that made us look twice.'

'Why?'

'The power tools at his home. The pathologist concluded the castration had been done with an electric saw. Everything in his workshop was tested but he kept his tools religiously clean and we only found one trace of blood on a sander and that turned out to be his.'

'Where is he now?'

'In Feltham prison. He got arrested for rape three years ago. He gets out in six months.'

Holly hadn't touched her food. Nor had Bishop.

'You're not hungry?' he said.

'No.'

He scrunched up his napkin. 'Come on, I can't remember the last time I walked along a beach.'

They mixed with the crowd heading to the sea.

'What were your first impressions of the murder scene?' Bishop said.

Holly took a second, reliving those feelings.

'He's not afraid of making a mess. Which suggests the killer is highly organised and will carry his full murder kit with him, including latex gloves, possible SOCO suit or equivalent and a full change of clothes. It looks as though he took her into the bedroom quickly.'

14

'To have sex?'

'To kill her straight away. I don't think this is someone who wastes time with small talk.'

'He could have killed her anywhere in the house. Why the bedroom?'

'The same as the previous two victims, it's a smaller space, more contained and therefore easier to control the victim. But I think he chooses the bedroom because it's more personal as well. It's the one place where we're supposed to feel safe in our homes.'

They were quiet for a while. Still walking.

'What about the victim?' Bishop said.

'Do we have a real name for her yet?'

'Just Vee.'

'I think she was a woman who'd spent most of her life fighting demons. Trying to make the best of a bad situation. She was strong, independent, and according to her diary was a regular at AA and NA. She seemed to be turning her life around, two hundred and seventy-eight days sober. There was nothing particularly personal in the diary or her house, as if she didn't really belong there, apart from the one photo of her with the young man found in the dressing table.'

'Lover or brother?'

'Either, or. What are the other working girls saying?'

'They're a tight bunch with the customary horror stories. They've all been helpful, but they're frightened they could be next. The local police have already brought in the usual suspects but so far every one of them has an alibi. There was a Volvo spotted in the area the morning Vee was killed that hasn't been traced. Apparently it kept circling then driving off.'

'Had any of the girls seen the car before?'

'No, but it was pretty conspicuous that evening, and if we can get a plate number we'll put it into ANPR. One of the girls saw the driver, but just described him as dark-haired and wearing a hoodie. She thinks there was another man in the back seat.'

'This was well-planned and the location was preselected,' Holly said. 'The killer would have followed her home from where she worked, not just once, but many times. He had to know for certain her daily and nightly routine, where she ate and where she bought her groceries, if she lived with someone or had a pet she had to come back to and feed.'

'He studied her?'

'With precision.'

'You think the killer knew her?'

'Yes,' she said. 'I do.'

Four

Holly and Bishop stood on Morley Street.

Two local plain-clothes detectives were talking to a group of the working girls. Some smoked, and those that didn't had their hands stuffed inside jacket pockets against the chill air. One of them looked over and made eye contact with Holly, then looked away.

'They're skittish,' Holly said.

'They think we're from immigration.'

A commotion among the girls. Choice language, pantomime gestures, and then one of them came over. It was Ulyana. Today she wore a black wig, but she'd still gone with the red lipstick. She told them she had been in Brighton for three years after leaving Portsmouth, trying to work on her own without a pimp.

'I've been stabbed three times, and I have no idea why these men attack me. Nika, one of the girls over there' – she pointed past her shoulder with a cigarette – 'was shot at last Christmas. Fucking *khuy-holova*.'

'*Khuy-holova?*' Bishop said.

'Dickhead.' She wrapped her arms around her body as she

spoke, shrugged but it turned into a shiver. 'We are all scared, you know?'

'I understand that,' said Bishop. 'How well did you know Vee?'

'She was like a mama-bear to me, she used to take care of me. She gave me condoms and told me how much to charge and what not to do. I don't have a bad word against her.'

'Did you know her real name?'

'Vee. That was it.'

'What's your real name?' Holly asked.

Ulyana shrugged.

'This Volvo that you saw,' Bishop said. 'Can you tell us any more about it?'

'Vee said she had seen it coming and going all night, but it wasn't one of our regulars.'

'Did Vee have regulars?'

'Some.' She shifted in her high heels.

'Do you know who they were?'

'No. We don't watch each other. We get our johns and then we go somewhere quiet.'

'Where?'

Ulyana pointed.

'Around the corner, over there behind the bank. We go where there's no lights, that's what the men want. They don't want to be seen.'

'Did Vee ever mention anything about her past? Where she was from?' Holly said.

'She never talked about the past, but she was clever.'

'Clever?'

'She could have got a job somewhere, you know? A proper job. She knew things that I would never know.'

'Like what?' Holly said.

'Like poetry and stuff. She would say things that were beautiful. She talked about love. Romeo and Juliet. She was romantic. She used to give me candles to burn at home.'

'Do you know if she was seeing someone?'

'Like a boyfriend? No. She'd been single for years. It's hard to find someone that isn't a dick, you know? She used to go out with a drug dealer, but I think he's dead now.'

'Do you know his name?' Bishop said.

'It was before I came here. Can I go now?' The girl sniffed and looked at Bishop. 'I want my knife back,' she said. 'They took it from me when they told me to speak to you.'

Bishop waved the two plain-clothes detectives over and took the knife off them. He opened it, folded it up and placed it in Ulyana's tiny hand.

'Don't kill anyone,' he said.

Five

Holly and Bishop agreed to meet Vee's sponsor at his home.

Robbie Sweep lived in a one-bedroom flat on Manchester Street, a three-minute walk from the beach. He was tall, over six feet, and in his fifties, sandy-haired and large, wearing jeans and a vintage Clash T-shirt. He smiled awkwardly as he took them into the living room, where tea and coffee was already waiting.

'This is horribly sad,' he said as they sat down. 'I've known Vee for three and a half years now and counted her as a friend. Vee was AA and NA, that's alcohol and narcotics, and yes, I was her sponsor for both. I was smoking crack at twelve, and drinking a bottle of Jack every day for nearly fifteen years, but then I got clean and I'm one of the lucky ones.'

'And you knew what she did for a living?'

'I have no judgements. She was a good person. When Vee first came to the rooms, she did what most people do, she poked her head in, had a coffee and a biscuit then disappeared for a week, sometimes a month. It's a cycle that a lot of people have to go through before they come back.'

Holly was content to let Bishop lead the questions and she watched Robbie throughout. He sat open-legged, arms across his lap, he seemed very relaxed.

'So as her sponsor, what did your relationship entail?'

'We spoke three or four times a week, sometimes for five minutes, sometimes for twenty. She would tell me how she felt and what she was doing.'

'And how was she feeling? Had you noticed a change in Vee in the past few months?'

'A change?'

'Did she seem more nervous or apprehensive?'

'No, it looked as if she was really getting it together. She was over nine months clean, which was huge for her, so we all thought this was the one.'

'What about a partner?' Bishop said. 'Do you know if she had anyone in her life?'

'I don't, sorry.'

'And when was the last time you saw her?'

'That would have been on Wednesday morning. There's an eleven o'clock meeting at St Peter's church just down the road.'

'Was the meeting busy?'

'About fifteen, twenty people. It's always like that, it's pretty regular.'

'Was there anybody new there or someone you saw recently, perhaps talking to her, that you hadn't seen before?'

'No, not that I remember. I mean the thing is, people come and go all the time so. Some people don't like who chairs the meetings, some people will feel uncomfortable with other people in the room if they recognise them from another an-onymous group, so it's a constant shift, to be honest.'

'But she was comfortable with you and the group?'

'She was. And we were comfortable with her.'

Bishop took a second and then:

'I know you pride yourselves on your anonymity, and this may seem a little inappropriate,' he said, 'but were there any men who knew what she did for a living and made advances to her within the groups?'

It was the first time Holly had seen emotion on Robbie's face. A flicker, but it was there.

'I think she would have said something,' Robbie said. 'A lot of people in these rooms come from abusive homes or relationships and they're not used to standing up to people, but Vee had found that strength. So no, I never noticed anything like that, and if she had been approached inappropriately, I think she would have dealt with it.'

'Thank you, Robbie,' Bishop said and stood up. All three shook hands and the big man walked them to the door.

'I don't know how long you are staying in town,' he said, 'but we're holding a vigil for her tomorrow night. It's open to everyone, we're going to light some candles and say some prayers.'

Outside, Holly and Bishop walked to the beach. There were no clouds and the sun was hot.

'You want an ice cream?' Bishop said.

They both got Mr Whippy vanilla ice creams with a 99 chocolate flake, then left the pebbles and found a path that led towards the pier.

'Brighton and Hove police already ran Robbie Sweep through the system and he's clean, but I'll ask them to get a few plain-clothes officers to go to the vigil and see if the killer turns up,' Bishop said. 'You never know, we might get lucky.'

It was his standard phrase, but Holly said:

22

'He's not coming back here, Bishop. He's done what he needed to do.'

Her eyes drifted down to the beach when there was a sudden breeze and she could smell the sea. The last time she had been here was with her parents seven months before they had been murdered when she was nine years old. They had all gone down to the Palace Pier and she had been dressed like a princess, walking in tiny flip-flops and getting dizzy on candyfloss.

'When's the autopsy?' Holly said.

'Nine o'clock tomorrow morning.'

Six

Holly was glad to be home.

She lived on the fifth floor of a block of Georgian flats in Balham, south-east London. Two bedrooms, two bathrooms and an open-plan kitchen and dining room. It was an area she had grown to love, with a literary festival, a comedy festival and the Bedford pub, which was a local institution. Once home to the likes of Eddie Izzard and the Clash, it stocked IPA and served a cracking Sunday roast.

This was the third case the Met Police had asked Holly to assist on. Normally, she lectured on Forensic Psychology and Criminology at King's College in London on Mondays and the rest of the week was spent at Wetherington Psychiatric Hospital, where she tried to get inside the minds of men and women who were lost to the normal world. There was no pill to cure the lust for cold-blooded murder, no antidote to help them tell right from wrong, but Holly had made it her mission in life to find the hidden truth behind the shuttered eyes of psychopaths. On the last case, which had seen her save a young boy's life, she had been called the Psychopath Whisperer by the press, an epithet she neither cultivated nor cared for.

Going back to Brighton had affected her emotions more than she thought it would, and after showering she found herself looking through a family photo album. Photos of her parents on Brighton pier and on the beach, smiling to camera. Her mother was wearing the silver and enamel butterfly necklace that her father had bought for her on their first anniversary. It had been her mother's favourite piece of jewellery and had been stolen on the day she was killed. Holly reached up to her neck, her fingers tracing the collarbone as if the jewellery were somehow there.

She put the photo down and moved across to three large shelves in the living room, all crammed with books on forensic science, criminology and psychology. There were home-made files as well, which she had created with newspaper cuttings and essays about serial killers that had caught her attention over the years: Dr Crippen, Hugo Schenk, Mary Ann Cotton, Jack the Ripper – their dark dreams, and the motivation to kill of those people who walked without conscience. Her fingers gently traced the spines of some of the folders and she hesitated at one labelled *The Animal,* then carried on until she found *British Unidentified Serial Killers.*

She pulled the large scrapbook down and sat at the dining table. The pages were glued with dozens of grainy newspaper photos of different crime scenes, page after page of press speculation and images of shadowy figures. She stopped when she came to an article dated 23 May 2013:

See No Evil
Met Police launch probe after sixty-five-year-old man found dead at his home

Police have launched a murder investigation after the body of a man, who has not yet been publicly identified, was found by officers called to a family residence in south London.

Police gave no details of any of the injuries, but stated it was a particularly violent crime and said a post-mortem examination is underway.

According to Detective Chief Inspector Eddie Walker of Scotland Yard's Homicide and Major Crime Command, specialist officers are supporting the man's next of kin. Officers have been deployed to search the nearby area, and are conducting house-to-house enquiries while closing off the street until further notice. No arrests have been made.

The next article was dated one week later:

The body of the sixty-five-year-old man who was killed at his home has now been officially identified as Stephen Freer, a doctor from Croydon. He was stabbed repeat-edly in the face and the eyes and horribly castrated. Detective Chief Inspector Eddie Walker says it is the most disturbing crime scene he has seen during his fifteen years as a Met officer and has vowed to do what-ever he can to bring this madman to justice. One man, who cannot be named for legal reasons, is helping the police with their enquiries. The deceased leaves a wife, Anne, and two children.

Various insights and articles followed for the next three months and as she turned over a page it was suddenly three years later when the next body was discovered:

12 June 2016

A murder investigation has been launched after a man was found dead in his bedroom in Sunbury-on-Thames last Sunday morning. Mike Thomas was a thirty-five-year-old art dealer who owned and operated a gallery in Sunbury. Officers from the Met Serious Crime squad attended at around 11 a.m. after receiving a call from his wife after she returned from visiting her parents in Cheshire. Neighbours were warned they could expect to see a heightened police presence in the area.

Early reports say the crime scene has eerie similarities to the unsolved murder of Stephen Freer, a doctor from Croydon who was found dead in his bedroom in 2013. Both men had been stabbed multiple times and were castrated. A childlike drawing that was apparently left at the crime scene and has since been inspected by forensic scientists is now believed to have been left by the killer.

Anyone with any information is asked to contact the Met Police on 101 and please quote Operation Devon.

Two weeks later:

A police spokesman has announced the Met believes the murders of Stephen Freer in 2013 and Mike Thomas in 2016 were carried out by the same killer. No connection has been found between the two victims, however, and the killings appear to be random crimes of opportunity. Detective Chief Inspector Eddie Walker, who headed the first murder enquiry three years ago, was due to retire this year, but is staying on at the helm of the investigation until the case is closed.

Holly made coffee and found cooked chicken in the fridge. She mixed it with salad in a bowl and started to eat. Above the fireplace in the living room hung an original oil painting by Harland Miller: 'Death – What's In It for Me?' She removed it from the wall and leant it against the back of the sofa. In its place she taped up the newspaper articles and the crime scene photos in order of their timeline: Stephen first, then Mike and now Vee. On the wall above them she wrote the timelines of the murders on the wall in a thick black felt pen and then printed off a map of Brighton and one of London and stuck them underneath. Above each victim she put the copy of their stickman drawings and compared them with their family photos. It suddenly dawned on her:

The stickman of Stephen Freer was bald like he was in real life. Mike Thomas had a goatee and so did his stick figure. Verity had scribbled red hair and the green triangle dress.

He's drawing them, she realised. Which begged the question – did he also draw himself?

The stick figure of the killer was always on the left and had a big head with big teeth, long arms and the knife was in his right hand. She wondered if the coroner had been able to deduce from the wounds whether the killer was in fact right- or left-handed.

She wrote on the wall:

Right-handed?

Mobile – does he drive? Volvo?

Man in photo with Vee – who is he?

AA & NA – candlelit vigil in Brighton tomorrow night.

Time between kills – strange – three years – killer in prison?

Then she drew an A4 sized square on the wall and put a question mark in the middle. Wrote the word **KILLER** above it. Stared at it for a few seconds then wrote underneath:

28

Deep-seated hatred of men and now women. The change of gender in target is unusual.

Male victims castration = emasculation and he takes their body parts as a TROPHY. His power over them.

What did he take from Vee? Was she sexually assaulted? Humiliation. Suffering.

She stopped and pulled away. Somehow she still had the smell of the blood in her nose.

'Sexual gratification? Yes.' And she raised her pen and went back to the wall.

Masturbation? Possibly, but would've worn gloves and condom.

'You know your victims' movements and where they live, and once inside their house you attack fast.' *Organised,* she wrote, and double underlined it.

All the victims attacked and killed face up, not face down. So you could watch them as you killed them? Or because you wanted them to be able to see you?

Why take that chance and risk being seen or recognised?

Because it's important to you.

She stared at the home-made incident board. An artist studying her first attempts at a sketch.

'You want to be seen,' Holly said quietly, 'So show yourself . . .'

Seven

The morgue was kept at a constant two degrees and Holly hoped she would never get used to the smell.

There were three steel tables but only one was covered in a white sheet. The walls were tiled as was the floor, with a steel gutter that sloped gently to the centre of the room. Angela Swan entered through swing doors, gloved hands held high.

'Morning, Bishop, morning, Holly. I made the preliminary examination last night, but there are a few things you should be made aware of.'

Angela was the chief pathologist for west London and had helped on both previous cases Holly had worked on. She was in her fifties with a sculptured face and her hair was brown streaked with grey. She turned her overhead mic on:

'It is Sunday the fifth of May 2019, 9.05 a.m., this is Angela Swan, DO, and in attendance is DI Bishop of the London Serious Crime squad and Holly Wakefield, forensic psychologist.'

She pulled the white sheet away and revealed the body underneath. Vee lay like a Carrara marble statue – white-skinned and glistening from head to toe after being cleaned. Neat stitches in her chest down to her waist from the Y-incision. A white towel had been draped across her face.

'Do we have a positive ID yet?'

'No,' Bishop said.

'The victim is to be identified for the record as Vee, that is V-E-E, no last name. The clothes and jewellery she was wearing have all been bagged and tagged: exhibits 53 to 59 – you will find detailed descriptions in my notes. Stomach contents showed she hadn't eaten anything after about eight in the evening, although she'd had a coffee at some point later on. Her blood alcohol level was zero. Urine samples revealed she had no STDs. Toxicology report says yes to chloroform and GHB.'

'We believe the killer used the drugs to subdue her,' Bishop said.

'GHB is usually swallowed in pill or liquid form, but sometimes it's injected. I found old track-marks on the insides of her elbows and between her toes but nothing recent. Chloroform, on the other hand, smells. It's sweet and pungent and you wouldn't want to drink it, so it's normally administered by a cloth to the mouth or nose, but there were no traces of any such fabric or material. No bruising around lips or residual finger marks against the back of the neck which means there may be another method of administration.'

'What effect would the drugs have had?' Holly said.

'GHB combined with chloroform?'

'Yes.'

'The chloroform would have knocked her out and the GHB would induce what's called a "G" sleep,' Angela said. 'Which isn't sleep at all, but a state of unconsciousness. GHB inhibits

31

the release of dopamine in the brain. At low doses, this results in a sense of euphoria, but the dosage administered to these victims would have left them suffering from dizziness, tremors and incoherence.'

'Would they have known what was happening to them?'

'If they were aware they would've experienced both physical and psychological fear, but they'd have been powerless to do anything about it. Their limbs wouldn't respond and they'd suffer from depressed breathing caused by lack of air moving in and out of their lungs.'

'They wouldn't have been able to shout for help?'

'No. They'd be screaming in silence,' Angela said, and turned back to the body. 'Moving on to the external examination of the victim: the body is that of a mature female, measuring sixty-seven inches in length, and weighing one hundred and twenty-seven pounds. She is fully developed but somewhat undernourished. I would put her age at between forty and fifty. Osteo-arthritis was prevalent in both hips and her left leg, a result of poor nutrition and overall health. Lividity was noted in the distal portions of the limbs; there is no peripheral oedema of the extremities.'

Angela brought the magnifier down and turned on its light. She ran her hands up and down Vee's arms, gently pressing the hard white flesh.

'There are two deep vertical scars on each wrist, highly likely to be the results of a suicide attempt some years ago – at least a decade I would say. There are dozens of other scars across her body, mainly found on her arms and legs, but also noted on her back and shoulders. These are consistent with bouts of self-harm and vary from hesitant two-centimetre cuts to deeper ones, the longest of which is on the inside of her left calf and measures twenty-three centimetres. Do we know what this woman did for a living?'

'She was a sex worker,' Bishop said.

Angela paused, her gloves halfway up the other arm.

'Surprisingly then, her sexual genitalia appear untouched. No FGM or assault marks of any kind. She had had sex the day she was killed, but whether with her attacker or not will be impossible to say as no forensic evidence was found.'

She angled the magnifier towards Holly and Bishop so they could see what she showed them next.

'The fresh cuts and abrasions evident on the back of her hands, forearms and upper arms are defensive wounds, which means she would have been conscious at the time of the attack. Where she made an attempt to grab the knife blade from the assailant, incised wounds are noted between the thumb and fingers of the right hand, across the palms and in the webspace between the bases of the thumb and index finger. There are numerous metacarpal fractures and abrasions, as well as five large bruises on her knees where she may have raised her legs to protect her abdomen during the assault.'

Angela stepped away for a moment, then said:

'And now we move on to the head.'

She pulled the white towel from Vee's face.

Holly felt herself look away, then forced herself to turn back.

Where the woman's eyes should have been were dark holes. There was a huge amount of discoloration and damage across the skin from the cheeks all the way up to the forehead. Vee's bright red hair had been tied behind her head into a bun with a tight net. She had a smoker's face – gaunt with tiny scars and spots, and her mouth was slack and open, her teeth yellow and stained.

'Her dentition is what one would expect of a heavy smoker.

She's had several fillings and three extractions and I've sent off X-rays to our forensic odontologist to see if he can help identify her.' She moved her hands up to the eyes and shot a look at Bishop. 'This is what you really want to know, isn't it?'

'It is.'

'Firstly, I would like to bring your attention to the trace evidence of adhesive residue I recovered from the lower right eyelash, consistent with electrical tape.'

'Electrical tape?' said Bishop.

'Normally this material would be used to bind a victim's hands or gag them, but in this instance it would appear the killer taped over the victim's eyes before he stabbed her.'

'See no evil,' Holly heard Bishop say, but she was thinking something else.

'Is it possible he didn't tape her eyes shut?' she said slowly.

'Why, what are you thinking?'

'I'm wondering if he taped them open.'

'Open?'

'So she would have to look at him.'

An uncanny silence followed until Angela broke it, her voice suddenly loud:

'I can only give you the facts, but yes, that could be one interpretation. Moving on – there is evidence of extreme trauma to the nasal bone, the glabella, supra and infraorbital margins and foramen and inferior nasal conchae. There is an irregular pattern of cuts on the insides of the eye sockets where the knife penetrated, and I counted a minimum of twenty stab wounds to each eye. Some of the cuts may be doubles or even triples that hit the same groove – it does happen, especially inside such a small target area, so we may never know exactly how many times he stabbed her.'

'Right- or left-handed?' Holly said.

'Right,' said Angela. 'The attack resulted in intracranial orbital stab wounds which caused the rupture of the globe, immediate retinal detachment, laceration to the extraocular muscles, optic nerve avulsion and lacrimal gland. Penetration into the cranial cavity occurred from the blade in both eyes via the optic canal with maximal bone fractures. The left side of the brain cortex was crushed, resulting in immediate intracranial haemorrhage. I removed the remains of what was left of both eyes, including the vitreous body, lens and optic nerve, but there was so much damage I couldn't even tell what colour her eyes were.'

'Brown,' said Holly.

'Thank you.' Angela paused to record this detail on the victim's chart. 'The weapon would have been a heavy knife. Possibly a kitchen knife or perhaps something larger, such as a hunting knife.'

Holly saw Bishop flinch by her side. He had his head down and was staring at his feet. He took a breath and looked up.

'Is it him?' he said to Angela.

'The use of GHB and chloroform is not the link, nor is the tape, which would indicate a slight shift in the MO. It's the ferocity of the attack to the eyes that is the giveaway. The grooves in the eye sockets caused by the knife are the exact same size as the wounds to the previous two victims, so it would appear to be the same knife. The same knife indicates the same killer.'

Angela took a step away from the table and her voice was as chill as the room.

'I'm sorry to be the bearer of bad news, DI Bishop, but I'm afraid your killer is most definitely back.'

Eight

Bishop led Holly through the incident room.

It was an amalgamation of open-plan offices and high-tech equipment compared to the last time Holly had been there – large television screens on the walls showed newsreel footage on a loop, and bodies moved constantly, loud voices mixed with the ping of emails and phone messages. There were a few familiar faces scattered in front of her, men and women who gave her a nod or a quick smile. Tired but somehow steely-eyed, and Holly wondered if they always took it home.

'Can I get everybody's attention, please!' Bishop shouted. 'Stephen Freer and Mike Thomas are cold-case murders from 2013 and 2016 and we are reopening them as of now. We have just found victim number three, a sex worker by the name of Vee who was killed in Brighton in the early hours of Friday morning.' A beat as he looked for faces. 'Sergeant Ambrose, take a team down to the archives and bring up everything we have on the two cold cases – that's Stephen Freer and Mike Thomas and I want summary copies for everybody.'

'Yes, sir.'

He motioned to a slim woman in her forties with neat clothes and not a hair out of place.

'Janet – Sussex CID in Brighton are expecting your call. I want a team briefing on victim number three in thirty minutes.'

'Thirty minutes!' Janet shouted as the room began to move.

Officers vied for Bishop's attention as they passed – 'Stick it on my desk, thank you, thank you,' he said as he grabbed the closest files and pushed open the far door in a glass-walled office and beckoned Holly inside.

'Welcome to my new glass elevator,' he said.

'I like it.' Holly sat in one of two 1960s Eames low-backed leather chairs opposite his desk. Bishop's normal office was on the second floor, with one window looking out onto a brick wall and an old desk and chairs. Here there was light from the outside world and everything was glass and metal. There was a tall filing cabinet at the back of the room and a fresh stack of files by his phone that probably hadn't been there this morning. The one thing he had brought with him was the pink orchid on his desk. It was in remembrance of Sarah, his fiancée, lost in Afghanistan. Bishop almost fell into his chair as he skimmed the reports he had just been given and dropped them on top of the others.

'You want a coffee?' he said.

'Thank you.'

He ordered a fresh pot with milk and hung up the phone. Glanced at his watch and rolled his shoulders back.

'How's the chair?' he said.

'Comfortable. I prefer this place.'

'So do I, but I mustn't get used to it. After this is all over, I'm sure I'll be back downstairs in the hobbit-hut.'

'I've got thirteen murder cases on my desk,' he said, 'seven manslaughter, some are at trial, some are being prepped and we're still trying to pass CPS requirements for the rest, but I'm going to need everybody for this one.'

He began making phone calls. Talking to DCIs, team management and employee schedulers, calling in favours. Holly was content to sit and focus on the autopsy she had just seen. If her theory was true, then the killer had taped Vee's eyes open in order to see her terrified reaction. He would have enjoyed watching the fear in her eyes as he inflicted the pain, but he hadn't punished her sexually, even though she had made her living in what some would consider an immoral profession. He was violent and deadly, but the killer was also very complex.

There was a knock on the door and an officer entered carrying a tray with the coffee, milk and biscuits. Bishop hung up.

'Take away the biscuits,' he said, 'I'm eating too much. Unless you want them, Holly?'

'I'm good, thanks,' she said.

The officer left. Bishop poured.

'Just milk,' Holly said.

'I remember,' and he handed over her cup.

'The tape around the eyes was new, wasn't it?' she said.

'Yes, nothing like that on the previous two victims.'

'So for the third victim, the killer has changed his MO and is getting closer to what he really wants, but Vee is the only one who wasn't sexually mutilated.'

'He ran out of time? Something spooked him and he decided to get out?'

'Possibly . . .' But she couldn't quite get her head around that yet, and perhaps neither could he, because he was staring at her and frowning.

'What?' she said.

'Do you definitely think the killer is a man?'

'It's highly probable. Eighty-five per cent of serial killers are male, and the level of violence would put this killer in a very small minority, regardless of gender. Were women interviewed in connection with the first two victims?'

'A few, but they all had alibis and some even said they would never be able to kill like this. It was just too extreme.'

'I agree. For now we should call the killer "he", but we shouldn't discount anyone. The killer takes his male victims' genitals as a trophy, but appeared to take nothing specific from his female victim. I don't believe that. This is his third victim; after all this planning and preparation, he will have taken something to remind him of his mastery, something he can touch and feel or look at when the urge strikes again.'

'What?'

'If not physically from her then something material. It's highly unlikely he went looking through the rest of the house, so it would have been from her bedroom.'

'Jewellery?'

'Possibly. It will be something small and intimate, something no one else would look at twice or even notice. Did she have home insurance?'

'No, so there'll be no inventory.'

'I'd like to have access to Vee's diary, I want to take that home and have a proper look through it,' she said. Then: 'DCI Walker was in charge of the original cases. What was he like?'

'Good and thorough. I liked him. Probably helped that he was ex-military as well – we served together in Afghanistan – so we had that bond between us. I don't think he went home for six months after the second body turned up. He slept in his office, which cost him his marriage, but I don't think he regretted it.'

'Are you going to end up sleeping here too?'

'Possibly. I hear the mice get lonely at night.' And then he lost his smile as the door opened and Chief Constable Franks entered. In his sixties, stooped and silver-haired, the chief closed the door gently but the look he gave Bishop stung his eyes.

'DI Bishop, is it true? Is it the same killer?'

'Yes, sir.'

'What are Sussex CID saying?'

'They're doing everything they can to help us, but we will be calling the shots.'

'Good. Miss Wakefield?'

'Sir.'

'Are you up to date with everything?'

'I think so.'

His face was strained, lips pursed.

'Good luck,' he said, and he exited.

Nine

'One minute,' Bishop said, and he watched his team settle.

The team consisted of forty-one detectives, two police constables and four police staff as well as himself and Holly. An incident board had been erected on one side of the room. It was a glass sheet on wheels with photos of the victims, their crime scenes and autopsies. Above it hung a projector screen. A female CID officer on the far side of the room slammed her phone down and swore. Tensions were running high already. They were about to get higher. Bishop looked for Holly and saw she had taken a seat on one of the desks to his left and he gave her a nod as he began to talk:

'Thank you, everybody,' he said. 'We're lucky to have DI Janet Acton joining us on this case, she will be deputy SIO. If you haven't met her, there she is.'

The woman gave a nod.

'And I'm sure most of you have heard of Holly Wakefield,' Bishop said, 'she's a forensic psychologist who has worked on a few cases with us, and she will be assisting with this one as well.'

Holly raised a hand to acknowledge.

'We're going to be moving at a fast pace,' Bishop carried on, 'and I need all of you to be up to date on these three murders. For those of you unfamiliar with the two London cases, I worked on both. They were frustrating, to say the least, due to the lack of evidence, and disturbing because of the violence of the crimes. When you read the full autopsy reports you will understand what I mean.'

He pressed his thumb on the clicker in his hand and the projector screen came to life.

'Stephen Freer was killed in Croydon in 2013, and Mike Thomas in Sunbury in 2016. They were stabbed in and around their eyes at least twenty times each and then they were castrated. The missing body parts have never been recovered. We had a few suspects, but nothing ever stuck.

'At each crime scene the killer left a calling card.' Another click. 'A rather bizarre stickman drawing which we've never been able to decipher. And now we have a third stickman drawing that was left in Brighton early Friday morning.'

'Is there a possibility it's a copycat?' from one of the sergeants.

'No, the coroner says the knife wounds are too consistent. This latest victim is a sex worker who went by the name of Vee, that's V-E-E, and that is the only name we have for her at present, so utmost priority is to find out who she is, what her real name is and where she came from. Because of the three-year gap between each kill, it's highly likely the killer was either out of the country or in prison, so we need to check recent releases across the UK against the timelines of all three murders, especially those criminals who are handy with a knife.'

'I'll take that, sir,' Sergeant Ambrose raised a hand.

'Thank you.' A beat. 'Janet, are you up to date with Brighton CID yet?'

He watched her hang up the phone. Before she had moved to the murder squad she had been a diamond-hard intelligence officer at GCHQ. He'd never worked with her before but her reputation preceded her.

'Yep,' she said as she stood up, and she kept a straight face when she talked:

'DI Swanson over at Brighton and Hove has sent me all the information on the case so far. They are broadcasting a constant news bulletin and everyone's email on this task force is now on their mailing list so if they get anything, we'll get it instantaneously. That works both ways. So let's start with what happened on Friday morning.

'The woman's body was found in her bungalow on Wellington Road in Peacehaven. The initial theory being that the victim had been followed home by a disgruntled john, but CCTV did not support this and we can therefore conclude that the killer was already waiting for her to come home or he had managed to get to her street avoiding all CCTV via either the new housing estate, which has no cameras fitted yet, or through the rough grasslands at the rear of her property.

'Her body was discovered at approximately 11 a.m. on Friday morning by her neighbour Rebecca Holborn when she tried to deliver a package that had been left with her by mistake. The front door to the house was unlocked. Brighton police interviewed her and neither Mrs Holborn or the other neighbours had heard anything unusual over the past few days: no arguments or disturbances, and on the night of the murder they were asleep.

'Looking at the victim, here's what we know. Vee worked on Morley Street, Brighton – an area known for prostitution – with about thirty other women. She was last seen walking home at about 2 a.m. Friday morning. She would have walked along the Marine Parade and Telscombe Cliffs, which run parallel to the sea. There is constant traffic there even at that hour; Brighton and Hove police have put up traffic signs requesting information.'

'Are they prepared to do a re-enactment?' Bishop said.

'I've already asked, and I don't know if any of you are familiar with Brighton but it's very busy at this time of year, so someone would have seen something.'

'Let's try and get the locals involved as well, and – sorry, Janet, hold on a second – who do we have here from Vice?'

'Sergeant Kenny, sir.'

'Our victim has been in Brighton for eleven years but she may have been like a lot of girls and started in London,' Bishop said. 'Ask around. A working girl by the name of Vee can't be that common and someone might remember her.'

'Yes, sir.'

'Carry on, Janet.'

'The victim was killed between two and four o'clock in the morning,' she said, 'so we are requesting CCTV footage of all Brighton to Central London train departures during that period in case that was the killer's exit route. We will be viewing trains stopping at Woking and every other station coming this way. We've also put in requests for CCTV on some of the major roads.

'Next stop is looking at local hotels and Airbnbs, checking on anybody who stayed in Brighton for up to a week before the murder. It's highly probable the killer went down to Brighton several times to find out Vee's routine and watch her. The killer may even have stayed there.'

'Where are we on the Volvo that was seen on the morning of the murder?' Bishop said.

'No trace so far. We're beginning to think it may have been stolen and the plates swapped.'

'Find that Volvo,' he said, 'make it the number one priority. Forensics at the victim's property please, Janet.'

'She was murdered in her bedroom on her bed. She was drugged with GHB and chloroform and stabbed repeatedly. You can see from the crime scene photos this was a particularly violent crime.' She clicked her clicker and enlarged photos appeared on the white screen: the body in situ on the bed with the cherry-red blood spatter.

'Over sixty different DNA samples and one hundred and twenty-five different fingerprints and partials have been recovered from the property. The possibilities of identifying the killer from that amount of prints and DNA is ridiculously small, and although we have started, it will take weeks or even months to work through every print and every sample. The ones not already on the police database will probably never be identified. That's it so far.'

'Thank you, Janet,' Bishop said. 'The killer never left any silent witnesses at the previous scenes, so I doubt very much he left anything here.' He clicked and the photo of Vee with the young man filled the big screen.

'This was found in the bedroom at the property. Apart from the crime scene and autopsy shots, this is the only photo we have of Vee. It was in an envelope hidden in her dressing table. It must have meant something to her. The photo is actually a low-resolution photocopy, so hopefully somewhere out there is the original. This boy or young man with her, who is he? What was their relationship? We find him, we identify her. Now the press are going to have an absolute field day with this – Kathy, what are we doing?'

Kathy Pembroke – severe hair and wearing octagonal glasses.

'Thank you, DI Bishop. Our focus is on getting information into the public domain about all three murders that will perhaps trigger a memory or someone's conscience. The appeal will be launched in collaboration with Brighton and Hove Police and will hopefully encourage witnesses to come forwards, which will in turn lead to possible suspects.'

'Try and get some fresh photos and quotes from Stephen and Mike's relatives as well,' Bishop said, 'it will remind the public who they are and increase the chance of getting information. At the same time, I think we should hold back on releasing the image of the stickman drawing that was found. It will give us an advantage when we start questioning suspects.'

'Agreed.'

'Beverly will be the family liaison officer; I want you to approach the relatives of Stephen and Mike again. I know it's always hard as I'm sure they don't want to be reminded about the murder of their loved ones, but it's important they are prepped before the press release goes out. Actually, Bev and Kathy, can you liaise with each other over this?'

'Yes, sir.'

'Thank you. Everybody else – any leads, we come back here and have a new briefing before any action is taken, understood?'

A sea of nods, but before they moved off, Bishop held them for a while longer.

'I just want to reiterate something: how hard we worked on the first two murders for nearly six years. I know each murder means everything to us, but this one, this one will mean everything to the cops whose shoes we are now filling. Especially DCI Walker, who is a good friend. Let's find this monster, okay?'

The task force moved off and he found himself watching them with a certain amount of pride. He looked for Holly and saw her at the incident board.

'Day one,' he said as he stood next to her. He could feel his stomach tightening as he lost himself in the stickmen drawings.

'You okay?' she said.

'Never thought I'd have to look at them again.'

And then he heard a voice he hadn't heard for years.

'Bill, you've put on weight, you fat wanker.'

He turned and saw a monster of a man in front of him. In his late fifties, he was six feet five, and at least two hundred and fifty pounds; he was solid and hard, a wrestler who perhaps hadn't been in the ring for a few years but still knew all the moves.

'How the hell did you get in here?' Bishop said, and the two men exchanged a handshake that ended in a bear hug. They pulled away and Bishop knew his eyes had gone a bit misty.

'Holly,' he said. 'I want you to meet my old boss, DCI Eddie Walker.'

'Less of the old,' Walker said. He shook Holly's hand and smiled. 'Charmed – Bishop's told me all about you.'

Ten

'Who was Cassius Spec?'

They were all sitting in Bishop's office and the two men were laughing at old police stories. It was amazing how a smile took away the tension.

'Come on, you started this,' Holly said. 'Seriously, who was he?'

'Cassius Spec,' Bishop began, then stared at his old boss. 'No, go on, you tell it.'

Walker leaned forward, still smiling.

'Okay, Holly. This is going back before I joined the murder squads, when I was still dealing with petty crime, all that sort of stuff. Imagine you've been away for the weekend to see your two children, then you come back home, open the front door and the first thing you notice is that the mail is not on the floor but neatly stacked on the hallstand. That's a bit weird, but you can't remember if the post came before you left on Saturday or after you left, so you let it go. Now, before you went to see your kids, you were in such a hurry you didn't have time to tidy up the kitchen, and you had a fry-up, so you know you're going to be walking into a mess of greasy saucepans, plates and coffee cups. However, the kitchen is now sparkling clean. You can even smell the bleach. You have a half-second of panic as you wonder if you've walked into the wrong house, and then you hear the tumble dryer going. That's an alarm bell, but Mrs Norris from next door has a key so maybe she came around to help out – but then you remember she's away in Cornwall with her kids so . . . you open the tumble dryer and there are men's clothes in there, but they are not your husband's. Underwear, socks, trousers and a cravat.'

Bishop laughed: 'I forgot about the cravat.'

'A bright blue paisley cravat. Now at this point you feel as though you've stepped into bizzaro-world. What the hell is going on? Nothing seems to be damaged and everything is very neat; the remote control, even the fruit bowl looks tidy, like the apples have been polished, but it's someone else's clothes in the dryer! You go up the stairs, a little nervous, but you don't feel threatened in any way, and then coming from your bedroom you and your husband hear gentle snoring. A bit wheezy. And you open the door and the lights are off and there's the shape of a body under your duvet and a head poking out the top resting on one of your pillows. It's a man, asleep. A stranger in your house. And you turn on the lights and say: "Excuse me, what are you doing in our house?"

'And the man props himself up in bed and blinks the sleep from his eyes and says:

'"Morning, Mr and Mrs Lynott, I put the mail on the hallstand and I think my clothes should be dry in a minute." And then he goes back to sleep. What the fuck!' Walker said.

'The guy's name was Cassius Spec. He was probably the worst burglar in the history of burglars. He got into the house

49

through a broken back door lock, stole fifty pounds from a biscuit tin in a cupboard, but then felt so bad, he decided to tidy the place up. Mrs Lynott said her house had never looked so clean. And the fifty pounds he stole he actually spent on groceries for them and stocked up their fridge. And he spent another thirty pounds of his own money on a saucepan because he'd burned theirs making himself scrambled eggs for breakfast.'

Holly laughed at the story, but it was the way Walker told it as well.

'Cassius Spec became a mini celebrity across London and we all wanted him to break into another house to see how much of his own money he would spend. We literally had a pool going. And he wore the blue paisley cravat at the trial. It was the one time the press came up with a decent headline,' Walker added. '"No Porridge for the Goldilocks Thief".'

'Bloody hell,' said Bishop, 'those were the days.'

'Good memories indeed,' Walker said, and he turned to Holly. 'Did Bishop tell you how we met?'

'No.'

'Out at Camp Shorabak in Helmand Province. He was coming back from a recce, I had just finished some R&R and we got put on a joint op.'

'Bishop was AAC, right?'

Walker shot her a look.

'Army Air Corps, then EOD, Explosive Ordnance Disposal for a while, then he went SF,' he said.

'What's SF?'

'Special Forces.

'Special Forces? You didn't tell me that,' Holly said to Bishop.

He shrugged and half-smiled.

'He didn't tell you he was SF?' Walker said. 'He plays dirty, this one. Did he tell you about our games?'

'What games?'

'Don't—' said Bishop, but it was too late.

'Afghanistan – what a shithole. Fucking sand, I can't stand it, and the boredom, Christ, there were weeks of waiting around being told to do nothing, so we whiled away the time playing cards and doing crosswords, and then we started making up our own word games.'

'Like what?'

'You know the army is full of acronyms, right? SF is Special Forces. CTC – Combat Training Centre, LZ – Landing Zone.' The big man smiled. 'Different versions; stupid but funny.'

'Like what?

'TU . . .'

'Go on,' said Holly.

'Please don't,' said Bishop.

'Tits Up,' Walker said proudly. 'Then there was S-O-S—'

'Save Our Souls?'

'Same Old Shit.'

Holly laughed.

'My favourite though,' said Walker, 'was D-B-F-K.'

'D-B-F-K?' Holly said, 'I have no idea.'

Bishop and Walker shared a look and spoke at the same time:

'Duck – Big Fucking Knife.'

They all laughed, and when it dried, Walker looked serious for the first time, and it was ominous how the atmosphere changed in the room when he said to Bishop:

'You going to catch him this time, mate?'

51

Bishop nodded slowly.

'Yeah, we'll catch him,' he said.

'What have you got to go on?'

'Not much. One suspicious car, one old photo from the victim, but no CCTV and no forensics.'

'Same MO?'

'Virtually identical, except he put tape around her eyes this time, so she had to watch him while he killed her.'

'Jesus.' Walker looked pale. 'Who's the coroner?'

'Angela Swan.'

'She's good,' he said. 'A bit stuffy, but she's on form.' There was a pause, and then he turned to Holly. 'Bishop told me you're good at this sort of thing. Your psychology – you can get into their heads.'

Holly felt herself nodding.

'I try,' she said.

'I have my old notes I made on the first two cases at home. Private stuff, just for me when this was all going down. I still take a look every now and then. I can give them to you.'

'That would be great, thank you.'

Walker looked relieved.

'And on that note' – he clapped his hands – 'I gotta go, dinner will be waiting.'

They said their goodbyes and at the door Walker turned:

'You guys should come over for a meal, Skyler loves to cook.' To Holly, 'I went through a divorce, got a new girlfriend now. Twenty years younger,' he laughed, 'but I'm not complaining.'

'Sure,' said Holly. 'That would be nice.'

'Sure,' said Bishop and he smiled too.

'Don't keep me out of the loop, Bill, I want to know when you're about to nail this guy.'

'I promise.'

Walker left and closed the door.

There were a few moments of silence.

'I like him,' Holly said. 'He's charming.'

'Charming? I don't think he's ever been called charming before,' Bishop said. 'Big fucker, I'll give him that. Going into a dark room back in Afghan, if anybody was going to get shot, it was going to be him.'

Eleven

It was eight o'clock, and Holly's flat was cold when she got home.

She collected her mail and let it drop on the hallstand then made herself a hot chocolate – her comfort drink after six o'clock ever since she had been a child. She leant back on the sofa and went through the cold-case files.

Stephen Freer and Mike Thomas had both been killed between 10 p.m. and 2 a.m. The two weapons that had been used were a heavy kitchen or hunting knife for the assault on the eyes, and a carpenter's saw for the castration. One of the crime scene photos at each room showed a wall socket by the bed that had been splashed with blood apart from a neat white square where the plug had been, and it was speculated that it could have been used as the power source for the electric saw.

American serial killer Ed Gein had removed human skin from his victims and used it to make everything from waste-baskets to chair seat covers, and Holly wondered how this killer was different. Neither man's testicles or glans penis had ever been recovered and the trophies would be stored, that much was obvious, but would he transform them into something else or would he keep them as they were?

At the back of each file was a detailed insurance form covering the house contents of each victim. Both the insurers and the families were adamant nothing had been taken from either Stephen or Mike's house.

Socio-economically both men were about the same. Stephen was married and had a mortgage, as did Mike. Stephen banked with Lloyds, Mike with First Direct. Credit cards were from different companies and building societies, they both had varying degrees of debt, and according to their bank statements neither of them had ever eaten in the same restaurant as the other.

Holly thumbed her way through the suspect list. Every killer, or possible killer, homophobic or otherwise, had been interviewed and released. The police had been through everything with a fine-toothed comb and nothing seemed to connect the victims or their crimes. She studied the notes for another hour, convinced that somehow like everybody else she had missed something.

Bishop called. She answered on the first ring.

'Hey,' she said.

'They just finished the candlelight vigil in Brighton. It was held at one of the churches and plainclothes managed to get some cameras inside. They think they got photos of nearly everybody who attended. It was very moving apparently, and turned into a bit of a street event afterwards. A lot of the working girls were there as well, paying their respects. We're going to run the photos through the police database to see if we get any hits on facial recognition.'

'What about the Volvo?'

'We've got CCTV but we can't make out the plates. IT are

going to try and clean up the images, but it's going to be hit and miss. The forensic odontologist got back to Angela but there was no match with the X-ray from Vee's teeth. When do you think you'll be ready with a profile?'

'I've just finished going through the files. Give me another day, I'm picking up Walker's notes tomorrow, I want to be thoroughly briefed before I come in.'

'Tuesday morning?'

'Perfect.'

They hung up at the same time.

She liked working with Bishop. It had been less than a year ago when he had first contacted her and asked for help on a double murder case, but it seemed like a lifetime. They worked well together and had shared more than most in the short time they had known each other. He had been responsible for saving her life on the Pickford case earlier in the year and now they had regular drinks and meals when time allowed, sometimes followed by a movie and always with the promise of things to come.

Before she had met Bishop and the Major Investigation Team operating out of Hammersmith police station she had been a dedicated introvert, quite content to live in the confines of her flat, study psychology and read, watch TV and take walks in the parks. Always by herself, but she didn't mind that. As a foster child she had learned to be self-sufficient and not to rely on anyone, and while that hadn't changed, spending time with Bishop and working with the police made her feel as if she had found a hidden part of her. A new family. She was getting out more and had even joined a gym after Christmas and was now kickboxing three times a week.

She was curious as to why Bishop hadn't told her he had

been Special Forces, but perhaps some things were best kept secret. Holly had her own secrets too, one being that her brother, Lee, was a convicted murderer and was one of her own patients at Wetherington Hospital.

Bishop was funny, thoughtful, loyal and truthful. And whether he knew it or not, she considered him her best friend.

Twelve

Holly spent most of Monday at King's College, leading a discussion with her students about the ways criminal behaviour could be influenced by genetic predisposition.

At five thirty she left and headed out to Barnes, west London.

Eddie Walker lived in a detached Victorian period house. The driveway was gravel and small, and the front garden neat. She pulled in behind a new Mercedes and rang the doorbell. Walker answered it quickly.

'Come in,' he said and smiled. 'Coffee or tea?'

The kitchen was country-style with wooden cabinets, a big pine table and painted white chairs. There was a shelf of books on cookery and photos on the wall, some of which had Bishop and Eddie together in desert fatigues.

'Do you miss it?' Holly asked as he passed her a coffee.

'Everyone does, no matter what they say. You're part of a massive family and leaving that family is hard. I went straight into the police force, so it wasn't too shabby, but others get a bit lost. Bill did all right; went into private security for a while, then applied for CID.'

'You have a lovely house.'

'Thank you. I was lucky: the kids had already left home, so when my wife and I split it was probably one of the friendliest divorces on record. She only lives about half a mile away. She still comes over every now and then.' A beat. 'Come on, let me take you downstairs.'

There was a side door in the wall at the back of the kitchen that opened at his touch. Wooden steps led into darkness and there was a cord that hung from the ceiling. He pulled it and a single bulb lit up overhead.

'I renovated the basement a couple of years go. It was a mess before, damp and untidy, now it's my office.'

She followed him down to a metal door with an electronic keypad. He pressed the access code and she heard the electronic bolts slide back with a click.

'Forgive the security, but I have a few things here that I like to keep safe.'

The door opened to a large room with a sofa opposite a wide-screen TV and stereo sound system. Walker went to the far wall and punched a code into another keypad and a hidden door clunked open.

'And this,' he said, 'is the epicentre of my old life.'

Another ceiling cord and the overhead bulb went on. The room was small with a desk and one chair, but there was no room for anything else. Case files, folders and stacks of paperwork piled high on the desk and floor, with tiny access paths between them. The walls were a 360-degree scrapbook of Stephen Freer and Mike Thomas newspaper cuttings, maps of London, suspects and speculation. The one thing out of place was a vintage film poster of *Cape Fear* by the desk.

The man was clearly obsessed. He said at the station he still

59

looked at the files every now and then, but it seemed to Holly as though he'd never really stopped working those old cases.

She realised he was watching her, waiting for a reaction.

'It's impressive,' she said.

'Thank you.'

She wondered if she was one of the only people who had ever ventured into this room. It reminded her of the murder-abilia she kept in the spare room of her flat: a collection of objects associated with murderers or their violent crimes. She had been collecting for over a decade, trawling auctions and private buyers across the world, and Bishop was the only other person who knew it existed.

'Old cases, old memories,' Walker said, and his eyes drifted back to the past ten years of his life. 'I still follow the news and watch new murder cases. Part of me wants to get back in there, you know?'

'Why did you retire?'

'I wanted to save the marriage, I wanted to make the effort, but it was already too late. I promised Esther I would come out early but when the second body turned up I stayed on. The last case killed everything and the marriage didn't stand a chance. I mean, we both tried, but it just wasn't going to work. Eventually, when Mike Thomas' murder got classed as a cold case, I came out and the marriage limped along for another three months.'

He gestured to the desk.

'Living in the past, but I still can't help myself. Every case I ever worked on, I brought home. That's why I have the security doors; there's information in here that never needs to see the light of day. All the murders were like jigsaws to me. Some with fifty pieces, some with five thousand, and I'd spend hours trying to fit them all together. It was a place I could work by myself, without other people offering opinions. Just me and a pen and my thoughts. Private notes and doodles, trying to get the old grey matter to look at something from a different angle, thinking out of the box. One of the things that used to infuriate my wife was when I came home in time for dinner and I'd still be making notes while she was pouring the wine. Autopsy photos on the dining room table while we were eating a Sunday roast doesn't make for good conversation. Maybe it did for the first three months, maybe even six because it was new to her, but after twenty years she got sick of it, and I don't blame her. I couldn't turn it off. It was a tap that just kept dripping.

'Sleeping was the worst, the thoughts were constantly there and I would wake up, pen and paper next to me on the bed-side table, and I would turn on the light and scribble notes and Esther would wake up and say "What are you doing?" and I'd say, "An idea just came to me. I think it could be him, this other suspect – I need to ask him another question." And she'd be like, "Give it a rest!" But I couldn't. So things spiralled and the relationship disintegrated, and I was hurt so I threw myself into my work, because the work couldn't hurt me like my failing marriage could, and that became my safe-haven. But the reality was I couldn't have solved any more, I don't think. Apart from this one.' He made his way to the desk and picked up a bulging file.

'This was the case that never went away,' he said. 'The bastard that wouldn't let go.'

Thirteen

The file was crammed with hundreds of papers.

'Most of the stuff at the front I'm sure Bishop has already given you – the summarised files on Stephen Freer and Mike Thomas,' Walker said, 'but the stuff at the back written on the yellow pad, those are my original notes. Take them and see what you think. Ramblings of an old man, probably, but there might be something in there that could trigger an idea.'

'Who do you think did it, Walker?'

He paused and shook his head.

'Someone smarter than me. And I've a feeling these aren't the only three bodies.'

'You think he's killed before?'

'I wondered for a while if he had lived abroad, maybe killed over there in the years we didn't hear from him, then when he came back to England, he couldn't stop himself so started again. I contacted Interpol, but they didn't have a record of any similar killings anywhere else in the world. Do you think he would change his MO if he moved countries?'

'Possibly, but with some killers the MO is as much a ritual as the killing. He has to follow the same steps because it feeds his compulsion. Watching the victim, waiting, biding his time until it feels right. What about Ralph McQuarrie – Bishop told me he was a suspect for a while.'

'He was, but he was never really up for it. He didn't have this level of extreme violence in him. He was a dickhead, beat up a few men, and I think he was gay deep down but he never showed it.'

'He's already in prison for rape.'

'Well there you go then, it's not him. No, there was something much deeper, much darker going on with these crimes, and to be honest I don't think I even scratched the surface, Holly. I've been there before and I've seen bodies, but this case I just couldn't get my head around. I can understand good and bad, right and wrong, and I know there are bad people and good people, but this was something I'd never seen before.'

He handed the files over. 'Take them all, use whatever you can and keep it until the case is solved. And you will solve it,' he said. 'I want Bill to keep me in the loop on this one – unofficially of course, I know I'm not allowed to get classified information. But if you think of anything or want someone to bounce ideas off, just let me know, I'm here for you.'

'Thank you, Eddie, I will.'

There was a noise upstairs and a female voice:

'Hello?'

'Ah,' he said. 'Skyler's back. Come on, let me introduce you to my other half.' He locked the security doors and took Holly upstairs. Skyler was in the kitchen, she had the kettle on and was getting two fresh mugs from the cabinet.

'Hello, love, who's this?' Skyler said.

'This is Holly, she's working on the new murder case with Bishop.'

Skyler smiled and shook Holly's hand.

'Nice to meet you, Holly.'

She was attractive with long blonde hair and bright blue eyes and Holly wondered if she was Nordic. There was something in there perhaps.

'Now,' Walker said, 'the big question is – who is going to cook tonight? You or me?'

Skyler smiled.

'You,' she said. 'Treat me. Do whatever you want, the kitchen is yours.' She whispered to Holly and winked: 'He thinks he's Masterchef . . .'

Walker heard her and smiled back.

'Red or white?'

'You choose, darling.'

He pulled out a Merlot.

'How was your day?' he asked as he looked for the corkscrew.

'It was okay. A quick flight. I'm a flight attendant, Holly. Short haul. Carrying those bags and putting them in the overhead racks for people does my back in after a while.'

Holly watched them talking. They worked well with each other and she suddenly felt like an intruder.

'I'd better get going,' she said.

'Would you like to stay? We have enough,' Skyler said.

'No, thank you, I have to get back.'

'Well, it was lovely to meet you, Holly. You should come over. Do you have a significant other? We could do a couple's night.'

'Thank you.'

Walker led her to the door and on the drive he said:

'What I just gave you, a lot of it is private but I don't care. Anything to catch this bastard.'

When Holly got into her car she put the files on the passenger seat and drove away. Whenever she stopped at a red light she would glance over at them, itching to see what was inside.

Fourteen

23 May 2013

Got the call today to a two-storey home in Croydon. A man – Stephen Freer – killed. Multiple stab wounds to face. Reminds me of a Jack the Ripper kind of madness. Never seen anything like this before. The anger is startling. Castration. Emasculation. A pissed-off lover?

Marcus Winn the coroner says the killer is right-handed.

A right-handed man who loves blood. Did he drink it? Is that cannibalism?

Got the forensic report back from the crime scene. No prints or DNA, but they found this weird stickman drawing in one of the bedroom drawers. Creepy – like a kid did it. They think it's linked – I agree.

Had to speak to the deceased wife today. Her name is Anne. That was horrible. She's a lovely woman with two kids to look after now. She asked me if she should sell the house. I told her I didn't know. I wished I could have been more helpful.

I'm getting heat from Chief Franks. He makes me feel like I don't want to catch the killer. He should try and bloody help and keep the press off my arse. Journalist called Andy Brooks is heading the wave of anti-police headlines. Had a meeting about him — we have to watch what we say in the incident room — there might be a leak.

The coroner brought me back in to tell me about the castration. Who is this crazy fuck?

We started to interview gay men with a history of violence — we are going with the theory that Stephen might have been homosexual, although nothing else points to this. The press are running with the story, Andy Brooks leading the way, which has understandably upset the family. I called Anne and told her we were just covering the bases, that's all.

Went on the beat today, showing Stephen's photo to bookies and some of the more heavy-hitting money lenders in town. None of them knew the vic and the man had no gambling debts. Another dead end.

Attended the funeral. Esther chose my tie for me. It was dark purple — I didn't have black, but it was okay, I think. I wanted her to come with me, but we decided against it. I'm not spending enough time with her. She hates my job. There were a lot of people there. I wonder how many will be at mine? Stephen Freer had had some good friends. Anne said hello to me after the service. I hadn't spoken to her for a week. She's lost weight. The kids looked as though they had lost weight too. The press were there — taking photos.

I had some plain-clothes detectives in amongst the crowd,

*but not at the wake. That was just me. It was awkward.
I left after twenty minutes. Felt I shouldn't be there eating
sausage rolls, I should be out on the street trying to catch
the killer.*

*Today marks 3 weeks in — we've now ruled out the gay-killer
angle and financial motives.*

*Thought we had a break with some CCTV, but it proved
to be a false alarm. We brought in five possible suspects and
I interviewed them all. The only one that might have some
heat is a guy called Ralph McQuarrie. He's got previous,
has no alibi and is a carpenter and owns an electric saw.*

*I'm a bit drunk tonight so I'm rambling . . . Why stab the
vic's eyes out? He didn't want Stephen to see him? Anonymity?
In case his victim escapes? Stephen had been drugged with
enough GHB to drop a horse — there was no way he was
leaving that bedroom. It has to be something else.*

*We're moving onto the theory that Stephen knew his killer.
The killer got into the house when his wife and kids were
away at her parents. He must have known Stephen would be
alone therefore he knew his routine. He's clever.*

*No link with Ralph McQuarrie and his carpentry
equipment came back negative for traces of Stephen's
DNA. SHIT!*

*No new numbers on the vic's cell phone. No emails to
new people. I interviewed some of his old school friends
today. Stephen had kept in touch with a couple of them that
I recognised from the funeral. They couldn't think of anyone
who'd have reason to kill him. He seemed like a nice guy.*

*We found some more CCTV from a local curry
house — again — nothing.*

The press are killing us.

Every night I say a prayer that this is a one-off and there won't be another one like this.

Three months now – I've got a great team and we are all working our asses off but haven't had any other leads.

Just had a gang killing in north London – they're happening every day now. I'm getting moved off the case. Not replaced – it's still mine – but other investigations are taking priority.

Anne called me twice. I'll get back to her tomorrow.

Fuck me – Esther and I are arguing.

Six months now and it's just me and a few sergeants. Nothing new to report. Dead end after dead end. After two years it will be classed as a cold case. I hope that never happens.

It's official – the Stephen Freer murder is now a cold case. I'll still make notes and hope something comes up but it's been handed over to a different department.

I hope I never see anything like this again.

12 June 2016

We have another one.

I got the phone call at 11.28 this morning. It's my day off but I'm about to leave for the station. Christ – I can't believe I have to go through this again. I never thought I would have to write in this journal for a second time. I thought whoever killed Stephen Freer was dead. That's why we – fuck . . . I need to go.

Spent the day at the crime scene, which was just bloody beyond words. It's the same MO – man murdered in his bed in his house with another creepy stickman drawing. The first was left in a chest of drawers, this one was on top of the dresser in the bedroom. This is his leave-behind – his signature. Son-of-a-bitch!

The vic is named Mike Thomas. He'd been castrated and there was nothing left of his eyes.

I showered three times when I got home.

I spoke to the second victim's wife – her name is Alison. Apparently they had been having a few marital problems and she was at her parents for the weekend. She came back on Sunday and found him at two o'clock that afternoon. He had been dead for at least ten hours. She can't help us, she was too upset to speak.

It's a pattern – he seems to attack when the rest of the family is away, which means he watches them and knows their travel plans? A close friend?

Had to go back and see Anne, Stephen's ex, to explain that we are reopening the case of her murdered husband. She seemed relieved and offered to talk to the new widow if it helped. I didn't see her kids.

For some reason I feel as though the violence is more intense with this one. Just a feeling. The new coroner is Angela Swan – she confirmed it's the same killer. I remember in 2013 I didn't think Stephen Freer was his first kill. These murders are just too well done. It's as if the killer has been practising somewhere.

A butcher? Baker? A candlestick maker? I'm drunk . . . Can't discount anyone.

No CCTV, no forensics again. It's the same nightmare.

This guy is a fucking ghost.

The killer does his research. Chooses victims who are CCTV free.

Again — access to the house, but no break-in.

McQuarrie has an alibi. FUCK!

Press release — hoping to get some answers — we need people to come forward.

Releasing images of the stickmen. Andy Brooks is a pain up the ass. Keeps misquoting me. Bastard. Press office have told me to keep my mouth shut.

I'm supposed to be taking early retirement but I'm going to stay on. This thing is in my blood.

Went to the funeral and said hello to Alison. It was awkward, she looked a mess. Poor thing is going through chemo. I had a massive argument with Esther before I went there, we're arguing again and for some reason I shared that with Alison. I don't know why. Alison was nice to talk to, I heard on the grapevine that her husband cheated on her. What a prick. I hope she recovers from this.

When I came home Esther wasn't here. I needed someone to talk to. Might as well go back to the station.

Things not good at home. Marriage is breaking down.

Nothing from the newspaper appeal.

Living at the station now and eating crap from the vending machine. No new leads.

Bringing more suspects in — but deep down we know it's not them. This guy has got evil written all over him. Some wanker had a tattoo of the stickmen drawing done on his back and sent a photo of it in to us — sold it to one of the

*gutter press. We arrested him — can't charge him for anything
but I want to smash his head in.*

*Three weeks now and how can there be no link between
these two victims?*

There has to be something.

THERE IS NOTHING.

This is going to be the death of me.

*Lost my temper and shouted at Geoff Atwick, the press
officer. He's a dick anyway, but I shouldn't have done that.
Sometimes I hate my job.*

Fuck me I want to catch this bastard . . .

That was the final entry.

On the last page was a list of forty-one possible suspects.
Walker had crossed all of them off one by one, until there was
nobody left at the end.

Holly put the pad down.

There was a deliberate sense of purpose with these murders.
The process of the kill, the selection of the victims, followed
by the stalking, was a special ritual with important steps that
might depend upon the location or availability of the victim,
but in general they would stay the same.

Holly had to work backwards like a film in reverse. Rewind
from the last murder scene and go back to the beginning.

Fifteen

Bishop had slept the night on the sofa in his office.

It pulled out into a bed and he had balled up his jacket as a pillow and didn't even feel himself going to sleep. He had been woken up at 5 a.m. by the cleaners. Now the rest of the murder squad were arriving like zombies.

Slurred voices shrugging off sleep and the strong smell of coffee. A sergeant entered the incident room carrying three boxes of cream doughnuts. Some rallied, others groaned and reached for the Gaviscon.

He took a coffee, even though he had already had two, and parked himself by the incident board. It had been updated with the crime scene photos of Stephen Freer and Mike Thomas. There was only one photo of Vee from the autopsy. Someone had drawn a heart in red pen above it. It was touching.

'Morning, Bishop,' from DI Janet Action, the deputy SIO, as she headed to her desk.

'Morning.'

He spotted Holly coming in with Sergeant Ambrose and wondered how she had slept. He thought his face probably looked as crumpled as his shirt as he shot her a quick smile. She smiled back. She wore dark blue jeans, a black T-shirt and black blazer. Her make-up was subtle and her light brown hair pulled in a ponytail. She looked beautiful. He realised he didn't need his coffee any more.

'Morning, everybody,' he said, 'let's go through the numbers please. It is Tuesday the seventh of May for those of you who have forgotten. Janet, start us off.'

'The two cold-case files of Stephen Freer and Mike Thomas have been reviewed by the Serious Crime squad and the CPS have granted permission to re-examine the evidence in relation to the new murder, that of the Brighton sex worker known as Vee. Both cases have therefore been officially reopened and the families and relatives have been contacted and warned of an increase in press coverage.'

'Kathy and Bev, did you talk to them?'

Beverly answered:

'We did. We went to visit Anne, Stephen's ex-wife, and she was very grateful and said she would do anything to help. Mike Thomas' ex-wife, Alison, doesn't want to open up old wounds. She's a little more reserved, has since remarried and is now Alison Paton. I think she just wants to get on with her life.'

'I don't blame her,' Bishop said. 'Janet?'

'We've uploaded all the cold-case information to a folder named Operation Hugo – and we have updated the telephone numbers for the witnesses where we could.'

'Where did we get the name Hugo from?'

'My dog, sir.'

'I like that,' Bishop said. 'Operation Hugo it is.'

Janet said: 'We are setting up interviews with both of the

first victims' friends and work colleagues, seeing if something in their memory has been jogged over the years. Hopefully, all of these interviews will be conducted this week. Since the murder of Stephen Freer was six years ago, a few of his old colleagues have left the surgery in Croydon and moved to different businesses across town. We're having problems tracking some of them down, and one of them died on a mountaineering expedition in 2015. Mike Thomas's art gallery in Sunbury was put into liquidation by his wife, but was then bought out by the trustees, so it's still up and running. We're facing the same problem with some employees who have moved on to other things, but we're doing everything we can. There were over thirty thousand pages of information collected per victim, and we are still in the process of reassessing the transcripts, witness interviews and bank account details etc, but at the moment we have come to the same conclusion as the original investigation: we cannot find a link between the first two victims.'

'In one way that's good,' Bishop said. 'It means we didn't miss anything. Moving on to Vee?'

'We still have no name for her yet, but I know Vice are working that angle hard.'

'Sergeant Kenny?'

The sergeant raised a hand: 'Couple of leads but nothing as yet. We're talking to Birmingham and Manchester as well, and we've started making enquiries on the availability of street GHB and chloroform, the latter being rather more unusual and harder to purchase. Nothing so far, but we'll keep trying.'

'Thank you.'

'DNA and prints found at the victim's home,' Janet said. 'We've managed to eliminate over fifty people so far, we are working our way through the others, and we have approximately thirty-five different partials that are not on our system.'

'No matches with the previous two crimes?'

'None,' Janet said, 'but we've got a couple of red flags from ex-cons who have recently been released back onto the street. The first is a Douglas Regus—'

'I know that name.'

'A convicted murderer, he got out three months ago. He has form for assaults against sex workers and one of the Brighton girls recognised his mugshot as the man driving the Volvo that night. We're trying to find him now.'

'Wasn't there a second man in the back seat?'

'Yes, no ID yet, but we think it was Douglas Regus's partner in crime, Gavin Lefton or Lefty as his mates call him. Both their files are on your desk.'

Bishop remembered him as a short fuse who lived on meth and drink.

'I thought Lefty was still inside?' he said.

'Convicted of rape in 2011, but he was out by 2013.'

'Can we tie either of them to Croydon in 2013 or Sunbury in 2016?'

'Not yet. At the beginning of 2015 Lefty was arrested for rape again and sent to Pentonville where he met Douglas Regus. The two shared a cell for six months and after getting out they went into the drugs business together and started running a county line in Harlow. As well as running up a lot of drugs charges, Lefty assaulted a sex worker in Brighton late last year and spent Christmas in Wandsworth, but he's back on the streets now. Current address for both is unknown, but we've got warrants out and we've already had a few tips from anonymous callers, so I think we'll get them in quickly.'

'If possible, I want them in custody by the end of the day.'

'Understood. We're extending the CCTV coverage on major roads and train routes from Brighton, and asking private businesses to share their camera footage in the hopes of getting a number plate for this Volvo that seems to have disappeared into thin air. All the private companies are being very helpful, but it's going to take time. We've actually had three officers on leave volunteer to come back early to help out.'

'Who are they? Are they here?'

Two female and one male officer raised their hands.

'Thank you,' Bishop said. 'Help yourself to doughnuts.'

A few smiles lit up the room.

'Airbnbs are being checked, as are the local hotels for any guests who paid cash and were out on the evening of the murder and came back in the early hours. So far nothing. The Brighton bobbies are being stellar and doing a great job. They're working 24/7.'

'Where are we on the analysis of the stickman drawing?' he said.

'The paper is an identical match to the original two pieces of paper, most likely from the same packet.'

'It's that old, it's not new paper?'

'No, it's the same quality and make as the previous ones, which is your standard white 80 gsm copier printing paper, bought from any one of a thousand retail stores and online. The crayons are made by Crayola – there are five colours used with each of the three drawings: black, scarlet, "radical red", brown and "burnt orange". The drawing found at Vee's had an additional colour on her skirt which was green, or "electric lime", which is its official name. Again – these can be purchased practically anywhere, so no chance of us tracing the source.'

From Bishop to the room:

'Does everybody have copies of these drawings? Good, print them out and have them close by, and I want them put on the bulletin boards on each floor.' He took a beat. 'The AA and NA candlelit vigil that happened on Sunday night – do we have the footage from Brighton police?'

'We do, one of the cameras broke so it's a lot less footage than we originally thought. We've pulled facial images though and are trying to match them up with anybody from the first two crimes, but it's not looking promising.'

'Okay,' Bishop said. 'What about the photo of Vee and the young man we found in her bedroom?'

'We've had the forensics lab examine it, but as it's not the original they can't detect the time code. Vee looks in her early teens, which would make the photo twenty-five, possibly thirty years old, way before iCloud and any type of social media, so we can't hack into that. That's it so far, until we can get a positive ID on our girl, we're stuck. A film crew will be filming the re-enactment of Vee's last walk home this Thursday night in Brighton – exactly one week after the murder – which will be shown on a special edition of Crimewatch Friday evening. The local press are really pushing this story and we've got a few nationals coming down as well.'

'That's good, where are we on the press, Kathy?'

Kathy stood, notepad and pencil in hand:

'They have made the connection with the two previous murders, which we expected, even without the release of the stickman drawing. Thoughts are now that we should release it.'

'What are Legal saying?'

'They're giving us the go-ahead.'

Bishop thought for a second.

'Hold off a while longer, I want to interview Douglas Regus and Lefty first. I've read some of the daily newspaper columns, but generally how are the press reporting it?'

'Some of them are being nasty as the latest victim was a sex worker, but the majority are taking a more sensitive approach. A few of the freelance reporters want to talk to you now you've been announced as SIO, and are asking for your number.'

'I bet they are. Quote whatever you think is appropriate – "following all lines of enquiry", etc, and remind them that all calls go through the press office. Is that it, everybody?'

It was.

'Okay, we are four days into this murder. I know you're pushing hard, but I need you to push harder. Our technology is better now than it was in 2013 and 2016, but this sort of case always boils down to hours and perseverance.

'I am now going to pass you over to Holly Wakefield, who is going to talk to you about this killer, this psychopath.' He looked over at her. Her eyes were so clear. She looked ready. 'Is that the clinical definition of what we're dealing with here?'

Holly stood up from the desk and nodded.

'Yes, he's a psychopath, DI Bishop. A rare breed. And I'm going to tell you all about him.'

Sixteen

Holly stood by the incident board, black Sharpie loose in her hands.

Her voice soft but strong when she spoke:

'I want you all to imagine, if you will, waking up in the morning, and your first thought of the day is not thinking about what the kids are going to have for breakfast, or do you need to fill up the car with petrol, or did I send that email last night? No, your first thought of the day is who am I going to kill next, and what knife shall I use?'

'This is him, this is our killer. He will then go through his workday like a ghost. He does whatever it is simply for the pay cheque, and he won't be stacking shelves somewhere, he will have a job with responsibility where people look up to him. He thrives on power over others. I worked on the Sickert case last year and Wilfred Sickert was a doctor, a figure of authority, someone you wouldn't necessarily suspect. Our killer may well be in a job that wears a uniform.'

'Wasn't John Christie a cop?' a plain-clothes officer with long hair asked.

'Yes, he was, a War Reserve police officer and he enlisted in the army and joined the Royal Air Force as well. Our killer craves this sort of authoritarian power and it's not something he can turn off. So who is he?'

She turned and wrote on the board:

A suffering soul.

Underlined it.

'This is the definition of a psychopath by German psychiatrist J. L. A. Koch from 1888, the same year Jack the Ripper became active in London.'

She carried on speaking, adding the pertinent points to the board:

'What happened to our killer to make him *devoid of compassion*, of *empathy* and *conscience*? How did he become this suffering soul? Well, unlike sociopaths, whose behaviour is learned, psychopaths are born.

'So he was born with no morality, no empathy, no conscience, but he was also born with *superficial charm*, an inflated sense of *self-worth*, a talent for *manipulation*. He will also be *impulsive, sexually promiscuous, narcissistic and a pathological liar.*'

She turned back to the room.

'Okay, I want to bring up a couple of interesting facts about how he acts in public that put his life into perspective.' She looked at the faces and chose:

'Kathy – imagine you're having coffee at Starbucks, okay?'

'Sure.'

'There's a mother with a baby sitting opposite you. The mother is feeding the baby and the baby is laughing. The mother looks over at you and smiles, what do you do?'

Kathy laughed and smiled.

'I don't know, smile back?'

81

'Yes, in exactly the same way you just did with me, because I smiled when I asked you the question, didn't I?'

'Yes.'

'That's called *mirroring*. Normal people, empathetic people, will imitate other people's expressions because we are all naturally attracted to people who share the same responses that we have. This goes back to the pack mentality of our caveman days. If they smile when we smile, and if they cry when we cry, then they are the same as us and they will not harm us and we will be safe.

'Now when the woman smiles at the psychopath he will not have that same reaction. He will feel nothing as he watches her and the baby smiling at him. You know why? Because he doesn't care. However, over the years the psychopath has learned that if he doesn't respond in the same way that others do, people will look at him differently, so what does he do? He needs to learn to smile at the right times, so it becomes an intimate game that he perfects over the years, because if he doesn't smile that would give the game away, wouldn't it? So he smiles and the woman with the baby in Starbucks smiles back and maybe he smiles even harder, but now he thinks it might look a little fake, so he quickly looks away and sips his coffee, but he got away with it, and the woman with the baby thinks, What a nice man. And that is how the psychopath has learned to blend in.

'He watches us, he sees what we do, sees how we react in certain situations and he will copy us. He will *mirror us and will have mirrored his targets*. Now, if you are very clever and very careful and if you study him up close, you will see these tell-tale signs. But if you don't have that opportunity, if he is just a friend in passing or someone you bump into at the supermarket or the pub every now and then, the glib attitude he has or the friendly wave as he walks away will be enough to convince you he is normal. And why wouldn't he be? He looks like us, he walks like us, he dresses like us. To all intents and purposes he is us, but of course he doesn't think like us.

'This next one is a bit of a party trick, but it's another fascinating insight,' Holly said. 'Psychopaths don't yawn when you yawn.'

'No, shit?' someone said.

'It's true. We all catch each other's yawn, don't we? Try it next time you have people over for dinner, invite the friend with the weird husband, and when you're talking, yawn a few times and see if he yawns back. If he doesn't, don't let him have dessert.'

There were a few laughs but it faded quickly.

'He will lie, manipulate and mirror people to get what he wants and that is how a psychopath lives his life. He works people out, knows what they need and gives it to them – whether it's companionship, affection, love or sex. So he has emotional intelligence but is devoid of emotion, it's as simple as that. And then there is the other side to him, an even darker side. Whereas we fantasise about love, about children, or winning the lottery—'

She pointed to the incident board and the crime scenes.

'He will fantasise about this.'

'He's fucked up,' Janet said.

'That's putting it politely, Janet. Yes, I'd agree with you there. The creation of this fantasy for this particular psychopath would have been established at some point in his childhood development. It could have been a traumatic event, it could have been abuse, the loss of a loved one, and if he could not cope with what happened or did not have the support around him, he would have developed feelings of hopelessness, self-doubt and an inability to connect or form attachments with others.

'Deep down, psychopaths are lonely people, and this is where the daydreaming and fantasies would have been created in these formative years. I've been hurt, someone needs to pay. I have lost love, I will make someone else suffer that same feeling. Daydreaming turns to fantasy, which is now a safe space for him, a substitute for the relationships he is becoming increasingly unable to foster. His fantasy becomes his go-to place when those feelings of inadequacy and hopelessness rise again, and eventually the fantasy turns into his reality, and that reality becomes murder.'

She wrote on the board:

MOTIVATION

'Anger is a powerful motivator. We know he's angry, so why did he kill? For financial gain? Stephen and Mike weren't rich, the inventory said no money or valuables were stolen and Vee was claiming benefits. Ideology? There is no evidence of that whatsoever. Power or thrill-seeking? Yes – he wants power over his victims, and he will get a thrill from this. A specific psychosis? He may suffer from delusions, visual hallucinations, and he's probably paranoid, which means he will be extremely careful and up to date on police procedure. A sexually based motivation? Possibly a case of sexual revenge as he castrates the men but strangely leaves Vee intact. So what do we have from the list?

'Sexually based anger, power over the victim, with a possible psychosis. This is someone who has a deep-seated hatred of men and women. A killer who wants complete control.

He would have experienced sadistic pleasure from torturing his victims. In the case of Vee, it appears he forced her eyes open with electrical tape so she would have to watch what he was doing.

'He wanted her to feel helpless – and I'm sure she did. He wanted them all to suffer, he wanted to rule over them, to gain back that power that he has lost. That power. What did he lose? You've all heard of the expression *hurt people hurt people*, so he has been hurt and that is what this is about and now he is playing at God.

'A psychopath's brain is wired to seek rewards at any cost. They are after the carrot regardless of the size of the stick, and I don't want to get into too much neurological detail here, but I think it's important for you all to understand this. A psychopath's brain can release up to four times as much dopamine in response to a reward as a non-psychopath's. Imagine the high they must get when they kill, which is why, once they start, they don't want to stop.'

Holly could feel the team's eyes locking onto her every word.

'He is highly organised and will carry a full murder kit to every scene. He is very strong. He can hold a hunting knife that weighs a pound and a half and stab someone nearly fifty times. One-two-three-four ... That's over one minute of constant movement with the arm.'

She rolled back her shoulders and put down her pen.

'So now that we know what goes on in his head, how he reacts and what he thinks. How the hell do we catch him?'

Seventeen

'At the moment he is an invisible man. Three kills and we have nothing.'

Holly went over to the incident board, lost herself for a second, then turned back to the room.

'But of course he is not invisible and in one sense we have everything we need because we have the crime scenes. So we have to work in reverse from these three crime scenes to try and piece together who he is.

'We know he has access to transport as he travels to his kills. Stephen Freer was killed in Croydon, that's here' – she circled it on the map with the black pen – 'Mike Thomas lived in Sunbury' – circling it – 'and Vee was in Brighton. Serial killers like familiarity, so does he know these areas? Yes. Does he live in any of these areas? No. Serial killers won't kill on their own doorstep, for obvious reasons.

'It's just under an hour by car from Sunbury to Croydon, and from Sunbury to Brighton it's maybe an hour and fifteen minutes. Generally a serial killer won't travel too far because it's simply too dangerous. They could get a speeding ticket after the murder, run a red light, have to fill up with petrol at a service station and get spotted on CCTV. But in these instances, the killer travelled a long way in order to choose someone to murder, which makes me believe these three victims cannot be random. If they are not random, it means they have been deliberately chosen, which in turn means our killer has a mission.'

She wrote *MISSION* on the board.

'A mission killer is pragmatic, a perfectionist who will plan his murders with great precision and will kill his victims quickly and efficiently. The kills here are exactly that: quick and efficient. They are also ritualistic, they take place on top of the victim's own beds, with their eyes shredded to nothing and the men castrated. He may see himself as an avenging angel, in which case by killing them he is absolving his victims of any sins or wrongdoings they committed in life.'

'He thinks he's doing God's work?'

'Possibly. Peter Sutcliffe was a mission killer, he said that God told him to rid the world of prostitutes. Herb Baumeister heard the same voices and targeted gay men.'

She took a second – keeping with that thought.

'He will justify his actions as being necessary to rid the world of people he believes to be undesirable. A sixty-five-year-old doctor, a thirty-five-year-old art gallery owner and now an unidentified sex worker believed to be in her forties. On paper they have nothing in common, but something binds them. They are all linked somehow. Janet, how many strangers do you invite into your home?'

'None, I never would, I have two kids.'

'So did Stephen Freer. They weren't there at the time, but these days as a society we generally keep our doors locked and our curtains drawn. There are two ways for the killer to enter someone's property: either he breaks in or he is invited inside. No sign of forced entry was found at any of the properties, so let's go with the second theory for now. If he was invited in, it makes sense that each victim knew him.'

One of the officers raised her hand. Holly hadn't heard her speak before.

'Sergeant Vronsky, ma'am. I was working the Mike Thomas case in 2016 with DI Bishop and we looked into all possible connections. Every single friend or acquaintance in his address book and on his phone was interviewed. Nothing.'

'I know, but I have people that I know or will recognise, but they're not necessarily in my address book. I think we need to cast the net wider. So when you go through the original transcripts, there may be a name in there that we need to look at again that for whatever reason was dismissed. Look for a name beginning with the letter V as well, because now we have a third victim, and with her comes a third circle of friends. I know we talked to a lot of the working girls in Brighton, have they told us any more?'

'Not so far.'

'Okay, because the killer would have watched Vee for some time, so he would have been in Brighton before. These murders would have been planned for weeks, probably months, and with each fantasy he would have refined the journey until it seemed perfect. But of course it wasn't perfect yet because he hadn't carried it out. And this brings me to an interesting point. I believe this killer would have had at least one practice run before he killed Stephen Freer in 2013.'

'So he's killed before?'

'Not necessarily killed – but I think he probably had a trial run with the drugs to see which dosage worked best. He may have used GHB by itself but found it wasn't fast-acting enough so decided to add the chloroform. It might be an idea to look at old cases where an attacker used a combination of both drugs to render a victim unconscious.'

'I'll look into that,' said Sergeant Ambrose.

'Thank you.' A pause. 'So we know our killer is on a mission, what else do we know?'

She moved over to the incident board.

'Keith Hunter Jesperson killed eight women and was called the Happy Face Killer,' she said and drew the symbol on the board.

'Jesperson was a truck driver, and drew the first smiley face on a truck-stop bathroom wall when two other people claimed his first kill. That pissed him off – How dare they. I killed this woman and I want people to know it was me – so he started drawing smiley faces at the crime scenes to let the police know he was the killer.

'Our killer leaves these stickmen drawings. These are his calling cards and they are unique to him. Like Jesperson, he leaves them at the crime scene because he wants us to know he is claiming the kill.'

Holly looked at the drawing found in Verity's bedroom. She pulled it down and held it up for everyone to see.

'It appears as if the killer is drawing his victims. We can see the similarities between the crayon pictures and the real-life people. The one on the left with the knife is the killer. Jagged lines of dark hair, no beard or moustache. He's tall, could be anybody, or maybe he is short and fat and is just drawing himself like this to throw us off. Watch,' and she covered the knife with her hand.

'We take away the knife and he's grinning like a kid.' She dropped her hand. 'We show the knife and he's grinning like a maniac.'

'Or perhaps the stickmen mean nothing?' said Janet.

'They'll mean something. Why go to all that bother unless it's important to him. Richard Ramirez, the Night Stalker, used to draw a pentagram at some of the crime scenes with the victim's lipstick. The Boston Strangler used stockings, scarves or underwear to strangle his victims and whatever he used he always tied in a neat bow and left it around their necks for the police to find. He has never explained himself. But if we look at these killers' victims it brings me to an interesting point – serial killers don't normally cross-pollinate to different genders. A man will kill men and keep killing men, like Denis Nilsen or John Wayne Gacy did, or like Ted Bundy he will only kill women. It's very unusual to suddenly switch from male to female, which means there must be something very special about Vee. He mutilated her face like the other two victims, but didn't go near her genitals. Why not? He respects the woman above all else? The mother, the sacred feminine? Or does he suffer from an Oedipus complex?'

'What is that?'

'It's a desire for sexual involvement with the parent of the opposite sex and a sense of rivalry with the same-sex parent, which would explain the castration of the first two victims. For men it's called Oedipus and for women it's the Electra Complex. Vee was a sex worker, so it might be worth going back to the original files to see if Stephen or Mike ever used prostitutes – which I don't think would have been in the original purview. Mike ran an art gallery – is there a list of all of the artists that sold there?'

'There'll be one somewhere,' said Bishop.

'Manet, Toulouse-Lautrec, Picasso all used prostitutes as their models. Did Vee ever model for any of Mike's artists at the gallery? Is that the connection between the victims? There must be a stock of canvases on their website. See if you can get an inventory and look for any red-headed women who have been painted. If there are any, contact the artist, do a check on them, and see if they can give you the model's name.'

'Will our killer have a psych record?'

'Extremely likely, and they may still be a regular at clinics. We need to find out if any self-admission patients have talked a lot about these crimes while they've been having sessions recently. Concentrate on London institutions, but don't discount some of the bigger ones like Manchester or Edinburgh. Check day-release schemes as well – are any of the patients showing a morbid curiosity about the murders? I think he will want to hide his past and he'll like his anonymity.'

'You think he's married?'

'Possibly, yes. He may well go home to a loving partner who will be oblivious to his secret life, just like Sonia Sutcliffe was to the Yorkshire Ripper. Next we need to check juvenile detention records. Go back to criminal records from early teens and younger. As a child he may have been violent towards a sibling or other children at school, and he may have tortured or killed animals for fun.'

'Seriously?' Thompson said.

'Poking out a puppy's eyes or setting cats on fire isn't an indication of a minor personality flaw – these are disturbing symptoms of severe mental illness. People who do this won't stop at animals, and many of them inevitably progress to violence towards humans. Before he killed seventeen people,

Jeffrey Dahmer practised his butchery skills by cutting up dogs and impaling their heads on sticks, Ian Brady killed his first cat when he was ten. Having said that, it's always hard to predict the age of a killer like this, but given the patience and maturity of the crimes I'd say he has to be in his late thirties to mid-forties, so focus on juvenile records between 1985 and 1995.'

'Sergeant Ingram, Miss Wakefield,' an officer raised a hand. 'I'll cover that.'

'Thank you, sergeant. Contact the UK Medical Register as well as the NHS.'

She turned back to the board and re-capped her pen.

'One more thing – something DCI Walker put in his notes when he was in charge of the investigation in 2013 – *A butcher? Baker? A candlestick maker? We can't discount anyone.* Take note of that. Okay, that's it for now,' she said. 'I'll email through my notes so everybody has a copy.'

'Thank you, Holly,' Bishop said. It looked as if he was about to say something else when a sergeant quickly put down a phone and stood up.

'Sir?'

'What?'

'The man who the sex worker in Brighton recognised driving the Volvo has just been arrested. Douglas Regus – they're bringing him in now.'

'Any news on the other one? Gavin Lefton?'

'No, sir.'

'All right, prep interview room eight. I want to be ready for him in fifteen minutes.'

Eighteen

Douglas Regus exuded hate. It seeped from him like poisoned breath.

He looked almost feral, sitting at the table in the interview room. He had thin straight black hair parted in the middle and his teeth were small, like milk-teeth, as if they had never fully developed. His eyes were dark and slitted. He was thirty-two years old.

His lawyer was called Eleanor Pope. She had instructed her client to say 'no comment' to everything but his name, which was exactly what Douglas was doing. Bishop was still asking questions:

'You understand why you have been brought in today, Douglas?'

'My client is fully aware.'

'Douglas?'

'No comment.'

'A working girl was murdered in Brighton last Friday – that was the third of May.'

'No comment.'

'The girlfriend whom you murdered back in 2011. Her name was Rose, wasn't it?'

'No comment.'

'My client has already done his time for the alleged crime, DI Bishop.'

'It wasn't alleged, Miss Pope. Rose was raped and murdered and your client took a selfie of himself holding the knife. She was a sex worker, wasn't she, Douglas?'

'No comment.'

'When was the last time you were in Brighton?'

'No comment.'

'Have you been to Brighton before?'

'No comment.'

'How about you, Miss Pope, have you ever been to Brighton?'

'I'm sorry?'

'Have you been to Brighton?'

'Yes,' a little flustered, 'but that's irrelevant to this interview.'

'Just curious,' Bishop said. 'I'm going to ask you again, Douglas. Have you ever been to Brighton before?'

'No comment.'

'It's a seaside town. Lots of sun, sand and bars. Quite a few working girls. London getting a bit rough for you? You thinking of trying to get some girls down there?'

'No comment.'

'Thing is, Douglas, one of the other working girls in Brighton recognised your photo when we showed it to her. She said you were driving a Volvo on the night of May third in the red-light district. You propositioned her for sex but said you wouldn't pay.'

'No comment.'

'That was the night the sex worker was murdered.'

'No comment.'

'She was brutally stabbed with a knife. And we already know that's how you like to kill women. We just want to make sure it wasn't you, that's all.'

'Singular, not plural, please, DI Bishop. My client has only killed one woman.'

'But we don't know that do we? Douglas?'

'No comment.'

'The sex worker's name was Vee. Have you ever heard of a sex worker called Vee before?'

'No comment.'

Bishop pulled out an autopsy photo and put it on the table. 'This is Vee.'

Douglas leaned back and closed his eyes.

'No comment,' he said.

'I didn't ask you a question,' said Bishop.

The silence ate up the seconds.

Holly had Douglas's file on the desk in front of her and was reading as she listened. He was a typical London gang member, brought up in a broken home with an absent father and an over-worked and neurotic mother. He had begun with petty crimes like shoplifting, accompanied by his two older brothers, and by the time he was nine he was already carrying a knife. He had been arrested over two hundred times since the age of twelve and spent twelve of the past twenty years behind bars at Feltham, Pentonville and Ipswich. He was a drug dealer and a pimp, had a protection racket and extorted money from local residents. This would be his life forever.

'For the record, Douglas has refused to look at the photo of the victim.'

'No comment.'

'You're getting ahead of yourself again, Douglas.' Bishop took the photo away. 'When was the last time you saw Gavin Lefton, or Lefty as he likes to be called?' Bishop said.

'No comment.'

'Were you in Brighton with Lefty on the evening of May third – that's last Friday?'

'No comment.'

'Have you ever driven a Volvo?'

A long pause and the silence made Holly look up. Douglas opened his eyes and leaned forward.

'No comment?'

'Are you sure, Douglas?'

'No comment.'

'Do you know where the Volvo is? We've been looking for it.'

'No comment.'

'Do you know where Lefty is?'

'No comment.'

'You met Lefty while you were in Pentonville prison, didn't you?'

'No comment.'

'The two of you shared a cell.'

'No comment.'

'He was convicted of rape.'

'No comment.'

'Do you know where he lives, because we would very much like to chat with him as well.'

'No comment.'

'Miss Pope, has your client been made aware again of the Criminal Justice and Public Order Act 1994?'

'He has.'

'Just to reiterate, Douglas,' Bishop said. 'All these no comments will allow a jury to draw their own conclusions if this ever reaches trial. Whether you have failed to mention a fact later relied on in your defence.'

'No comment.'

Douglas swallowed and Holly caught sight of his tiny teeth again. They reminded her of a hamster. He had a cold sore on his lip, a big one, and his nails were bitten down to the quick. Rose, the woman he had murdered, had been stabbed once in the chest. The blade had pierced her heart and she had been dead in less than a minute. They had both been high on meth. Not only had Douglas taken a photo of himself with the murder weapon, but he had sent numerous text messages to his contacts telling them what he had done and asking for advice.

Holly had had enough.

'It's not him,' she said. 'He's violent enough and he hates women, but he doesn't have the cognisant reasoning.'

Douglas's eyes widened and he looked at his lawyer.

'I would prefer if Miss Wakefield would refrain from summarising my client's intelligence.'

'I'm just stating the facts, that's all. You should be grateful, he could be facing a triple murder charge.'

Holly saw Bishop smile for the first time that day when he turned back to Douglas:

'No comment?'

Nineteen

Douglas Regus was free to go.

He seemed confused when he left with his lawyer.

'I think you hurt his feelings,' Bishop said.

'Good.'

The hunt for Lefty and the Volvo was still on, but Holly wasn't holding her breath. It seemed like a dead end, and she didn't think either of them had anything to do with Vee's murder, but she knew the police had to follow it up anyway and eliminate the two men officially. She and Bishop were passing the main reception when someone called out:

'DI Bishop?'

The man wore a poorly cut crumpled dark blue suit. He was fat – beer and nachos fat – and looked to be sixty, maybe sixty-five, it was hard to tell. He offered his hand.

'Andy Brooks, freelance reporter.'

Andy Brooks, Holly thought – the journalist DCI Walker mentioned in his notes.

'I left a few messages with the press office, but they never got back to me.'

He was out of breath and sweating. Holly wondered if he might drop dead.

'How can I help you, Mr Brooks?' Bishop said.

'It's how I can help you, DI Bishop. That's what's important.' He wiped his forehead. 'Can we go somewhere private? Maybe your office? There's something you need to see.'

They walked through the incident room.

Holly noticed Andy glance surreptitiously at the incident board more than once as they walked. In Bishop's office he asked for water rather than coffee and downed a cup quickly and got a refill. Then he reached into his shoulder bag and pulled out two sheets of paper with two slightly different stickman drawings. He put them on Bishop's desk and took a step back.

'What do you think?' he said.

'How did you get hold of these?'

'They were left outside my house on the twelfth of August 2016, three months after Mike Thomas was killed. I'd been covering the story, selling a few pieces to different editors and I knew exactly what they were.'

Holly examined them curiously. The drawings looked similar to the ones on the incident board: the victim's eyes were reduced to black and red scratches and on both, the killer was on the left holding a bloody knife and the victim on the right. In the first one the victim appeared to be male with brown spiky hair — but on the second drawing the victim was a lot smaller. Almost—

'Is that a child?' said Holly.

'I think it's a girl,' said Brooks. 'It looks like she's wearing a skirt and she's got pigtails or something. I don't know if you guys did a missing persons search back then?'

'Do you still have the envelope they came in?' Bishop said.

'I threw it out – I didn't even think about it. So what do you think?'

'Are these the originals?'

'Yeah.'

Holly put on a pair of latex gloves and held one up. They were similar to the others and the colours looked right, but they were messier, less controlled.

'It's hard to tell,' she said.

'Did you show these to DCI Walker?' Bishop said.

'Yeah, and he had them analysed.'

'And what did forensics say?'

'Inconclusive, but that doesn't mean they're not by the killer, right? It just means they couldn't be definite. Look, I know you have victim number three, the sex worker in Brighton, but I'm thinking there are two more bodies back in 2016 that nobody ever found. The killer sent these to me to say, "Hey, I've killed before – why haven't the police found the bodies?" Maybe putting these on the news might help flush out the killer?'

'How?'

'I don't know. He wants the bodies found, right? Maybe that's why he sent the drawings to me in the first place: he wants the publicity?'

'Then why come to us a second time when the forensics test has already come back as no good?'

'Maybe they got it wrong back then? Maybe the tests have got better in three years, I don't know. Walker wouldn't help me last time and he missed a trick, and I want to work with you. I help you, you help me. I want access to what you're doing, you know? Maybe I can ride along with you when you go and talk to people?'

'This isn't a reality show.'

'We all want to see this killer caught, so let's work together. Look, I've had an offer from a national newspaper for these drawings, so let's get these in tomorrow's rags and then we can see what happens.'

'I wouldn't recommend publishing them,' said Holly quickly. 'We don't know enough about him yet. A serial killer will leave calling cards so he can claim the kill. If these are fake, then he will know someone is imitating him and taking away his claim.'

'So?'

She turned to him. His eyes were wet like a fish.

'I don't think that's a good idea,' she said. 'Because if they're not by him – you're going to piss him off.'

'Isn't that a good thing?'

'You really want to piss off a psychopath?'

He shrugged, annoyed.

'Look, I read books; this guy isn't interested in us, he just wants his name in the paper and a headline. So if they are fake and a couple of kids did them for a joke, no harm no foul. How long will it take to do another forensic test?' he said.

'Twenty-four to forty-eight hours,' said Bishop.

'Christ, it's not like the films, is it? Maybe you can speed it up a bit? Come on, Bill, I hear good things about you.'

'I'll get them tested again,' Bishop said, 'but until we get the results, I don't want any newspaper printing them, okay?'

Andy Brooks smiled but it wasn't pleasant. He stared at the drawings for a few seconds as if weighing something up, then he nodded.

'Sure. I'll leave them in your capable hands and wait for the phone call.'

101

He left the office and Holly got up and closed the door behind him.

'I don't trust him,' she said. 'Walker was vehement about Andy Brooks and said the reporter was trying to destroy his career. Did Walker ever mention these drawings to you? They weren't in his notes.'

'No, but if it was just between the two of them I wouldn't have seen them anyway.' A beat. 'I'm going to give him a call.'

Bishop put it on speakerphone – no reply, so he left a message. He gloved up and picked up the two new stickmen drawings, studied them for a second then dropped them on his desk and rubbed his eyes.

'What do you think?' he said.

'This is the killer's calling card – I don't think he would take them from the murder scene and send them to someone; it doesn't make sense. He wants us to find the bodies – if he did this, he would probably give us an address to go to as well.'

'It doesn't fit the MO, does it?' he said.

'No.'

The phone rang. It was Walker.

'Andy Brooks just paid us a visit at the station,' Bishop said.

Walker almost shouted:

'Brooks? That guy's a fucking dick!'

'He brought us a couple of stickman drawings for us to look at.'

'Piece of shit! We had both of them tested and forensics said the results were inconclusive and he still threatened to publish them.'

'Do you remember what was wrong with them?'

'Something to do with one of the colours that was used. There was half a yellow or orange crayon found underneath the chest of drawers in Stephen Freer's bedroom in 2013. A blood-sniffer dog located it the day after the body had been moved. The orange matched the colours used on both the drawings found at the crime scenes, but didn't match the Andy Brooks examples.'

'That's pretty conclusive.'

'I can't remember where the review is, but it will be in the original case files – 2016 I think he brought them in—'

'That's what he said.'

'So it will be logged online. Are you going to test them again?'

'Due diligence, and we have the third drawing now.'

'His are fake, I'm telling you.'

'What do you know about Andy Brooks?'

'He's dodgy as hell. He was one of the journalists caught up in the 2011 Leveson enquiry. You remember that right? The phone-hacking scandal.'

'I remember.'

'Son-of-a-bitch – he had a wife, Penny, I think her name was, and a mistress and a massive coke habit. He ended up in a clinic, and when he got out he went freelance and sold fake news and celebrity gossip, made a fortune, but most of it went back up his nose.'

'How come you know so much about him?'

'He tried to destroy me in the papers, Bill! He kept misquoting me – dogging me – he was a nightmare, so yeah, I did my research, I got some dirt on the bastard as well. I was hoping he'd smoked himself to death, but obviously not.'

'All right, well thanks for the callback, I'd better crack on with this.'

'Let me know what happens.'

'Will do.'

Bishop hung up, called forensics and Holly watched him as he slipped the two drawings into an envelope. He pulled up the original case files on his computer.

'Walker was right,' he said. 'The wax crayons were Crayola, but forensics were concerned about the use of a different shade of orange on the Brooks pictures. The drawings left at the Stephen Freer and Mike Thomas crime scenes were analysed and according to the colour chart had the colour "burnt orange" in them, and the two Andy Brooks handed in had the colour orange. The first is an eight count, the latter's a sixty-four count – whatever that means. To the naked eye there's not much difference, but under a microscope they're worlds apart.'

Twenty

Holly went to the canteen on a sandwich run and by the time she got back to the incident room Bishop was in his office talking with three men.

One of them was Sergeant Kenny from Vice, the other two she didn't recognise. The door was closed. Holly pushed past desks until she spotted Janet Acton.

'What's happening?'

'Vice think they have a lead on Vee,' the DI whispered. 'Apparently she *was* a sex worker in Soho before she went to Brighton, but there seems to be a problem.'

'What?'

'The girl who said she knew Vee is part of an undercover immigration operation and can't be taken off the street.'

'They have to, this is important.'

'I think that's what Bishop is telling them.'

Raised voices could be heard, and at the end of it, Bishop exited his office, looking grim as he took Holly's arm.

'We can eat later, let's go.'

*

Bishop drove fast into Central London and parked at Charing Cross police station on Agar Street.

They walked in silence; Holly could tell he was thinking ten steps ahead. The informant was expecting them.

'Here we are,' he said.

It was an open doorway between a dry cleaner's and a Lebanese restaurant in Green's Court. The corridor inside was well-lit and led to a set of carpeted stairs. There were two red signs inside that said *MODELS*. Bishop had explained what they would see on their way over. This open doorway was known as a 'walk-up', it gave access to a flat above which got around the prostitution laws of the Street Offences Act of 1959. They would not reveal their true identities for fear of disclosing the undercover informant.

Bishop pressed a bell. A female voice answered:
'Yes?'

'Gerald Blackwell and Catherine Jones,' Bishop said.

'Second floor.'

'I'll go first,' Bishop said, and led the way.

On the second floor there was a single door with a hand-written name on a piece of paper – *Grace*. Another bell which Bishop rang. The door opened and revealed a small Chinese woman with braided hair.

She gave them towels and pointed a finger, which they followed to another door. No bell. Bishop hesitated and the woman behind said: 'Go in.'

He turned the handle and they entered.

It was like walking into bubblegum – Holly had never seen so much pink. The walls, the bed, the carpet and the woman with her pink hair, her lingerie and her transparent, towering heels. Everything smelled like popcorn. The woman wore performance make-up and Holly guessed her age to be forty plus. She was on the other side of slim.

'Gerald and Catherine, right?'

She was pure London cockney and suddenly the pink wasn't quite so girly.

'Yes.'

'Shut the door, you can leave the towels on the bed. There's nowhere to sit unless you want the bed? I'll stand, I need to give my back a rest.' She crossed to the door, opened it a crack and looked out. Closed it and took a fresh pack of Marlboro and lit up. Bishop and Holly stayed standing.

'You've got two minutes,' Grace said.

'Tell me about Vee.'

'I never knew her real name, she was always just Vee to me. I first remember seeing her in '98. Her red hair – that was her trademark. She was like Pretty Woman. She was strung-out back then – bad on crack, but she was sweet.'

'How old was she?'

'Seventeen, eighteen when she got here.'

'From where?'

'She wasn't London that's for sure, and she wasn't up north, no accent at all really, but she spoke well, like posh, but maybe that was all part of the act. She worked by herself for a while – we were all still on the streets then and in the back of the sex shops. I teamed up with her for a couple of months, I'd watch her back and she would watch mine. During the day she used to love to see the matinee shows in the West End. I'd go with her and we'd sit in the peanut seats. She loved it, she was like a kid again. She was a stripper for a bit as well, worked at Ye Old Axe in Shoreditch, but only for a few weeks. She couldn't keep off the drugs, that was her downfall. Then she disappeared from London for a couple of years, I don't know why, and when she came back, she had changed.'

'In what way?' Holly said.

A pause and Grace took a sip of something from a black cup.

'Quieter, more out of it. Dunno, it was hard to make her smile.'

'Do you know where she went?'

'No, but we all travel quite a bit. Sometimes to avoid the law, sometimes to pick up new clients.'

'Were there any clients you can think of that might have wanted to hurt her?'

'Clients? No.' She took a long drag. 'When she came back, she found a new pimp.'

'Do you remember who?' Bishop said.

'Reggie Cross – he's dead, died of AIDS in 2003.' She checked her watch. A frown. 'She was with him until he died, then someone else came on the scene.'

'It wasn't a pimp called Douglas Regus was it?'

'Never heard of him. No, this guy was a dealer. Nasty piece of work from Croatia.'

'Does he have a name?'

'He does.'

A silence.

'Come, on, Grace,' Bishop said. 'The girls in Brighton mentioned she might have been seeing a dealer, but they thought he was dead.'

Grace sniffed and shook her head. Her eyes shone. The facade was slipping.

'One question first,' she said, 'was it as bad as they said it was in the newspapers?'

'Yes,' said Bishop. 'I'm afraid it was.'

She nodded as if she already knew and put her cigarette out.

'The pimp's not dead,' she said. 'His name is Stefan Spenski and he's in Wandsworth prison.'

Twenty-one

'Have you heard of Stefan Spenski?' Holly said.

'No. I'll get a rap sheet from Vice and sort out a Visitor Order for Wandsworth prison. We'll go and talk to him tomorrow morning.'

They had stopped in a restaurant called Rabbit near Seven Dials in Covent Garden. Wooden benches and chairs, easy on the eye décor with wild seasonal produce. They ordered lunch and water for them both.

'Sergeant Kenny said they've had reports of a red-headed woman matching Vee's description working in Portsmouth as well before she moved to Brighton,' Bishop said.

'London first, Portsmouth and then Brighton,' Holly said. 'She's been working her way along the coast, I wonder why? And for two years she disappeared.'

'She may have gone abroad. Without her real name we have no chance of tracking her movements; she could have gone anywhere in Europe.'

They paused for thought as the starters arrived. Aubergine

humus that was rich and tasted smoky. Holly brought him up to speed on Walker's files.

'He has a room in the basement still dedicated to the case. He still goes through the files every now and then. I don't think he can let go.'

'I don't blame him. He spent nearly six years of his life on it. Apart from the intense dislike of Andy Brooks, was there anything else you found that might help?'

'He had a few thoughts, but they're all circumstantial so far.'

For a split second Holly had a vision of Andy Brooks as their killer, but physically he was all wrong and he wasn't exactly a figure of authority. She moved on: 'I met Walker's girlfriend,' she said.

'What's she like?'

'She's nice. She invited me to dinner. Asked if I had a significant other – I don't – but I was thinking maybe we could go there together. Not a date night obviously.'

'Obviously not a date.' Bishop smiled. 'Friday next week?'

'Sounds good to me,' and Holly smiled too. 'I want to talk to Walker over a bottle of wine and try and get some more intel about you.'

'*Intel?* Fuck me, you in the military now?'

Holly grinned. 'I want to know why you never told me you were SF?'

'You've started using our acronyms as well?' He laughed. 'We were a small ODA team – that's Operational Detachment Alphas – with twelve members. I was the officer in charge of mission and logistics planning.'

'Was Max part of that team?'

Holly was referring to the ex-army sergeant who had saved her life on the Pickford case.

'He was. He's been through some pretty bad shit. It's never a particularly pleasant story.'

'No, I didn't think it would be.' Then she said: 'It's your birthday next week.'

His face lit up enough to show he was pleased she had remembered but then:

'It's Sunday, but I won't be doing anything.'

'I know.'

He didn't make eye contact, just shrugged his heavy shoulders and made a big deal about filling up the water glasses. He'd already told her last year he refused to celebrate his birthday because his fiancée had been killed on the same day. Holly wondered if he still thought about her every day. If he still loved Sarah as much as Holly still loved her parents. They might be gone but her feelings hadn't changed – if anything, they had grown stronger. They would never be replaced. Perhaps neither would Sarah.

The main courses arrived. The plates were hot, the meat sizzling and she was trying to trace her own steps when the talk drifted away from the case, and Bishop asked:

'Who was the first psychopath you met?'

'Officially?'

'Yeah.'

'I was twenty-three years old and I had just finished my doctorate in forensic psychology at Bristol University. As part of the graduation process I was given the opportunity to conduct an assessment interview on a man called Donald Sharp. He had been found guilty of raping and murdering a woman named Lucy Clemments on Clapham Common in 1999. I don't know if you remember the case?'

'No.'

'He was convicted and spent six years in Feltham prison. Now, I knew all about clinical psychology and the application of psychological theory and practice in relation to the criminals, the court, the victims, but I had never been hands-on. This was my first proper interview. I was nervous, I wanted to make a good impression, I didn't want to let anyone down.

'When I first entered his cell he looked at me and I felt like I was his next meal,' Holly said. 'One of the scariest things I have ever seen. His eyes pinned me to the wall. I sat there pretending to read my notes for a few seconds and in those first moments something interesting happened – his eyes suddenly switched from predatory to caring and he asked if I needed a drink and was the seat comfortable? I said I was fine, thank you, and the seat was fine, but thank you for asking. I felt a little of the tension drain away. After all, this was a man who had a violent history of rape and murder, but according to his doctors he had turned over a new leaf. He had recently been examined by the review board and independent clinicians, and I had been granted the interview so as to give me experience of a present-day rehabilitation.

'He apologised if he appeared fidgety, and said he was nervous because I reminded him of his younger sister. He was thirty-five years old, attractive, and I think I actually blushed when he said that. His sister had been in a skiing accident two weeks before and he was desperate to see her again. She had been a lifeline to him during his time in prison. I was starting to relax. If *he* was nervous, how did he think *I* felt?' Holly paused and smiled. 'The truth was, he wasn't nervous, because psychopaths have no fear, it's an alien concept to them. He didn't care if I was thirsty or if my chair was comfortable, and he didn't have a sister. He lied to me about everything to get me to relax, and it worked. I transferred my trust to him. Because when we are at ease, we lose our edge, and if we lose our edge we lose our ability to see the predator in front of us. I realised afterwards that I had been manipulated before the interview had even begun.

'Donald Sharp was released two weeks later and within three months had raped and murdered another woman, Belle Rashimon. He was rearrested and is due to be released in 2024. Apparently, he's a changed man. Again. He will rape and murder when he comes out, that is a fact, as he cannot stop himself. More importantly, he doesn't want to.'

Bishop nodded and watched her for a while.

'This guy won't stop, will he, Holly?'

'Never,' she said, and felt herself go cold. 'Everybody has a pattern, no matter how contrite. We get up in the morning, we drink our coffee, we read the newspaper and check our emails. That's our routine. We all do it, and this killer is no exception. We need to get inside his head and learn his routine and why he chooses the victims.'

'Unless they're random.'

'If these killings are totally random and there is no pattern then we really don't have much chance of ever finding him. He'll be careful, and by following reports in the press he'll know exactly where we are in the case. He will binge-watch the news, because the coverage will be exhilarating. And he will be closer than we think.'

'What do you mean?'

'He may be outside watching this station as we speak. He'll know we're in here talking about him. He may even call the station with a soft lead that he read about in the papers and pretend to help, or he might follow one of the officers home and bump into them "by accident" – *sorry, didn't see you there* – and then he'll be on his way home all the time thinking, I was right in your hands, but you missed me. See you later, sucker . . .'

She finished talking and found herself watching him. She would never be able to forget his eyes. Dark blue like the sea in the falling sun.

The coffee arrived. He poured in cream and sugar and stirred.

'Interesting profile you gave earlier,' he said.

'Interesting case.'

He nodded, then yawned.

It made her yawn back.

'Just checking,' he said, and smiled.

Twenty-two

When Bishop dropped Holly off, he drove straight home.

He lived in a Georgian terraced house off Duke Road in Chiswick, west London. After he left the military, he had stayed at STOLL in Fulham for two months, an estate that helped veterans find their feet when they first came home, while he looked for somewhere more permanent. This coincided with his parents downsizing, so with his army pension and money left over from their move they had helped him buy the house. He had been there twelve years now and still couldn't get used to coming home. Home had always been a tent, a cabin or bunk bed on a different continent in extreme weather, but the old bricks here felt good to his touch. Sometimes it felt as if the clay, the sand and the lime had been standing there just waiting for him for over two hundred and fifty years.

He poured himself a whisky and lit a cigarette, then sat in the living room in a chair that faced the television. He didn't know where the remote was, but he didn't care as he didn't watch much TV unless it was a documentary, and he stayed away from the news, so instead, he read. The living room had six shelves either side of the fireplace and each shelf was crammed with books. His bedroom was the same and there were more books stacked in his office. He went to the library and borrowed at least half a dozen books each month on topics he knew nothing about, which could range from eighteenth-century English porcelain to how to fly a kite in Japan. He saw it not only as a challenge but a way to take his mind off the cases. He knew some of the murder squad officers spent hours in the garden at the weekends to forget what they had seen during the week, but Bishop read. He always had at least a dozen books in a stack by his bed, and at night he had his ritual: he would turn on the Radio 4 shipping forecast, lie on his left side and read until he only had one eye open.

Then he would try and sleep.

But sleep was always sporadic.

Whisky, sleeping pills, other drugs. He'd had his fair share over the years, but had turned a corner recently and he had Holly to thank for that. She had come into his life less than two years ago, but every time they worked a case he looked forward to seeing her. There was a spark and he knew it. Something he had never expected to feel or see again after Sarah had been killed. When he had come back to Civvy Street, it had been recommended he see a therapist about the death of his fiancée. He had gone to a few sessions, but had been half-drunk and hadn't been an entirely willing patient. Now he felt different and had started seeing one again for the past six weeks – a Dr Young.

He had some expensive pieces of art in the living room, but there was only one photo hanging on the far wall and it was a photo of Sarah. It was large, black-and-white, with sand dunes and mess huts in the background, and she was dressed in camouflage, wearing her beret with the Army Air Corps insignia. It had been taken in Afghanistan two years before she had been killed.

Dr Young had suggested that he take it down.

He had, three weeks ago, and then had put it back up after five minutes. It felt somehow as if he were cheating on her. He had talked about how it made him feel with Dr Young, and she had urged him to try again. He had, and each time he managed to keep it off the wall for a little longer. Last night he had slept with it resting against the couch and put it back after breakfast. Tonight he would do the same thing.

He knew he had changed now he was out of the military. Back then he was obsessed with his job, now he understood that sometimes you had to take a step back for the sake of self-preservation, and in that respect he knew he wasn't like Holly. On every murder case she turned her flat into a living incident board, but he couldn't do that here. He had to leave the mayhem at the police station because if he didn't he would think about nothing else and he would go insane.

The last few days had been hectic – with clues, suspects and interviews, but murders were like the seasons, they came and went, except this particular one was a road he had already walked, and for the first time since he'd taken over the MIT he could feel the pressure mounting. What could he do to solve this case that DCI Walker and the others hadn't tried? What did he bring to the table? He briefed Chief Constable Franks on their progress once a day, sometimes twice if he felt it was necessary, but there was an unspoken message in the silence between the phone calls and the frustration was building.

He was happy Holly was back on the team. Not only was

118

she one of the smartest women he had ever known, but he liked her more each day. The two of them worked well together and he wondered what she was doing right now. Not smoking and drinking whisky and about to read a book, that was for sure. He picked up the hardback with a sigh and realised he must have been really out of it when he chose this one.

The Knitters Almanac.

According to the bookmark he was on page 57, tackling double-knits and warp knits, but he couldn't remember a single thing he'd read. He flicked the pages absently – there were a few illustrations further along – something to look forward to.

Had it really come to this?

He took another hit of whisky, turned back to page one and started reading all over again.

Twenty-three

After Holly got home, she called Wetherington Hospital to change her shifts until further notice.

The case would be taking up all of her time and the hospital were always happy to oblige, but it also meant she wouldn't get the chance to see her brother. Lee was doing well on his new meds; they had switched him back to Risperidone, which seemed to control his anger, but his mood swings were still volatile and now he had a problem with balance.

She asked to talk to him, but he refused, and the last time she had visited she had suggested he write to her, but since then he had been put back on suicide watch and wasn't allowed any sharps. She missed him horribly – they had been so close before their parents were murdered and they had been separated by the foster care system – and after this case she promised herself she would see more of him.

She thanked the hospital and hung up, feeling slightly empty, made herself a hot chocolate and began to review the case files again.

She noticed an article written by Andy Brooks in her

scrapbook about the second murder victim, Mike Thomas, and his wife, Alison Paton. According to the reporter, Alison had been having chemotherapy for breast cancer at the time of the attack.

She googled the murder on her Mac and found another article Brooks had written claiming Mike had had numerous affairs while he was married to Alison. His wife denied the allegation, but Holly opened up Walker's notes – there was something she had seen there – *I spoke to the second victim's wife – her name is Alison. Apparently they had been having a few marital problems and she was at her parents the weekend he was murdered* – and Holly wondered if that was what the marital problems were? Her husband's infidelity? And perhaps that was why Alison didn't want the press talking to her again, because she didn't want everything to be rehashed on social media.

Another article stated she had remarried within the year and was pregnant. She was in remission from the cancer and she and her second husband were excited about the start of their new life together. The article was a year and a half old and Holly wondered if the pregnancy had been a success.

She found the case notes on Alison and read her witness statement: she had been visiting her parents in Cheshire the weekend Mike had been killed, and returned on Sunday night to find the body. Holly noted the new address she had moved to, it was in Cheam in Surrey.

She called Bishop.

'What are you doing?' she said.

'Reading.'

'The case files?'

A pause.

'No ... something far more depressing.'

Holly smiled, then:

'Alison, Mike's wife. I think we should talk to her.'

'She may be a little reluctant.'

'Walker thought she may have been having marital problems, and the press said her husband had been having an affair. Was it true?'

'I don't think we followed that line of enquiry. You think if he was seeing another woman she could have been a witness to something?'

'It's always possible.'

There was a long pause, then he said:

'I'll set it up for tomorrow afternoon.'

'Thank you. Enjoy your book.'

They both hung up at the same time and she stared at the copies of the stick figure drawings on the coffee table. She passed them from hand to hand, a puzzled look on her face as though recalling a memory. There were lines at the edges of some of the pages, right angles and squiggles that meant nothing to her but could have meant everything to the killer. She re-arranged them together, turned them over, picked up the one of Verity: dead on the bed with her big head and teeth and a crude attempt at a triangle dress.

She took a sheet of A4 paper from the printer and drew a figure of herself. The head first, then a stick for the body, arms and legs, then three lines in a triangle to make the dress. It was too narrow, so she rubbed the dress out, but the pencil lines left an impression in the paper so she started again. With a red pencil rummaged from a kitchen drawer she scribbled some blood and stared at it, semi-satisfied.

She held it up to the light then put it aside and started to read Vee's sobriety diary. It was mishmash of AA and NA

meetings, locations, times, telephone numbers and sponsor initials.

Meet RS – 2 o'clock – St Peter's church.

RS – Robbie Sweep, her AA sponsor? It had to be.

*I'm not perfect with or without alcohol. Bad mood today – condoms
and dickheads.*

Two days later:

RS call and chat. Coffee. Felt shit.

Cryptic clues amongst the scribbles and looping circles in
black biro.

Love me or hate me – both are in my favour.

Days turned to weeks and then months amongst the sched-
ule of meetings, and on every day were written the words – *All
it takes is faith and trust in myself.* The same quote for 278 days
until the morning she had been murdered. Good days and bad
days always have their triggers, Holly thought. What made
you so determined to stay sober and drug-free this time?

Holly read the autopsy report again and noted Angela had
concluded from the scars on Vee's wrists the suicide attempt
had been at least ten years ago, if not more.

Holly ran the tips of her fingers over the inside of her own
wrist. She had tried it once. Stared at the silver blade of the
kitchen knife and counted the seconds. No one cares. No one
cares. If am the one doing the pain then it isn't anybody else
doing it to me. Nobody will even notice. I want the voices in
my head to go away. I have had so much trauma and nothing
has been resolved. My heart is lying in the middle of the road
and everybody walks past and nobody sees it. There is no way
out. It will be very peaceful and I will just fade away.

And as she had pressed the blade into her skin, her foster
mother, Maureen, had walked into her bedroom.

'Dinner's ready,' she had said, and had paused at the door and come back inside.

'Don't do it, love,' she said. Holly could remember her voice as if it were yesterday. 'You're not broken, Holly. None of us are really broken.' She had sat next to Holly and put an arm around her, leant back and stroked her hair. 'I'm not going to take the knife off you, because I know that won't stop you. But I'm not going to leave this room without you. How does that sound?'

Holly had started to cry and they had lain like that together until the next morning.

She picked up her phone and called her surrogate mother. It went to answer machine.

'Maureen, it's Holly,' she faltered for a second. 'I don't call you enough, I know I don't. But I just wanted to say I love you and thank you for everything. Not a day goes by that I don't think of you. Speak soon.'

She put the phone down, and for a moment could fix her eyes on nothing. The incident board above her fireplace was blurry and she suddenly realised it was tears and wiped at her eyes irritably.

Twenty-four

Holly woke with memories of Maureen and a message from Bishop.

The Volvo had been tracked down to a field in Surrey. It had been abandoned and set on fire and the VIN number revealed it had been stolen a week before Vee's murder and the plates had been swapped. Bishop was going with forensics to the abandoned car, but in the meantime he had organised a Visitor Order for her at Wandsworth prison to visit Vee's pimp, Stefan Spenski.

She arrived thirty minutes early, having taken the Northern Line to Tooting Bec and then the number 219 bus to the County Arms pub; after that she walked the rest of the way. The prison was built in 1851, refurbished in 1989 and was one of the largest prisons in western Europe, holding a maximum of 1628 prisoners.

Holly passed through a metal door and entered a large rectangular room with rows of bolted-down plastic chairs. There was a receptionist behind a glass panel and several doors to her right. Holly had a pound coin for the locker and put away her handbag and phone and took a seat on one of the chairs. Visiting started at 9 a.m. and the waiting room was already busy. Brothers, sisters, mums and dads; there were babies and toddlers too, the latter playing an enthusiastic game of tag. One of the babies started to cry, which set off the other one, then the toddlers looked like they were about to join in when the receptionist called:

'Holly Wakefield?'

Holly went up to the counter.

'Prisoner's name and number?'

'Stefan Spenski, 207789,' Holly said.

'VO and ID, please.'

She handed over the Visitor Order and her driving licence.

'Have you been here before?'

'I have.'

'No personal belongings allowed past these doors. You can use the lockers to store items. Do you have a pound?'

'I've already done it.'

'You are allowed to take a maximum of thirty pounds sterling through and any essential baby items.'

'Yes.'

'You are only allowed minimal physical contact at the start and end of your visit. There will be no long or passionate embraces or kisses as they are not permitted and may result in your visit being terminated. Do you understand?'

Holly hadn't planned on any passionate kisses but said:

'Yes.'

'Once seated, the prisoner is not allowed to leave his seat and move around the visits hall. There is a tea bar where you can purchase hot and cold drinks and snacks for yourself and your prisoner. The prisoner can only eat these items during the course of the visit. There is a toilet and children's play area. If you need the toilet, you will be accompanied by an officer and searched before and after you go. If the prisoner you are visiting needs the toilet then we will terminate the visit. Understand?'

'Yes.'

The receptionist kept the driving licence but handed back the VO and pushed a button. A metallic thunk and one of the doors to her right opened and Holly went through to a corridor. Ahead was the main prison and she was searched and patted down by a female guard, then asked to go through the metal detector. She was patted down again on the other side then told to open her mouth. To her right, watching her intently, was a passive drug detection dog. Kept on a lead at all times they were trained not to bark at visitors but simply wander over and sit quietly next to someone when the smell of illegal narcotics was detected.

After the all-clear, she made her way through another door and along a corridor that had a mirror-like floor and smelled of disinfectant. Another guard greeted her at the visits hall, checked her VO and sent her through. The prisoner was already seated and Holly recognised Stefan Spenski from his mugshot.

He was forty-three and virtually hairless. A bald head, bald arms, yet somehow he had an attempt at a beard. A stag's antlers – fluff on his chin. A narrow face with a mulberry-coloured birthmark on his left cheek.

Bishop had sent his file over and she had read it on the way.

Spenski was a man who liked to make money. He also liked to be in the presence of women he could control. He had started pimping in Lambeth, south London, when he was in his early twenties, having spent three years sharing a cell on drugs charges with a pimp who had imparted the knowledge to him. On his release, he had moved to Portsmouth and had been there ever since. His motto was 'let the whore do the time and the pimp pay the fine', and it was always hard for the CPS to pin anything on him because he had very little contact with his stable of women. He always led with his hand, not with his dick, so took money but rarely slept with his women, that way he could put them in debt straight away and they would be his. A vicious cycle that few women ever managed to escape from.

Holly pulled out the chair opposite and was about to sit when:

'Coffee would be nice. Milk and sugar,' Stefan said.

He spoke good English with barely an accent. Holly went to the tea bar, bought him a KitKat and a packet of Marlboro as well. She laid them on the table and took her seat.

He picked up the tea and slurped it with relish like a child, lit a cigarette and opened the KitKat. Then he took a big bite of chocolate and a hit on the cigarette. He was doing everything at once. Cramming the experience in, worried he might be done any second and have to go back to his cell. He noticed Holly watching him.

'It's staff-training day every Wednesday. That's why they're always short-staffed on the wards, so we're kept in. I've got an hour, I'm going to use it,' he said with a mouth full of choco-late. 'Where's the cop? I was told there would be two of you.'

'Just me, Stefan.'

'And you're a shrink, right?'

'That's right.'

'You're pretty for a shrink.'

Moving on.

'You were told what happened to Vee?'

The mulberry birthmark got darker.

'My cellmate tried to read me the gory details, but I told him to shut up. Have you found the killer yet?'

'No, and we're hoping you can help. We need more information about her.'

'I don't know much. She was one of the smart ones, which meant she kept herself to herself and never talked about her past. A lot of the girls don't want us knowing stuff, we know about them we get leverage, so the smart ones keep their mouths shut.'

'Where did you first see her?'

'King's Cross. I came down from Portsmouth and spotted her red hair from a mile away. Thought she could be good, and she was. She was a kid, working the streets like a pro, but she wasn't. She was living at St Mungo's, you know it?'

'No.'

'Homeless shelter on Birkenhead Street. We were introduced but she didn't take to me. I came back a year later and she had disappeared.'

The timeline seemed to match Grace's account.

'Do you know where?'

Stefan took some tea and brushed his lips with the back of his hand.

'There was talk she had a kid, but it might have been a rumour. Happens a lot, though. It was probably a john if it was true, you know what they're like, an extra fifty quid if they don't use a condom. Maybe she'd come off the pill – had to give her body a rest and it was just bad timing. Then when she came back she went with a pimp called Reggie something.'

'Reggie Cross.'

129

'That's right, but after Reggie died she needed security and I provided it. I took her back with me and set her up in a flat in Portsmouth.'

'And she never talked about her child?'

'Never. Like I said, maybe it was just a rumour.'

He finished the cigarette and lit another. Looked over as the door to the hall opened behind Holly. Footsteps and chatter as a family made their way through the tables and chairs and found a spot at the other side of the hall. All of a sudden Holly had to raise her voice to be heard.

'We're trying to find out her real name.'

'Vanessa, Valerie, she changed it all the time.'

'But it always began with a V?'

'That's what I'm saying. She was in Portsmouth working for me for six years then she said she wanted to move on so she paid off her debt.'

'Her debt?'

'Drugs. She had a habit and I kept her high.'

'How did she pay it off?'

'She came up with the cash. I thought she was holding out on me but the other girls said she had another income.'

'Do you know what from?'

'Knitting fucking socks? I don't know. Maybe she had a sugar daddy, but I got my money.'

'How much?'

'I'm not telling you, but it was more than a working girl can earn in five years. The debt was paid, that's all you need to know. Then she left me for Brighton.'

'Do you know why she chose Brighton?'

'No, and she never contacted me again. I went to try and find her a few times, but she had changed her number. I like the sea air, but I'm not welcome in Brighton – there's people there that don't like me – I don't know why.' He smiled, but his eyes were cold. 'Let me ask you a question, shrink-wrap. I get a lot of letters from women, you know? Fan mail, if you want to call it that. Why do they do that? Write to me in prison when they don't know me.'

'Some are just curious; some genuinely want to help.'

'Sending photos of their tits? That doesn't help me. Helps them.' He tapped the ash into the KitKat wrapper as Holly removed two photos from her jacket and placed them on the table.

'Stephen Freer and Mike Thomas,' she said.

'Are these the first two victims?'

'Yes. One was from Croydon, the other from Sunbury. Do you know if Vee ever had any clients in those towns?'

'Not when she was working for me.'

'Never?'

'Maybe when she was working for Reggie?'

He looked at her curiously. Another cigarette died.

'When I get out of here, I'm gonna find this killer for you,' he said.

'We're going to find him before that, Stefan, trust me.'

He drank air from the empty cup and lowered it to the table as if he knew their conversation had come to an end. He finished his KitKat in one bite.

'When's the funeral?' he asked.

'Next week.'

'Send some flowers.'

'I will,' Holly said.

Twenty-five

The Volvo was a charred husk.

Bishop watched the car from the edge of the field. There were two police vans next to it and a tent had been erected. It was usually a pasture for cows and there were discs of dried cow shit everywhere. The DCI in charge was a woman he had never met before, DCI Lawrence, and Bishop got the feeling she never missed a trick. She was shaped like a box, but moved like a hare, and was hacking over to him now.

'Did SOCO show you the head?' she said.

'No.'

She turned and shouted at the field:

'Pete? Bring it here!'

A SOCO suit shuffled towards them carrying a sports bag. He nearly tripped on a cow-pat when he got close.

'It was found behind the passenger seat,' DCI Lawrence said. 'Open it up then, Pete.'

The SOCO did and inside was a charcoaled human head.

'Gross, right?'

'I doubt very much it's connected to our case,' Bishop said. 'Very different MO.'

'Good, because we think the head belongs to a seventeen-year-old-boy by the name of Gregor McMillan. He hasn't been seen since Saturday and his brother posted on social media that he couldn't contact him. His body parts were identified yesterday, they were found in two bags in a forest in Tufnell Park. He was a known drugs runner, probably killed as a warning by his rivals. It'll be some time before a proper ID, but I'll let you know.'

'Thank you.'

They both stared at the car for a while.

'Why were you searching for this Volvo then?' she said.

'A sex worker in Brighton was killed last week and the Volvo was seen in the red-light district the same night.'

'What night?'

'Thursday night, Friday morning. We had trouble tracking it, but we'll pass on all the CCTV. We've already interviewed the driver, Douglas Regus, but there were two of them in the car. The other one was a guy called Gavin Lefton, who we haven't managed to find yet.'

'Lefty?'

'Yeah – you know him?'

'I think we've already got him.'

'You have?'

'He was picked up last night in Battersea on a possession charge. Hold on.'

She grabbed her phone. Speed-dialled:

'Dispatch, this is DCI Lawrence. Do we still have a Gavin Lefton in custody? . . . We do?'

Bishop felt his heart skip a beat.

'Great,' said the DCI. 'Keep him there and get the CPS to hold off on the drugs charge, we might be able to get him for murder. I'm in a field full of shit with a very nice DI from Hammersmith MIT who has some CCTV of him along with a Douglas Regus in the Volvo so it looks like we can charge them both … Bring Mr Regus in as well, please. Thank you. Will do.'

She hung up.

'You want to come back to the station for the interview?' she said.

'No, thanks.'

It was looking more than ever as though Douglas and Lefty were involved in a drugs spat and had nothing to do with Vee's death, which discounted their only real strong lead.

'The murder of the sex worker in Brighton you're investigating,' DCI Lawrence said. 'It's not connected to the cold-case file that's been reopened is it?'

'That's the one,' said Bishop and he felt suddenly weary. He was starting to get cold despite the sun and he thought it best to make a move.

'Thank you, DCI Lawrence,' he said.

'Thank you,' she said, and they shook hands, then added: 'Good luck with the case.'

He nodded and started to walk back to his car.

Everybody was saying that to him now and it was really starting to annoy him.

Twenty-six

No sooner had Holly got back to her flat from Wandsworth than Bishop came to pick her up.

They updated each other as he drove.

'And Spenski had no idea who the father might be?' Bishop said.

'He wasn't even sure if the rumour was true. If Vee did get pregnant, she never mentioned the baby to him.'

'And he doesn't know who this sugar daddy was?'

'All he knows is she managed to pay off her debt.'

There was a silence as they both thought things through.

'And Douglas and Lefty are off the suspect list?' she said.

Bishop nodded.

'Never seen a burnt head in a bag before,' he said as he pulled over and parked. They were in a residential housing estate in Plumstead, south London, about forty minutes from Holly's flat. He opened a file and handed it over.

'Alison Paton was thirty-three when she married Mike Thomas. She's got a couple of DUIs and has been to Refuge a few times, do you know it?'

135

A woman's shelter with locations across the UK.

'While she was married to Mike?' Holly said.

'Before they were engaged. We spoke to her about it at the time of his murder, it happened once when she miscarried and then again when she said Mike hit her, but when she was questioned about it, she changed her mind and refused to press charges.'

'He sounds like he was a bit of a shit.'

'You talk to her, ask the questions.'

'You're not coming in?'

'I think she'll respond better to you.'

Alison Paton was forty-three years old with light blonde hair.

She was wearing a white T-shirt and black track pants when she opened the door. The tension in her body was pronounced, one tight turn of the screw and she might snap. She smiled but it was a struggle.

'Holly Wakefield?'

'Yes.'

'I've got the two little ones with me, but they're fine. Come in.'

It was a small semi-detached with tiny rooms and lots of doors. There were wedding photos with her new husband on one wall in the living room and fresh flowers on the coffee table.

'Do you want a drink?'

'No, thank you.'

There was a boy, perhaps six or seven, who watched Holly walk into the house as if she were from another planet.

'Your snack is on the table in the other room, go on.'

'Mum . . .'

'Do it.'

He trotted off.

'I'm step-mum to him,' Alison said, 'and this little cutie is mine.' She smiled and scooped up a baby from a cot and sat in an armchair. Holly took a seat on the sofa opposite.

'What's your daughter's name?'

'Ruth. I was in remission when I got pregnant – I didn't think it was possible.'

'And how are you now?'

'Strong and enjoying life. It's so different when you have something to look forward to. Are you sure you don't want a drink?'

'No, I'm good, thank you.'

'How can I help, Holly?'

'I know you've been informed of another murder by the same man who killed your husband. We were wondering if there was anything else you have remembered or thought about that could possibly help with our enquiries?'

'It seems like a lifetime ago, to be honest, and I don't really remember what I wrote in my statement. I'd just been through chemo – there was a lot going on at the time.'

'Of course,' Holly said. 'Do you remember DCI Walker?'

'Yes, I liked him, he was a gentleman. Is he working the case now?'

'No, he's retired. I met up with him earlier this week and he gave me his case notes. There was something in them that I wanted to ask you about. It's sensitive, but it might be impor-tant, I hope you don't mind, but he mentioned in one of his entries he thought you might be having marital problems. Was that true?'

Alison paused and Holly saw the woman's lips tighten around her next words:

'Every relationship has its ups and downs.'

A beat and Holly hated herself for asking but had to.

'Alison, was Mike cheating on you?'

The woman shrugged, her eyes unflinching.

'Because if he was,' Holly said, 'there might be someone out there who knows something or saw something that could help us.'

'A witness?'

Holly nodded.

'If she was there when my ex-husband was murdered, she must be one of the luckiest people alive.'

'Why is that, Alison?

'Because if the killer had caught them in bed together perhaps there would have been two bodies instead of one.'

Alison's whole demeanour changed and the baby sensed it and started crying.

'Come on,' she said, 'it's feeding time. I'm sorry I can't help you more.'

'Thank you, Alison,' said Holly as she was shepherded to the door. She managed to pass her card over.

'My number is on there if you think of anything that could help.'

'Say hello to DCI Walker from me.'

'I will.'

Holly turned and walked away. She didn't hear the front door shut behind her.

Bishop's car was waiting for her at the kerb.

'How was it? He said when she opened the door and sat inside.

'Difficult.'

He nodded and started the car.

138

Twenty-seven

Holly sat on one of the desks in the incident room as Bishop took the daily update:

'Most important piece of information,' he said, 'is that we can remove both Gavin Lefton and Douglas Regus from the incident board as they are no longer suspects in our case. The good news is they are both going to go down for an unrelated murder, as there was a head found in the back of that Volvo. Surrey CID send a massive thank you to the night owls here for helping trace that car.'

A round of applause.

'So, by the numbers please, let's go through each point and see where we are at. Sergeant Ambrose first.'

'We looked at the art inventory of Stephen's gallery and there were two portrait artists who used redheads as their models. Both of them could account for their whereabouts and neither of the models they used was Vee – they're what's called life-models and are both alive and well.'

'Janet?'

'We're still no closer to finding out Vee's real name. We

contacted missing persons, but if no one has actually reported her missing, then we're onto a loser from the start. It also means, if she is not missing as such, perhaps her loved ones or family do know where she is, they just don't know she's dead or haven't connected her death with the body found in Brighton. We're thinking of increasing the media coverage, maybe put the photo that was found in Vee's house of her and the young man in the press? We might get a hit.'

'That could work,' said Bishop. 'Kathy, can we do that?'

'Yep, we could run it in conjunction with the stickman drawing, if we're okay to release it.'

'Let's do it. Her former Portsmouth pimp, Stefan Spenski, suggested she may have given birth to a child during the two years she went missing from London, so can we start looking into birth certificates during that period with a mother called Vee.'

'What about adoption agencies?'

'Yes, good idea, it would have been 1999 or 2000 around then. Work on the London adoption agencies first and then cast the net wider. Also, Spenski said she had paid off her debt to him, which was apparently quite substantial, and that's when she moved to Brighton. He used the phrase sugar daddy, someone else she was close to, but couldn't back it up with anything. Did we talk to the other sex workers in Brighton about that? If Vee had someone taking care of her financially, that wouldn't have gone unnoticed.'

'We did ask them if Vee had any regular clients. She did, and all of these have been eliminated.'

'Maybe it's not a client,' Bishop said. 'Maybe it's a customer who wants to talk or take her out to dinner and just helps. It does happen. Tick the box. Trains from Brighton to London?'

'CCTV footage had been time-coded,' Janet said, 'we're just not sure exactly who we're looking for, that's the problem, and it's the same with the roads. Until we get a registration plate or a name to match ANPR, it's impossible to move forward.'

'Airbnbs and hotels?'

'Dead end, and nothing on the photos from the vigil at Brighton.'

'All right,' Bishop said. 'Kathy, have we heard anything more from Andy Brooks?'

'No.'

'Just to make you all aware,' Bishop said. 'He's a reporter who a few years ago had a – shall we say – fall from grace when he hacked a few phones he shouldn't have. He's claiming to have two stickmen drawings that were sent to him in 2016. We think they are fakes, as did DCI Walker back then, so just be careful on the phones with things you say, okay?'

Mutual nods.

Ambrose spoke again:

'We got quite a few names pop up for using chloroform and GHB before 2013. All of the offenders are known to us and only used it to knock out their victims while they burgled their house or shop. None of them have any previous for assault, ABH or GBH.

'Day-release patients from psychiatric hospitals have all been interviewed and none of them correspond with all three dates, and the ones that match the single dates have no connection to any of the others, so unfortunately that looks like another blank.'

DI Thompson raised a hand.

'I had some weird chats with the NSPCC and RSPCA regarding kids who drew violent pictures or have had violent episodes with knives in the past or who tortured animals, but again it's needle-in-a-haystack time.'

'Juvenile records, Sergeant Ingram, where are we on that?'

Ingram stood and read from his notes:

'On a lot of the searches I hit the same stumbling block as DI Thompson when it came to researching 1985 to 1995 on the DBS checks. If the applicant was under eighteen years old at the time of the criminal conviction, they were classified as a minor and the offence would have been removed from their record after five and a half years; cautions are even less stringent and are removed after two and a half. The records that never clear are the serious sexual or violent crimes, and I've had three names appear that fit the violent criteria you gave us, Holly.'

She eased herself off the desk.

'Who are they?' she said.

'Two are in prison on murder charges now, but one, Dustin Eccles, racked up a list of over sixty offences ranging from burglary to assault when he was a kid. He's used a crowbar and a knife and liked to start fires. When he was thirteen he got charged with shooting three cats and a dog in Battersea Park with an airgun.'

'Any abuse against children or the elderly?'

'No – but seventeen domestic abuse charges against his wife and girlfriends from his past.'

'Was he ever with social services?'

'On and off for nine years until he was sixteen.'

'Was he a bed-wetter?'

'A what?'

'A bed-wetter.'

'I don't know.'

142

'Find out if it was ever noted,' Holly said. 'Bed-wetting after the age of fifteen, starting fires and torturing or killing animals are what's known as the triad of homicidal tendencies. They're warning signs that can sometimes be regarded as a precursor to later criminal behaviour that includes serial and sexual murder. Was he ever interviewed for either of the first two cases?'

'Yes, he was. Eccles was thirty-three at the time and was two years out of Pentonville after a rape charge. We brought him in for the Stephen Freer murder, but his wife gave him an alibi.'

'What was her name?' Bishop said.

'Samantha Eccles.'

'That's right. Sammy and Dustin.'

'Do you remember him?' Holly said to Bishop.

'I do. Skinny little bloke, but he's a cold bastard.'

Sergeant Ingram pulled a photo from his file and held it up. It was passed from hand to hand until it made its way to Bishop. He gave it a cursory glance then handed it to Holly. The man was sleek and sinewy, five foot ten inches tall and with a face making it hard to determine where the scars left off and the wrinkles began. He was fifty-two years old.

'We brought him in for the Mike Thomas case as well,' Bishop said, 'but again his wife gave him an alibi and we could never prove he was near the crime scene.'

'I made some preliminary enquiries this morning,' Ingram said, 'And the mobile phone tower coverage puts one of his phones in Brighton on the night of the murder.'

Holly saw Bishop's head snap up at that.

'Which one?'

'Registered to him ending in the numbers seven-two-six-seven.'

143

'That's a bloody good lead,' Bishop said. 'Thompson, put this to the CPS and see if we can get a warrant.'

'Did you pull his psych report?' Holly asked.

'I did.' Ingram passed it over and Holly speed-read while the rest of the team carried on the discussion.

Dustin Eccles was smart, angry and had been diagnosed as a paranoid personality with sociopathic tendencies. He was known as a fire-starter when he was a child and classified as a pyromaniac – he enjoyed watching things burn, but there was no evidence of pyrophilia – sexual satisfaction from setting and watching fires. When he burgled people's homes he often defecated there or urinated – not unusual for a thief entering someone's house, partly because of the excitement and tension it generated, but that was a red flag to Holly because the psychopath they were looking for wouldn't get nervous and there was no urophilia with any of the victims so far. Apart from the airgun shootings in Battersea Park there was no more mention of animal cruelty in the report. She looked up and got Bishop's attention.

'He's a possible,' she said. 'I don't think he's a psychopath, but it's worth bringing him in. He may be well hidden though, because he does have a paranoid personality.'

'What is that?' said Sergeant Ambrose. 'I'm paranoid most days.'

'That's because nobody likes you,' Bishop said, and the room laughed. 'Well done on this, Sergeant and thank you, Holly,' he added. 'Do we have his current address?'

'We do.'

'I want a team on him immediately, and I want to know what he's been doing for the past month. Is he still having to report to a parole officer?'

'No,' Ingram said. 'Not since last year.'

'Okay, good. He becomes our new person of interest – and get the police armed response unit on stand-by. The moment we get that warrant, I want us through his front door.'

He turned to Holly and looked as if he was about to speak when Chief Constable Franks caught their attention from the doorway.

'DI Bishop, Kathy and Holly. My office, now.'

Twenty-eight

'Fuck,' said Kathy.

The press officer was looking at the preview for tomorrow's headline in one of the daily newspapers and it wasn't good. Andy Brooks hadn't kept his word. He had sold the images of his two stickmen drawings, and they were splashed over the covers and the centre pages as well as a blurry photo of the incident board. The headlines carried the message:

Serial killer is a child-killer – victim drawn with pig-tails and a dress

Police incompetence as they refuse to investigate two other killings

Profiler Holly Wakefield says 'A serial killer will leave calling cards so he can claim the kill.'

'Can they get away with this?' Holly felt a cold lump in the pit of her stomach.

Kathy was already making notes on the sides of the pages and her phone was buzzing continuously.

'The editor sent over the transcripts of a conversation he had with both of you, supposedly in your office, DI Bishop. They have your quote, Holly, which by itself doesn't harm the investigation, but it's the story that goes with it.'

'If he has a transcript, does that mean he recorded everything we said?' from Holly.

'It happens all the time.'

'Shit – apologies, everybody – I fucked up. Will this kill our press release?' Bishop said.

'I suggest we hold back on it. Don't release the drawing found at Vee's or the photo of Vee and her mystery beau. It's six o'clock, we may still have time to print a counter story, it's just a question of what we say. He mentions an orange crayon in one of the articles.'

'Yes, that was the bone of contention with the 2016 forensic results when they were deemed inconclusive – it was all down to a shade of orange the killer had used on the previous two drawings,' Bishop said.

'When will the forensics results be in?'

'Tomorrow afternoon.'

'Well, the clock is ticking,' Kathy said. 'We can say something like – "SIO DI Bishop, who is investigating the triple murder, had doubts about the drawings' authenticity when they were first seen in 2016 and still believes they are fakes to this day. Andy Brooks came to Hammersmith police station on" – what day did he come in?'

'Yesterday – Tuesday.'

'"Tuesday the seventh of May, and was advised not to release the drawings to the media until the forensic testing had

147

been completed. He chose to ignore that advice. We would welcome a dialogue with him as we believe he is the disseminator of fake news.'"

'Have they broken any laws?' Franks said.

'Legal are looking at the possibility Brooks may have contaminated a crime scene – if we can class your office, DI Bishop, as a crime scene because of the evidence inside. By law, all crime scenes are closed to the media. Was he invited into your office?' she asked Bishop.

'He sort of invited himself,' Bishop growled. Holly had never seen his jaw so tightly clenched.

'And he would have seen the incident board?'

'It's an open-plan office, he walked right past it. That's when he would have got the photo.'

Kathy took a second, then:

'Journalists have the right to photograph and report events that occur on public property, but this police station is private property, or rather property owned by the government, so we may be able to get him on charge for trespassing, but it's flimsy at best, and it's not enough for them to retract the story or get an injunction. Have you spoken to him since he came in, DI Bishop?'

'No, why? You think we should call him?'

'It wouldn't hurt.'

Kathy dialled the number and put it on speakerphone. As it was ringing:

'By law you have to tell him you're recording the conversation,' Kathy said, 'although I'm sure he'll be recording it as well.'

It kept ringing then went to answer machine.

'It's Andy Brooks. Leave a message.'

'Andy, it's DI Bishop at Hammersmith MIT. We understand you have sold the stick figure drawings you showed us
to a national newspaper. This is my direct number. Call me at
your earliest convenience.' He hung up. 'Slimy piece of shit. No
wonder Walker wanted to kill him. Worst-case scenario, Kathy?'

'We're already in it,' she said. 'The story is going to run
tomorrow, along with Brooks' allegation that there are two
more victims we haven't told the public about – and one of
them is a little girl.'

Holly and Bishop retreated to his office as the chief was
prepped for a live press conference and Kathy tried to control the fire.

'Have you had this happen before?' Holly said as she closed
the door and sat.

'A couple of times. We're always under scrutiny by the
press, which is fine, but this is a different fight, it's one journalist cashing in. I don't want it to hinder the investigation
and I don't want to damage the public confidence in us, but
Christ – some of them will think there are five murders now,
Holly. Five murders, and we still have nothing. This case is
the recurring nightmare. It happened to us back then and it's
happening again now.'

She watched him for a while then said:

'What else can we do?'

'Don't answer your phone. The press will already have your
number and some of them might try and get another quote. If
you do answer – just say no comment.'

Holly couldn't believe it had come to this so fast, and
they sat in uncomfortable silence until her phone buzzed. It
made her jump.

'Unknown caller.'

'Let it go to voicemail.'

She did and then played it and put it on speakerphone.

'Holly, this is Moira Drake. You need to call me as soon as you get this.' She left her number and Bishop asked:

'Who's that?'

A voice Holly hadn't heard for years, and that cold feeling in the pit of her stomach was back.

'After my parents were murdered I was assigned a victim liaison officer,' she said. 'One that specialised in children, more like a social worker and friend. Her name was Patty Longborn and she retired about ten years ago and then Moira Drake was assigned to me. The last time I spoke to Moira was when she took over my case.'

'Do you need some privacy?'

She shook her head and dialled the number. Moira picked up after one ring.

'Holly?' The woman's voice was shrill.

'Yes.'

'Thank you for getting back to me and I'm sorry to be the bearer of bad news, but I've just been made aware that Sebastian Carstairs has a parole hearing tomorrow morning.'

'What?'

'The Parole Board has fast-tracked the process. It's an emergency session so I need you to meet me at the Royal Courts of Justice at ten o'clock tomorrow morning. You need to have your victim statement at hand to be read in front of the judge.'

'My God, how did this happen?'

'I don't know yet – I'll have more details tomorrow. Ten o'clock?'

150

'Yes, I'll see you there,' Holly said.

The line went dead. She turned to Bishop.

'The man who killed my mother and father is up for parole.'

Twenty-nine

Holly kicked her shoes off when she got home.

She found a half-empty bottle of Malbec, poured herself a glass and leaned back on the sofa.

'I don't have time for this, Bishop,' she had said before she left the office.

'Make time.'

'What's the point? He's never going to get out.'

'It's important, Holly, you have to say your piece.'

He was right and she knew it. He had told her to take the day off tomorrow and concentrate on what needed to be done. The possibility of parole for The Animal had been a dirty whisper Holly had buried in a box decades ago and the suddenness of the phone call made her feel sick.

She had been nine years old when she had come home from school and found her mother and father dead in the kitchen. The Animal had been standing over their bodies sweating from exertion. Thick arms hanging. Knife in one hand. The searing anger inside him, a living thing.

That had been twenty-seven years ago and she had followed

the reports of his incarceration and knew his lawyers and psychiatrists had been working hard on his behalf. According to one of them, Hedley Phelps, Sebastian was a reformed man. Olanzapine and Aripiprazole were miracle anti-psychotics and the intensive CBT therapy sessions had produced incredible results. They had no idea who he really was though, thought Holly. *I do. I saw him that day and I will never forget. He didn't kill her and she'd never found out why. A moment of clarity when he saw her innocence? Nine years old. What a start to the world.*

Sebastian Carstairs had been caught by the police two weeks after murdering her parents, and it was during the trial that she devised her plan for revenge. As she watched him in the courtroom, she didn't hear the legal jousting or the testimonies. All she imagined was his chest under his jacket and his beating black heart. Before the verdict had been announced, The Animal had been led by his lawyers past the press and it was there that Holly had tried to kill him. A nine-year-old girl wielding a fruit knife had made a wonderful front-page photograph, but the blade had missed his heart and lodged in his ribs. As he had fallen to the floor, his lawyer, Alastair Simms, had caught him and in turn Animal had grabbed hold of Holly and pulled her down with him as gently as if he were putting her to bed. She had felt his breath on her cheek when he whispered:

'I've been waiting for you, Jessica.'

That was her real name – Jessica Ridley, but after her parents had been killed she had been moved into foster care, witness protection and granted a new identity.

She didn't get to choose her new self, but she liked the name Holly. It reminded her of Christmas, and from that day forward she was told to forget the name Jessica for her own safety. For a nine-year-old, it was like having a secret identity, a superhero nom de plume. Last year she had confessed this to DI Bishop when they were working their first case together, and he, Sergeant Ambrose and Chief Constable Franks were the only ones at Hammersmith police station who knew her real identity. There was a legal file sealed deep in the bowels of victim-relocation but, apart from that, Jessica Ridley was as deeply buried as her parents. Not a day passed, however, without Holly remembering who she really was and what she was capable of.

The Animal had been four hours in surgery after her attack, but had survived the attempt on his life. He recovered, and six weeks later one of the tabloids ran the headline *The Animal Is Alive and Walking Tall* after one of their photographers managed to get a photo of him in the exercise yard at Broadmoor. The Animal was six feet three inches in height, very thin, but with big hands.

She walked over to her shelves on criminology and found the home-made folder she had put together on The Animal. She pulled it down and wiped the dust off its cover – a blur of newspaper articles and photos, colour alternating with black and white. The dizziness stopped on a page with a black-and-white rendering of an artist's impression of the killer – a shadowy figure dressed in black wearing a balaclava and holding a knife. The banner at the top of the page read: *What We Know So Far!* The riffling began again and stopped on a series of grizzly crime scene photographs from seven of his victims. Riffling – stop – a photo of an old farmhouse taken from the front garden. Riffling – stop – the headline at the top: *Two more dead in The Animal killing spree.* The date – 9 March 1993.

Holly's hands were cold.

On 9 March at approximately four thirty in the afternoon, Mr and Mrs Sayles of 35 Chestnut Terrace in Oakley, Hampshire, were enjoying a cup of tea when the doorbell rang. They weren't expecting anyone, but friends and neighbours would often pop round to say hello and catch up on local gossip. Mrs Sayles answered the door and almost fainted when she saw the little girl standing on the steps. The girl was covered in blood and crying. Mrs Sayles called for her husband and the two of them immediately took the girl inside to the kitchen. They thought she might have been involved in a terrible car accident, but when Mr Naylor went outside, the street was empty and quiet.

The husband and wife started to wipe the blood off the girl using tea towels and there was mess everywhere. 'We thought she was going to die,' said Mrs Sayles. 'We were trying to talk to her and the girl kept saying "I don't know what to do. I don't know what to do."'

And Mrs Sayles told her, 'You're okay, pet. Whatever happened, you're safe here. Nothing can hurt you here.' And the girl kept asking for her mummy and daddy.

'She wasn't a local girl,' Mr Sayles, who works at Ford car plant in Basingstoke, told our reporter. 'The village is quite small and we know everyone – but then Harriet Wallace, our neighbour, came over because my wife had called, and she took one look at the girl and said she might be the daughter of the new couple who had moved into Beech Tree Farm after Christmas. I drove over there straight away. I wasn't scared at all. At this point everybody thought it was just an accident. I'd been to the farm before, on and off over the years; it's a big old stone building in an L-shape with barns and stables out the back. When I got there it was unusually quiet. I couldn't hear any of the animals and the front door was locked so I went around to the back. The kitchen door was open and I just walked in.

'It was like something out of a nightmare. Out of a horror movie. You don't think you'll ever see anything like that in real life.

'There were two bodies and blood everywhere. Like a slaughterhouse. I ran from that building as fast as I could and I don't remember driving back to Oakley. All I remember is coming into our house. The police had arrived by then with an ambulance, and I saw the girl sitting with my wife, who was holding her hand. The girl had been cleaned up, she was a pretty little thing, and my wife had given her some biscuits and made her a mug of hot chocolate. The girl was holding it so tight her fingers were white, and she wouldn't speak and we still didn't know her name. She kept looking around as if she was trying to find something.

'My wife asked me what I had found at the farm but I just shook my head. I couldn't tell her, not in front of the girl. I told the police where I had been and what I had seen and then all of a sudden a dozen more police turned up and some of them had guns.

'The police wanted to take the girl's clothes as evidence and even though our two children have left home we've kept all their old things, so my wife managed to find a blue dress that fitted her. She was shivering so we made her another hot chocolate. We didn't really know what to say. It's not as if we have training in anything like this. Then the police took a statement from us. The girl wanted to go back to the farmhouse, but the police wouldn't let her.'

'We felt so very sad,' Mrs Sayles said. 'And then a policewoman came in and started to talk to the girl. She was very good and the little girl seemed to respond to her and they hugged each other. I never found out the policewoman's name . . .'

'Yannis,' Holly whispered under her breath. 'Constable Yannis Marie.'

Yannis had been killed five years later in a botched armed robbery and Holly never had the chance to thank her. She hadn't kept in contact with Mr and Mrs Sayles either. They had tried with her, sent her a birthday present the year after and a Christmas card through the foster agency, but then she had gone into witness protection and all of her old life had vanished into obscurity. She thought one of them had died from heart complications a few years ago, but couldn't remember which one. She should have made more effort. They had been an integral part of her life, as had Maureen, her surrogate mother, and the other girls she had been brought up with in the foster home.

Holly closed the folder and put it back on the shelf. It would be her parents' ruby anniversary next week and she should buy them flowers.

She went to bed and was still awake two hours later.

Thirty

There was nothing quite like a dawn raid, and at four o'clock Thursday morning, Bishop was wide awake.

'Police – open the door!'

He had seen one of the sergeants next to him jump he had shouted the words so loudly, and he had immediately thought of Walker and the times they had kicked down doors in Afghanistan. This was so different. They might get a gun, a knife or a knuckle duster, but they wouldn't get an RPG or a landmine or a tripwire that would click and explode a kilo of Semtex the moment they walked in. He had called Walker before he had left the station and spared a thought for his old friend who was sitting at home waiting for the next update.

'Open the door! Armed police!'

Armed Response Officers turned to Bishop and he said:

'Go!'

The door was hit with a battering ram, but after two smashes and no movement, Bishop knew the door was reinforced. A lot of drug dealers did that. It stopped the police from getting in and gave them enough time to flush stuff down the toilet, throw it out of the window or swallow it.

'Windows – use the crow-bars!'

And within a couple of seconds there was a smash and a tinkling of glass around the rear of the property.

Move, move, move!

Bang-bang on the front door.

But there was no way it was going to open, so everything shifted around to the back and Bishop followed the noises. Shouts coming from inside the house – a young woman's scream – and he hoped nobody was going to get hurt. By the time he got through the side gate and made it to the house, the Armed Response team were conducting their initial sweep and one of the officers had opened the rear door. Bishop walked through the kitchen, the hallway. All the lights were on, and in the living room a woman and two men were sitting cross-legged on the floor – the woman looked out of it – an officer was kneeling next to her trying to get her to respond. The one that was making the noise was upstairs so Bishop went to the second bedroom on the left. There she was – Samantha Eccles – skinny as a rake, short spiky silver hair – spots all around her mouth.

'Look, I'm not resisting,' she said. 'You don't need to handcuff me.'

'We have to,' said the officer. 'It's procedure.'

'I'm not resisting, look at me, I'm shaking, I'm not going to do anything, I'm not going to run away am I? I'm just a little girl.'

Little girl.

Her arrest record flashed through Bishop's head. She had stabbed three people in the past two years and bitten off someone's ear.

'Cuff her,' Bishop said.

159

'You fucking pig.'

Yeah, yeah, I've heard it all before.

'How many phones do you have in here?' he said.

'That's my phone that white one, you can't take that!'

'Yes, we can, how many other phones are in the house?'

Forensics were already moving in, picking up things in their white gloves and putting them in evidence bags.

One of the sergeants had pulled out a black backpack from underneath the bed. 'I think there are phones in here, sir.'

'How many?'

He tipped it up onto the bed. There must have been twenty phones scattered over the bedcovers.

'Have they got SIM cards?'

The officer opened one up.

'This one has. Looks like they all have.'

'Seven-two-six-seven are the last four digits we're looking for. That's the phone that will link him to Brighton.'

Bishop back to the girl:

'Where is he, Samantha?'

Her eyes went ferrety.

'Don't know. Haven't seen him, sorry, and you can't just come in here, it's my property, and you haven't got a warrant.'

'It's not your property, and yes we have a warrant. Do you know why we're here?'

'No.'

'We need to talk to him about a murder. If he's responsible, he won't get away with it this time.'

'It weren't him, he was with me.'

'Yeah, you have a habit of saying that, don't you. Is he still hitting you?' She didn't even flinch. 'Well if you're protecting him or involved in any way you'll go down for this as well and you'll never see the light of day again. We just need to find him. When was the last time you saw him, Sammy?'

'Don't remember.'

'Did he stay here last night?'

She pouted and her eyes drifted upwards.

'No,' she said.

Bishop looked up, there was a square wooden loft-hatch in the ceiling.

'Get a ladder,' he said quietly to one of the officers.

They took Sammy out of the room and she didn't protest. She had the handcuffs on now and five minutes later the room had been cleared and a ladder had been borrowed from a neighbour. Bishop put it under the loft. He hated doing things like this. Nothing worse than getting your knuckles rapped by a baseball bat if someone was waiting for you. One of the firearms team handed him a pair of ballistic gloves and he put them on. He climbed the ladder and slowly pushed up the trapdoor.

'Dustin, we're coming up!'

No response.

He lowered the trapdoor.

'Identify yourself if you are up there!'

Nothing.

He flung the door open and pulled himself up in one fluid movement. Had his torch all ready and was waving it around the darkness.

'Dustin? Are you in here?'

He looked past the beams and floating dust. Somehow lofts were always bigger than you thought. Hiding places stacked with boxes and asbestos on the crawl space between the rafters. The place stank of damp and mildew and there were holes in the roof where he could see the sky.

161

Two sergeants came up behind him and went the other way. After a few minutes it was obvious the suspect wasn't there. Bishop climbed down to the bedroom where one of the officers told him:

'We've found a knife and a machete in the other bedroom – forensics have already taken them.'

'All right, good. Keep looking and start door to door.'

Thirty-one

It is being reported that The Animal is dead.

Sebastian Carstairs, who killed nineteen men and women – one for each letter of his name – has been murdered by the daughter of one of his many victims, just two days after his release. The Broadmoor Parole Board who granted licence to The Animal have promised to hold a full enquiry. Witnesses say he didn't scream for mercy – neither did he shout for help – he merely accepted his fate, like a rabbit caught in the jaws of a fox. The woman who stabbed him in the chest handed herself in to the authorities immediately after the killing and has yet to be named.

Holly propped herself up in bed.

The dream had been so real. She had stabbed him! She had felt the knife arcing into his chest, a slight twist of the handle as it had touched his ribs, then the blade had eased slowly into his tar-like heart with the grace of a falling angel. His final breath bubbling and liquid-like as if he was blowing through a straw. Did all victims dream like this? Revenge. Bloody night sweats.

She turned the bedside light on, stared at the ceiling, then turned it off again and tried to sleep. Bitty and broken with legs and arms hanging outside of the sheet that had replaced her duvet a month ago. The windows were open and the world longed for rain but the humidity hung like a dead animal.

She shivered into the bathroom and showered, eyes squeezed shut. Dried her hair and got dressed. It was 5 a.m. when she went to the living room, still dark outside with the faint hum of distant traffic.

At 6.30, breakfast became a silent but hurried affair, and after applying a touch of make-up she got in her car. The red MG purred like a lounge cat.

Early Monday morning and the traffic was sparse, so the drive to Norwood Cemetery in south London only took thirty minutes. She parked in the street, entered through the main gate and walked across the grounds. She had the whole place to herself. Armies of gravestones and pockets of trees. Black birds flew overhead, watching her curiously.

She found her parents' white marble headstone, a rectangular block with two carved hearts and their impressed names. Holly had chosen red roses for their ruby anniversary and she laid them on the grave. She sat in silence with their memories and wished her father was there to hold her.

'I've got you,' he would say as he wrapped his arms around her. When she was too tired to talk but didn't want to go to bed for fear of missing out on something, or if she was simply crying, she would feel the comforting embrace and let her head fall back on his chest. 'I've got you,' he'd whisper into her ear.

There had been so much quiet after her parents had been killed. Moments of nothingness in her bedroom at night and sometimes she craved the same. She pulled out a dog-eared pink envelope from her jacket pocket. There was an old letter inside she had written when she was a child. She unfolded it and leaned against their gravestone. She read it out loud. It always helped:

Dear Mum and Dad

I hope you are both well. Don't worry about me. I'm in what's called a foster home. I'm making new friends and everything is going to be all right. I have so many questions for you and don't know where to begin. I want to know about the sky, and the sun and the stars. I want to listen to the waves on the beach again, but I want you to be there with me. Maybe you can still hear the waves where you are? When I get older I'm going to try and find out exactly where you are. Heaven is a big place apparently. Like space. It just goes on and on. And I guess you can travel from side to side and up and down and I hope you can see me. I wave up at the sky every now and then and I imagine you waving back. You both have your arms around each other and are smiling. Sometimes when I look up I can't see you and I don't know where you have gone. I've been told that you are always there but sometimes I don't believe that. I went for a walk the other day by our old house. I wasn't allowed in but they let me walk in the fields around the back with a policeman. He held my hand and we saw a rabbit. We tried to catch it but it was too fast and disappeared into a blackberry bush.

When we walked back there were butterflies everywhere,
and I thought of you both. I want to know why butterflies
chase you when you walk in fields. Maybe they're fairies in
disguise, like the ones we used to have at the bottom of the
garden? I love you from a thousand miles away. I always
will. I'll write again next month.

   Please write back.

   Jessica

   Age nine and a half

'God bless you, Mum and Dad,' Holly said. She folded the letter and slipped it away. 'I still love you from a thousand miles away.' She caught a violent memory of their bloody bodies and struggled to get up. Pushed against the head-stone as a black bird cawed nearby. It watched her and she watched it back.

Then she kissed the grave, toughened her soul and walked away.

Thirty-two

Holly's expression was blank, as if nothing around her existed, not even Moira Drake, her victim liaison officer, who was escorting her through the corridors of the Royal Courts of Justice on Fleet Street.

Moira was thirty-six and sweating in a cream-coloured suit.

'How was your journey, Holly?' She didn't wait for an answer – 'Some idiot was chasing his dog on the Central Line at Marble Arch. Did you get caught up in that?'

'No.'

'I've been here since seven,' Moira said.' I'm hoping it will have cleared up by the time I leave.' She checked her watch and quickened her pace. 'Let me go through the rules. I know you know them, but legally I must. This is an oral parole hearing for the case of Sebastian Carstairs who was convicted of killing nineteen people, including both of your parents. You are allowed to talk for five minutes about how the crime affected you at the time and how it has affected you since. How the prisoner's release would affect you—'

'Do I call him that? The prisoner? Or do I use his real name?'

'He was dubbed "The Animal" by the press. Do not refer to him as that. Are you comfortable calling him by his real name?'

'Yes.'

'You are allowed to speak about how the prisoner's release or move to an open prison would affect you, your family, friends or community. You are *not* allowed to talk about whether you think the prisoner should be released.'

'Even though I am more than qualified to make that professional judgement?'

Moira shot her a look.

'Because of the background of your case I have no knowledge of who you really are. Your anonymity is still the court's upmost priority. I am impartial in these proceedings and have no wish to know what you do as a profession. You are simply a member of the public I am escorting to and from the witness box. I'm not going to get into a debate with you about this. You cannot talk about you on record. Not only will it be viewed unfavourable by the board but may give clues as to your current profession and risk your anonymity being exposed. Sebastian Carstairs has his own psychiatrists. The board will listen to them and them alone.'

'Understood.'

'Left up here.' Moira's heels clicked on the shiny floor. On either side were corridors leading to different courts and clerks in black gowns and white wing collars whispered to each other by stone columns.

'You are not allowed to discuss or give long or vivid descriptions of the original crime. And neither are you allowed to

168

make any threats or critical comments to or about the prisoner or the Parole Board. Understood?'

'Yes.'

'The panel can use your victim personal statement to understand the impact of the crime on you. Decide what questions to ask the prisoner based on your statement, to ascertain his feelings of remorse and or empathy.'

'He has no remorse or empathy.'

'He's—'

'—A narcissistic psychopath.'

The first pause of the day from Moira and then – 'The board can also assess and use your statement to decide what the prisoner can and cannot do if he is released, these are known as licence conditions. I am also required to ask if you have any other information that will help the Parole Board make a decision.'

'If they let him out, I'll kill him myself.'

Moira – face ashen.

'No threats, remember?'

Holly was matching Moira's stride now. She just wanted to get this over and done with.

'Why are we wasting our time?' she said. 'The Animal has to serve nine consecutive life sentences. He's never getting out.'

Moira's silence unnerved her.

'Moira?'

'You should be aware the Home Secretary has become involved in this case. The Parole Board are pushing for leniency on compassionate grounds.'

Holly stopped walking. Her jaw clenched.

'What?'

'He has cancer.'

'Cancer?' Holly thought she had misheard. Realised she hadn't: 'What sort of cancer?'

'Pancreatic cancer, stage four. It's metastasised to his bones and his brain.'

'Why wasn't I informed?'

'Personal details of all prisoners are strictly confidential and any—'

'How long has he got to live?'

'The doctors think two months, three at the most.'

'And that's why we're here?'

'Yes.'

Holly took a breath.

'Is he in pain?'

'That's irrelevant.'

'Not to me it's not.'

Holly interlocked her fingers until they hurt. She started walking again. Moira struggled to keep up.

'He started treatment four months ago, Holly. The cancer has spread fast. He wants to spend the last days of his life on the outside.'

'I bet he does.'

'The Parole Board panel makes a decision based on whether a prisoner is still a risk to the public. If he is deemed a risk he will stay incapacitated until such time as his lawyers and doctors believe he has made sufficient progress and may be referred to a Parole Board in the future for another hearing. If after this hearing, however, he is deemed to be low risk or zero risk as a result of his illness, then he will be granted parole.'

'When will we know the Parole Board's decision?'

'It normally takes between two and three weeks.'

Moira managed to stride ahead, stopped and turned at a plain wooden door.

'We're here.'

She unlocked it and pushed it open. A bright windowless box. One table, one chair, a camera facing the chair and a television screen to the right. Moira made sure everything was working as she talked:

'Have you prepared the victim statement?'

'I have.'

'Would you like me to read your victim statement on your behalf?'

'No, thank you.'

She brought Holly a glass of water from the cooler.

'Would you like me to be here in the room when the interview takes place?'

'No. How long do I have before we begin?'

Moira checked her watch.

'Other witnesses and family members have been reading statements since eight o'clock this morning. They should get to you in about fifteen minutes. If things get too much or you change your mind at any point during your video interview, you can cut the link by flipping this switch. I will be outside.' She turned to leave but stopped in the doorway when Holly asked:

'Does he know I'm here?'

'Yes.'

Thirty-three

The TV monitor in front of Holly buzzed and came to life.

A woman appeared on the screen wearing a grey suit, a wood-panelled wall behind her. She said nothing and seemed preoccupied, as if watching an event out of view. Then the television went black. Five seconds later it returned to life and the woman was staring directly down the lens at Holly.

'We'll be with you in about one minute.'

Holly nodded.

'Can you answer, please? Test the levels for sound.'

'Sorry. How's this?'

'That's good.'

'Do you have water, enough to drink? Tissues?'

'I'm fine. Thank you.'

'If you go over your five-minute time limit a flashing red circle will appear on the top right of your screen. This will give you another twenty seconds then the feed will automatically be cut. Is that clear?'

'Yes. Can you see me?' Holly said.

'No. The screen is blank and we have no visuals in the

courtroom. I have no idea who you are, I just hear your voice and you will not be seen by anyone. Anonymity is key here, you are simply assigned a number, as are all the other witnesses.' She paused to listen to someone through an earpiece, head tilted to one side, nodded, then turned back to Holly. 'When we get close to your time, a clock will begin to count down from twenty seconds on the bottom of your screen. At five seconds you will be introduced by Judge Wasserman as Witness Number Fourteen.'

'Is there a witness number thirteen?'

'No, there isn't. The judge will then ask if you have a statement to read. Do you have one prepared?'

'I do.'

Holly unfolded a sheet of paper and held it like a love letter in both hands.

'Judge Wasserman will then remind you of your five-minute time limit and will ask you to go ahead when ready. Your time will start when he finishes speaking. The countdown clock has begun. Can you see it on screen?'

'Yes.'

Eighteen seconds ... seventeen seconds ...

'Take a deep breath. You'll be fine.'

When Holly read out the letter she tried to keep her voice flat and impersonal. There was a secret to getting through witness evidence. Just pretend you're reciting a shopping list.

Red wine, one bottle. And that's when I came home and saw the bodies. *A bottle of Irish whiskey as well.* My father had been decapitated, my mother killed by a single stab wound from a ten-inch blade to the heart through her back between her ribs. *Lemons. Do I need lemons?* And Sebastian Carstairs was standing in the kitchen, knife in hand, watching me as if I were a – *I should probably get some salmon for dinner* – as if I were a curiosity. *What goes with salmon? I can't think straight today. Concentrate, Holly.* I wet myself when he spoke to me, I was so scared and I thought I would die. *I should get some broccoli and perhaps some pasta.* His eyes were dead as if the fuse had burnt out, as if I didn't exist, and in a way I didn't. I don't know why he didn't kill me and some days I hate him even more because of that. *Bananas and kefir would be good for a dessert.* Because every day I still lose a little part of me. A speck that I can never get back, as if I'm somehow slowly dissolving and no matter what I do I cannot stop it until there will be nothing left. But I can stop it. I can ask you, Sebastian Carstairs' Parole Board, to consider not just how his release will affect my life, but the lives of all the other people he has already altered forever.'

Maybe some Green & Black's chocolate as well for a treat.

'I've just been told he has cancer. I didn't know that until now. I don't think ...' Holly drank some water, cleared her throat and continued. 'I don't want to talk about him and his disease. It's a waste of my breath. I want to talk about my parents. I want you to hear their voice.

'Not a day goes by when I don't think about them. I used to have nightmares, but not any more. Now I remember my parents fondly and I think that's the best way to survive what happened. When people die a normal death, old age, their time has simply come, their relatives always remember that day, don't they? Today's the day Uncle Stan passed away. He had a good life, a long life, lived well and went peacefully in the end with his family and friends by his side. I choose not to remember the day my parents were murdered. Why should I light a candle on that day, it will never shine bright enough, and if anything it will just illuminate him. The man who did this – Sebastian Carstairs. So I celebrate other days that my parents had together. Their birthdays, their wedding anniversary. This would have been their fortieth year together. That's the ruby anniversary. These are the days I choose to remember.'

She showed the camera a photo of her mother and father with their arms around her, all three of them were smiling.

The red circle started to flash.

'My memories of them are fading faster than the photos I have in my home. I didn't think that would ever happen. When I went into foster care, I vowed never to forget things about my parents but sometimes I do. Silly things, but it annoys me. I make diaries now when I do remember something important, an event, a holiday, a joke that made us all laugh, I write it down so—'

The screen clicked off and went black.

'—so it will be remembered. Forever.'

Thirty-four

'You want to talk about it?' Bishop said.

Holly handed him a cup of coffee and sat next to him on the sofa in her living room. She had a mug of hot chocolate for herself. It was ten o'clock and the sun was setting.

'No, it's fine. I wasn't expecting it, that's all,' she said.

'Even with the cancer the chances of parole are slim to none. If he is released, there'll be strict licence conditions and he'll be under permanent house arrest. There's no way he will ever be allowed out on his own. He'll have to have an escort wherever he goes, probably 24/7.'

'It's not enough,' she said, shutting her eyes hard. 'Let's change the subject. Dustin Eccles – what did you find at his house?'

'A machete and a knife,' Bishop said. 'The knife had one spot of blood on the blade. They're both with forensics, we'll know within twenty-four hours.'

'What about his wife? Samantha, right?'

'Sammy, yeah. She not talking, she's still saying no comment to everything. He has friends and family he can manipulate, so we've got teams knocking on their doors tonight, and tomorrow morning we'll pay a visit to his mother.'

'Do you know her?'

'I've been there a few times. She's got to be in her eighties now and swears like a trooper. She makes me blush.'

'I can't imagine that,' Holly smiled. 'And what does the mother say about her son?'

'She knows he's a bad one, but she's his mum. She'll protect him, up to a point. He'll hear that we've been there, so it might flush him out.'

There was a moment of silence between them, not uncomfortable, and she noticed his eyes drift to the incident board above her fireplace.

'I forgot you always did that,' he said. 'I try not to think about the victims when I get home.' He turned to her, his face almost childlike. 'Do they ever speak to you?'

'Sometimes.' And she wondered if he dreamt about them like she did.

'What do they say?'

An image in her mind of her mother and father lying dead on the floor.

'They scream,' she said softly. 'And nobody knows the sound of their true scream until they're about to die.'

The sun had disappeared and there were shadows everywhere, but she couldn't take her eyes off him. 'And they feel betrayal.'

'Betrayal?'

'At life being taken away from them. It's always very cold and bloody and painful, and that final second seems like an eternity.'

He put his cup on the coffee table and moved forward.

'Holly—'

His phone rang. He checked the number and answered it. Listened for a while:

'That's good news,' he said. 'Thank you, Sergeant Ambrose.'

He hung up.

'We've found a birth certificate for a baby girl who was put up for adoption during the 1999–2000 time period with the mother's name listed as Vee. We have an appointment with the foster agency tomorrow at noon.'

Thirty-five

They parked on Napier Terrace.

The foster agency was called Carestrom and their appointment was with Ellie Nunn. The building was large and cool, and they only had to wait a few minutes before they were ushered into her office. She had everything ready and her reading glasses reflected the stack of files in front of her.

'Yes,' Ellie said, 'the baby was born on the seventeenth of June 1999 to the mother whose first name was Vee, no last name given. We were contacted on June twenty-first by the mother about the adoption. That would make Juliet twenty years old now.'

'Juliet?' Holly said.

'That was the baby's birth name.'

'Do you have contact details for her?'

'We do, but we cannot give them out. We would have to contact Juliet and see if she will be willing to talk to you. You understand this is always a very delicate matter.'

'Her mother has been murdered, unfortunately,' Bishop said.

'Oh, how horrible.'

But she wasn't shifting.

'Is there mention of a father?'

'No, there isn't,' Ellie said. 'It says here the baby was removed from the family home due to concerns and was placed into short-term foster care to begin with.'

'Does it say what the concerns were?'

'The mother was a sex worker and a drug addict. She actually volunteered the child herself for protection and its own welfare.'

'Protection?'

'The mother didn't think the child would be safe with her, whether through her own actions or employment, or perhaps the behaviour of a partner. The baby was granted an emergency short-term placement for two weeks that turned into two months. During that period we looked into numerous adoptees who were being assessed. We found a family for Juliet and she stayed with them for six months, but then the mother died unexpectedly and the father didn't feel as though he could cope, so she was brought back to us again. We then looked for a longer term arrangement, which we found.'

'Can you tell us who Juliet was finally given to?' Bishop said.

'Again, this is confidential information. I will have to contact the adoptee and see how she feels and if she is willing to come forward and share this information.'

'We are trying to find Vee's killer. It could be very important.'

'I am aware, DI Bishop, but so is the welfare of our children.'

When they got back to the station Holly spent the rest of the afternoon getting updated.

Janet was in Brighton preparing for the response from the

re-enactment that was going to be broadcast that evening and everybody was hopeful the phones would be ringing non-stop. The team had their own dedicated number for Operation Hugo that would appear at the bottom of the television screen.

DI Thompson was following up leads in the search for Dustin Eccles.

'His mother swears blind she hasn't seen him for weeks,' Thompson told her. 'We've put the place under surveillance as well as two of his other hang-outs, but it's like he's always one step ahead.'

She asked if the forensics had come back on the Andy Brooks stickmen drawings.

'The results are the same as the findings in 2016. The shade of orange doesn't match with the broken piece of crayon found at the Stephen Freer crime scene that was used on the first two drawings. The argument from the newspaper is that it doesn't prove the killer didn't do them – he just used a different crayon.'

'The killer wouldn't have sent the drawings to the press – he would have sent them to us,' said Holly. 'I still think they're fake.'

'So do I,' said Thompson.

Bishop came in carrying coffees and Holly joined him in his office.

'Any response from Andy Brooks yet?' she said.

'I've left him three messages, but he's hiding away.'

Bishop had the two drawings from the reporter in a folder and he tossed them over to her. She took them out and gave them a cursory glance before she turned her attention to the stickmen drawings Bishop had put up in his office. They were taped to the glass wall by his door and the light streamed in from behind.

'These are the originals, right?' she said.

'Yes.'

She studied each one. The brilliant colours, the bold outlines and her eyes ended on the image of Verity lying on her bed with her bright green triangle dress and the grinning killer on the left. There were three lines by the killer, an impression in the paper Holly hadn't seen before when they were on the desk, but now the light was shining through it was quite clear.

'Did you see this, Bishop?'

'What?'

She pointed at the almost invisible lines in the paper.

'The killer drew Verity on the left to begin with – you can see the outline of the dress where he rubbed it out.'

Bishop nodded and said:

'He made a mistake or changed his mind. The other two drawings both have the victim on the right.'

'Yes, but I wonder why that's so important to him?'

'Don't know.'

She was distracted by it, but couldn't work out why. She wrinkled her nose and turned away.

'Go home, Holly. Get some rest,' he said. 'When we get the bloods back from the knife we found at Dustin's, I'll let you know.'

'What time will you be in tomorrow?'

'Early,' he said, and Holly wondered if he was going to stay overnight in the office again.

At home, she fixed herself something to eat and turned the television to *Crimewatch*, and the re-enactment. A quick introduction from Janet Acton and the police search for the killer and then the programme began:

'Brighton – at between one and three o'clock in the morning on Friday the third of May, a sex worker made her way along Marine Parade towards her home on Wellington Road. She was wearing black leggings, a blue skirt, a white T-shirt and a thin black jacket. Perhaps her most distinctive feature was her red hair.'

The woman they had chosen for the Brighton re-enactment was a redhead like the victim and was probably a local actor. The camera shots were documentary style, jumpy and fast cuts as 'the sex worker known only as Vee' waved goodbye to her sex worker friends and started walking towards the sea and then took a left onto Marine Parade. Now the camera was a static shot that followed the woman along the coast as cars passed by.

Holly watched the phone number come up at the bottom of the screen.

'Did you see this woman?'

She wondered how much Andy Brooks got paid for the drawings as she felt herself drifting off to sleep.

Thirty-six

Andy Brooks rose from his chair and paused the re-enactment on his big-screen TV.

He left his plate of fish and chips half eaten, walked over to the window and lit another cigarette in an endless chain as he stared out at the darkness. He was wearing a brown smock top and tracksuit pants, the only thing comfortable in this heat. Sometimes he caught sight of a fox by the trash at night; the little bastards got bolder every year. He coughed and tossed the cigarette out and watched the orange tip glimmer until it died.

He went into the bedroom and changed his oxygen tank. He had sleep apnoea, which meant he stopped breathing when he lay down and had to keep his head raised. The house was ex-council, he had bought it in the early noughties as a transition property, but he never got around to transitioning, and after his wife left him, he just didn't see the point. Nothing had been changed from the day he set foot in here nearly twenty years ago.

He fell back into the chair and drank from a frothy beer can that had just been popped. Picked at the chips and grabbed the remote control. He pressed play, but kept the mute on. The TV was directly in front of him and he watched it like he was caught in a tractor beam. Vee walking along Marine Parade, dragging on her cigarette. He lit up and did the same.

The phone rang and he let it go to answer machine. He thought it might be DI Bishop again but:

'Andy – it's Penny,' the female voice said.

He pulled himself out of the chair and fumbled for the receiver.

'Hey, Penny.' He said and realised he sounded out of breath.

'Congratulations! You're in every bloody newspaper!' Her voice was raspy. He used to love watching her smoke.

'I told you, love! I'm back and this is the big one. I'm helping the police – we're like the dream team, me and them.'

'So is it true then? You really know the killer?'

'Yeah. I mean, I don't know them, but they contacted me, you know.'

A pause and he could hear her smiling.

'Doesn't that scare you?' she said.

'No, why would it?'

'I don't know – they send you the creepy drawings – it's weird.'

'It is weird, but it's the new normal. So are we up for lunch then?'

'Yep, you're paying,' and she laughed.

'I don't mind that, I never did.' That was true. He played with coke but he was also generous to a fault. 'What day is good for you?'

'Monday.'

'Monday then. Let's get the week off to a good start, maybe go out for a drink after?'

'Awright, big-boy.'

His old pet-name was back and he smiled.

'I gotta go, Penny. I'm watching this re-enactment to see if I can get any more clues for the police.'

'All right then – see you Monday. I'll book a table somewhere nice.'

'Wherever you want.'

He hung up and squeezed back into his chair. Rewound what he had missed and pressed play again. He got caught up in the silent images, and five minutes later he almost had a heart attack when he heard a noise from the garden. The security light came on and he saw the top of one of his old metal bin lids see-sawing on the concrete path. It was the foxes. He got up and stood at the window until the security light went off. He went to sit down, but something caught his eye in the hallway.

There was a white envelope on the carpet by the front door.

A4 size, no stamp or address, so it had been hand-delivered. He went over and picked it up, opened the front door and looked left and right. His was the last house on the street and there were only a few streetlights. It was dark and quiet. He shut the door. The envelope hadn't been there when he had come in an hour ago, and he hadn't heard the letter box go so he had no idea how long it had been there. He caught a glimpse of himself in the hall mirror: overweight, receding hair, grey. He made another silent promise to get his act together – tomorrow.

He tore off the top of the envelope with his stubby fingers. A bank statement? An electricity bill? A credit card offer?

It was a stickman drawing. All in orange.

Andy Brooks looked utterly stunned and his thick brow knotted together.

The figure on the left had a big grinning head and was holding a knife that dripped blood. The figure on the right was comically fat and lay on the floor. It looked upside down with his head by a wall and there was a broken plant pot with twigs next to the orange crayon head.

A tiny ripple of fear tugged at his gut as the security light in the back garden came on again.

Another noise and he hefted his huge body over to the window. There were sweat stains across his back and under his armpits. The bright spotlight cast a shadow through the darkness of the trees. He couldn't see anything but felt jumpy and turned to the phone and dialled 999.

RINGING. RINGING. RINGING.

'Police. What is your emergency?'

Andy hesitated and glanced back outside as the security light snapped off. He would have to give his name and then DI Bishop would be informed and it would all go horribly wrong.

'Hello?' the voice said.

He hung up and cradled the phone like a child's toy. He was being stupid, the stick-drawing was a prank, that's all. Very few people knew where he lived. Penny did and some of the old-school reporters, but they hadn't visited for years. Who could have sent this to him? He had boasted about selling the drawings the other night at the pub on the way home, maybe that's what it had been. Telling the locals he was making loads of money, buying rounds for all of them as they got pissed on his cheap cider and excitement. That was it. They had obviously got together as a joke, grabbed some paper and borrowed some crayons and drawn the shitty picture for him.

He went back to the hallway, the drawing still clutched in his hand. His heart was racing as he checked the chain again. It was secure. He turned away and caught another look at himself in the mirror. He looked ghastly.

There was a knock at the door.

He almost shit himself. It was the night of a thousand surprises.

'Hello?' he said.

He wanted it to be the guys from the pub. Maybe they had brought him another bottle of scrumpy? He heard a voice, but it was very low and monotone. No emotion and no change in inflection.

'I can't hear you?' Andy said.

'Could you open the door, please, sir.'

He recognised the tone.

'Oh, of course. I just called you guys. Hold on.'

Fuck – I hope it's not DI Bishop.

He pulled back the chain.

The door swung open and a figure dressed in a full SOCO suit stepped forward and sprayed something in his face. It stung his eyes. He gagged and fell backwards, toppled like a felled tree and smashed into the carpet. He had the wind knocked out of him, tried to get up and shout but something slapped into his belly. Slapping in and out of his stomach like a red-hot poker and then there was that gagging sensation and he vomited and tried to turn over but something was stopping him, a weight on his chest and the red-hot feeling in his stomach wouldn't stop.

And then something hit him in the face like a freight train.

And he tried to summon the strength to use his arms, but

he had forgotten how to use them. And plastic fingers fumbled over his eyes, there was a ripping noise and he couldn't blink. He was suddenly warm all over and tried to curl up in a ball to protect himself, but he couldn't because his hands and feet weren't working and then the heavy weight on top of him shifted.

He's moved away, Andy thought. A jolt of cognisance when he realised he might not die. Why has he left me? Maybe he wants to rob me. He can have anything he—

He wanted to shout but nothing came out.

He was having difficulty breathing. His chest and throat felt as though they were closing up. A squeezing sensation, a narrowing and tightening of his airways.

There was an angry buzzing coming from somewhere. Like a bee caught in a bell jar. What was that? He felt hands tugging at his track pants. Pulling them down to his knees and the figure in the suit hovered over him, eyes cloudy and dead. He sensed something was about to happen to him. Something terrifying.

Dear God ... no.

His mouth was stretched open to scream but it turned into a shallow rattling sigh. He inhaled his terror as the buzzing noise got louder and he wanted to shout, but no matter how hard he tried he couldn't make his throat work. He almost passed out and maybe the noise was fading or was he fading now?

Fading into oblivion.

Thirty-seven

The knock on his office door woke Bishop at 3.45 a.m. and he stared bleary-eyed at the sergeant standing by his desk trying to comprehend what was being said to him.

'You want me to do what?'

'In the incident room, sir, you might want to come and look at this.'

Bishop pulled himself up from the sofa and followed the sergeant.

'More dashcam footage from Brighton?' he asked.

'No, sir.'

He had managed three hours' sleep, having spent the majority of yesterday evening answering the phones after *Crimewatch* showed the re-enactment in Brighton. There had been over four hundred calls and a lot of people walking or driving on Marine Parade had remembered seeing Vee before she turned into Wellington Road. All witness accounts and camera footage had so far pointed to her being by herself.

It was a skeleton crew in the incident room and the team had patched the police station CCTV onto one of the big screens. It was dark outside and the floodlights at the main entrance made the picture glare.

'What am I looking at?'

'There, sir.'

A figure paced backwards and forwards by the iron-railed entrance, going out of frame then coming back in again.

'He's been there for nearly twenty minutes.'

'Do we know who it is?' said Bishop.

'We managed to grab a screenshot when he came closer. He said something, but we haven't got audio, so we don't know what, but we think it's Dustin Eccles.'

'You're joking?'

'No, sir, we're not.'

The figure came back into view and stood by the main gates with his hands above his head.

'It is him.' Bishop said. 'He's giving himself up. Who's down on the station desk? Get them outside now with two other officers.'

'Do we need armed response?'

'No, we don't need to be heavy-handed. Just get everybody inside on alert.'

The officers were ordered outside and Bishop watched the events unfold on the screen. They opened the gate and talked to the man. He raised his hands higher with his head kept neutral and then they led him off camera and into the station.

Bishop met Dustin downstairs at the booking desk as the suspect was getting cautioned.

'You took your time,' the man said. 'I almost ran out of fags.'

'Dustin,' Bishop said. 'Lovely to see you again. You know we've been looking for you then?'

'Yeah, my mum said you people had popped by. I knew you'd never find me so thought I might as well come in. I need a lawyer and I want to make a statement.'

Thirty-eight

Holly was woken with a phone call ten minutes later.

'Bishop?' she said. There was a crick in her neck where she had fallen asleep on the sofa and her body was cold.

He told her what had happened with Dustin Eccles.

'That's unusual, isn't it?' she said.

'It is and it makes me suspicious. He's already asked for a lawyer and says he's going to read us a statement. How soon can you get here?'

'Half an hour?'

'All right, depending on how long his lawyer takes, we may have started the interview by then. Come into the observation room, I'll make sure we're in number three so you can watch.'

When Holly arrived at the police station the interview was already under way.

In the observation room, she put on the headphones and turned on the mic that was fixed in the ledge in front of her. Nobody was talking, the lawyer was studying a sheet of paper and Dustin sat to his right. He was smaller than she had imagined him, but the creased face was there and his eyes were hooded and unblinking.

'Bishop, I'm here,' Holly said.

She saw him nod softly – a sign he had heard her.

Dustin's lawyer shuffled the papers.

'And the mobile phone tower coverage is the only disclosure you're prepared to give to us right now?'

'That's correct,' Bishop said.

Bishop hadn't told them about the blood on the knife yet.

'How much more can we expect?' the lawyer said.

'At least one more disclosure.'

'Okay. My client has prepared a statement and I will now read it on his behalf.'

'Please proceed – we're recording video and audio,' said Bishop.

'Mr Dustin Eccles of 25 Redgmont Road, EC17, has come to Hammersmith police station voluntarily to help with the enquiry into the murder of a sex worker in Brighton last Thursday night/Friday morning. My client wishes to state for the record that he had nothing to do with this heinous crime. He was not in Brighton on that evening/early morning and has not been to Brighton for at least six years as far as he recalls. He understands you have cell-phone tower evidence that his phone was in Brighton on the night in question, but that was the phone he lent to his wife, Samantha Eccles, of the same address who we believe you already have in custody. She will verify this story. She went to Brighton as part of a hen-night with seven other ladies from London who will all testify to this.

'I would also like to reiterate that my client had no part in any of the previous murders, namely Stephen Freer and Mike Thomas. He has been brought in and asked to account

194

for his whereabouts on each occasion and on each occasion he has been released and no further action has been taken. Tonight, having heard of the raid on the house that he shares with his wife, he decided to perform his civic duty and come to Hammersmith police station to clear his name for the third time. He hopes that if there is another murder of a similar MO he will not be brought in. My client understands he has done wrong in the past, but once again insists that he had nothing to do with these crimes. Signed and dated by my client and witnessed by me.'

'Thank you,' said Bishop. 'This is DI Bishop terminating the interview at four forty-seven a.m.'

Holly and DI Thompson were gathered in Bishop's office.

'How long before we get the bloods from the knife?' Thompson said.

'They're fast-tracking it, but it could be another eight hours,' Bishop said. 'Him coming here makes me think he had nothing to do with the murders.'

'Maybe it's a double bluff?' said Thompson.

Holly shook her head. 'He's violent and paranoid, but I agree with Bishop. I think he came here because he wants people to know it wasn't him. Clearing his name before any enemies think about taking the law into their own hands. If the drawings in the newspapers are to be believed, he killed a young girl. That never ends well.'

'He's using his wife as his excuse again, so we need to go through all the CCTV of Brighton, but instead of looking for him, we need to be looking for her.'

'I'll tell the troops.' Thompson was about to leave when the duty sergeant knocked and entered.

'DI Bishop, something just came in for you.'

The officer handed over an A4-sized envelope. It was folded over with an elastic band and Bishop pulled the band off and let it drop on his desk. Holly stared at it for a while then inched closer.

'Bishop?'

'What?' he looked up at her, but she had seen something he hadn't.

'The back of the envelope,' she said. 'Don't touch it,' as he moved a hand forward. She grabbed a pencil from his desk and flipped it over.

In the centre of the envelope was a drawing of a very tiny stickman.

Thirty-nine

Everyone in Bishop's office had been given forensic gloves. SOCO had been brought in and were observing.

The duty sergeant who had signed for the envelope was asked to come back and was grilled. The envelope had come from one of the regular couriers who delivered to the station. Where was it sent from? We're tracking that address now, sir.

'As fast as you can,' Bishop said as he weighed the package in his hand. 'There's definitely something inside, and whatever it is it's small and light.'

'You think it's a prank or do we need to get bomb disposal in?' Thompson asked.

'What's your take on it, Holly?' Bishop said.

'If it's a prank then it will contain something trivial, perhaps not even related to the murders,' Holly said. 'Something someone will have sent to either annoy us or confuse us. If it has been sent by the killer,' she paused slightly, 'then I don't think he wants to hurt us. We're not part of his mission, remember? But I think he'll want us to see what's inside.'

Holly felt herself holding her breath as Bishop cut along the top of the envelope with a pair of scissors. He peeked in and pulled out an orange-coloured wax crayon that had been broken in half. She wasn't sure what she had expected, but felt herself staring at it as if it were a religious object. She heard Bishop say quickly to SOCO:

'Take the envelope, check for prints and saliva, but I need to keep the crayon.'

He picked up the phone and got an internal line.

'This is DI Bishop on the third floor. I need a clearance officer to go into the archives for me and find an evidence bag from the 2013 Stephen Freer murder case. It will be catalogue number 397-D. As soon as you can, please.'

He passed the broken crayon to Holly and her eyes caught a thousand details of it at once. The crystals and impurities inside the sloping edge of the orange and the smell of paraffin reminded her of school.

The clearance officer arrived a few minutes later carrying evidence bag 397-D. He went to pass it to Bishop but:

'No. You reach in and take out what's there,' he said. 'Then you pass it to me.'

The officer reached his gloved hand inside and Holly saw a flash of orange as he pulled out another broken wax crayon. Bishop shot her a look when he next spoke:

'This evidence was never disclosed to anyone.'

The briefest hesitation and Holly passed her half crayon back to him and Bishop put the two pieces together. They fitted perfectly.

'Like two halves of a penny,' he said.

'My God, he's leaving us clues now,' from Thompson.

'Not a clue,' Holly said, 'a message. This is the orange

he uses for the drawings and he wants us to know he wasn't responsible for the two that Andy Brooks gave us.'

She rubbed her eyes and found herself looking past everybody into the incident room. People were gathering around one desk. She couldn't tell whose it was, but all eyes faced the same direction. An officer in the group put down a phone and headed towards them.

'Bishop?' Holly said.

He followed her gaze just in time to see the door open and the duty sergeant enter. He was out of breath:

'The parcel was ordered for a pickup outside a house early this morning in east London. It's 22 Eastbourne Crescent, sir.'

'Should I know that address?'

'It's where the reporter lives, sir. Andy Brooks.'

Forty

Bishop parked on the dirt track.

Holly got out and stood for a while by the car, taking in the neighbourhood. Andy Brooks lived in a small detached bungalow at the far end of the street. There were five other bungalows further to the left. Nothing to the right but trees and the edge of a forest and beyond that fields of wild flowers. Apart from the birdsong it was unnaturally quiet.

The bungalow looked more like a static home with a wooden frame, plastic cladding and double-glazing. Holly followed Bishop onto the small porch as he rang the bell.

'Mr Brooks? It's DI Bishop here with Holly Wakefield.'

Nothing. He knocked on the door.

'Andy?'

There was a garage to the left and a narrow cement drive-way with an old BMW.

'He's home,' Holly said and cupped her hands and looked through the living room window. Silhouettes of a sofa and a fireplace and the reflection of photo frames on shelves. She looked at Bishop and shrugged. Followed him around the side of the house to the gate which was overgrown with weeds and covered in hanging ivy. They pushed past into the back yard where a bin bag had been pulled from one of the bins, its contents spilled on patches of dead grass.

There was a security light above the sliding glass doors that led to a kitchen and living room. Holly cupped her hands again and saw a big-screen TV and a large chair with blankets and pillows. There was a plate of food on the floor with a dozen or so empty beer cans.

'Bedroom?' Bishop said.

She followed him over to two small sliding windows about four feet off the ground. The curtains were drawn. Bishop pushed down on the metal rim of the window and it scudded to one side. He pulled back the curtains and stuck his head in.

'Jesus Christ.'

'What is it?'

'It stinks.'

They both put on latex gloves.

Bishop managed to squeeze through the frame, got a leg down and hopped inside. He offered his hand and Holly grabbed it and followed him into the bedroom. There was an oxygen tank on one side of the bed, raised pillows and a massive indentation in the mattress where Andy Brooks would have lain.

'Andy?' Bishop shouted.

Walking on threadbare carpet into the living room. Fish and chips on the floor by the chair. Holly stared at the television.

'Bishop?'

He looked over and she nodded to the TV screen. It

had been paused on the Brighton re-enactment from the night before.

'He was watching it,' she said.

Bishop's phone rang. He answered it.

'Yeah, we're here now. No sign of him, we're looking.'

He walked into the kitchen. Holly glanced up at the ceiling. She didn't say anything but her eyes narrowed. Tiny splashes of purple on the white paint. Blood spatter? She turned and followed the trail. Bigger splashes, darker, almost black, and then she went around the corner of the living room into the hall and looked down.

'I've found him,' she said.

Forty-one

Angela Swan needed help getting through the bedroom window.

She couldn't use the front door because the body was blocking it and the back door was jammed shut and she didn't want to wait for the team to break it down. Holly walked her to the scene. Three other SOCOs followed, taking photographs and video.

Andy Brooks was on his back, bloated purple and foul-smelling. His head looked up at the ceiling with two ragged holes that used to be eyes. His stomach was in ribbons, his arms by his side, legs straight and flat with both ankles turned out as if he had fallen asleep on a beach. His track pants were discarded in a heap by the door. The pathologist stared at the body for some time.

'Yes,' she said, and there was a glimmer of excitement in her voice. 'But this is quite different from the others.'

'Same killer though?' Bishop said.

'Undoubtedly. He came in' – she shot a look at the front door – 'and started stabbing straight away, walking forward at the same time. The tails of the elongated blood spatter indicate the direction of travel. The victim has been stabbed multiple times in the stomach – note the large lacerations from a heavy blade. I'll know the exact number when I get him to the lab. There appears to have been internal organ damage as the lower intestine is visible. He has been castrated.' She glanced around and pointed underneath the hallstand. 'There's a plug there. The killer may have used that one for the electric saw.'

Her hands moved across the face, fingers gently touching.

'The victim's eyes were taped open, as per the previous victim from Brighton. There are numerous cuts and abrasions to the orbicularis oculi and the procerus, and lateral damage to the nose. Heavy bruising where the hilt of the knife has made repeated contact with the cheekbones. I think they are probably both fractured. The eyes have been rendered indistinguishable from the flesh, mucosa and sclera. Preliminary examination of the eye sockets shows the killer has not removed the tape. Well, that's very interesting.' She stood up. 'I wonder why?'

'I think he panicked,' Holly said. 'I think he panicked and left. This was badly planned compared to the others.'

'Do we have any idea who the victim is?' Angela asked.

'He was a reporter,' Bishop said. 'Andy Brooks.'

'Ah, yes, the journalist everyone is talking about. Hold on a second.'

She was examining the inside of Andy Brooks's mouth with a flashlight. 'There's a cut on his lip. He might have bitten himself during the assault or our killer has turned into a biter. It's only a nick but it ruptured the lip and bled. Slim possibility, but if it was the killer we may be able to get DNA or a partial cusp or incisor measurement.'

'Time of death?' Bishop asked.

'At least twelve hours. It's a hot room.'

'Was he alive when he was castrated?' Holly said.

'Yes, but probably unconscious. The amount of blood loss would indicate his heart was still pumping. Any sign of the genitals?'

'No.'

'Then we can conclude the killer took them when he left.'

Angela rested her hands on her hips. Suddenly she saw something and pointed to the left hand.

'There – he's holding something, look.'

She pulled pliers and tweezers from her tool kit. Crouched down and tried to prise the fingers apart.

'He's gripping it tight, which would have been caused by a post-mortem spasm, ATP and all that malarkey. In cases of a violent death you keep hold of things and it looks as though that has happened here.'

She pulled a piece of paper free. It was a corner piece that had been ripped from a page. The edges were red from blood but the middle was clean and white where the thumb and palm had pressed together. She held it up. It was white paper with a thick orange crayon line running through the middle of it.

There was silence for several seconds. Holly gazed at it contemplatively. 'Part of a stickman drawing,' she said.

'Yes,' said Angela. 'The question is – where's the rest of it?'

Standing still they looked around as if it would suddenly appear.

The smell was getting too much and Holly walked away into the living room. The drawings were always left at the scene after the victim was dead, so how did Andy get his hands on it? Did the killer walk in and say, *Here you go – this is for you?* She put her hand over her mouth and swatted away a fly, then silently watched the SOCO team dusting for prints.

They never seemed to talk.

Forty-two

'I need a beer,' said Bishop.

'I need two,' said Holly.

They were at the Bedford pub near Holly's flat. There was a live band booked for the night and she could hear someone hitting the drums and the ballsy first notes of a mic test. Bishop got four bottles of beer and they sat by themselves in a booth. She allowed herself a breath, then dropped her eyes to hide her frustration.

'I could have saved his life,' she said, angry at herself.

'Andy Brooks?'

'Yes. I don't think I did enough, Bishop. I don't think I warned him properly. Rule number one – you do not piss off a psychopath. I should have been more insistent when I told him not to use the drawings, I should have told him this might happen.'

'You did.'

'No, no, I didn't.'

'He wouldn't have listened anyway. You weren't to know, Holly, it's not as if—'

She cut him off, impatient to speak:

'Imagine something so precious to someone that it must never be mocked. It must never be ridiculed, because a psychopath will react differently to you and me. Someone hurts me, I get sad or annoyed, but I shrug it off and get over it. Someone hurts the psychopath and blood will spill. This kill was a mistake, mark my words, it was rushed and infantile in its approach – it was just wrong. Stabbing the stomach? He was so lucky he got that first blow in. And this killer is strong, Bishop, if Andy Brooks had been ten years younger or fifty pounds lighter, he could have put up a real fight. Were there traces of GHB and chloroform present?'

'We'll get the toxicology back tomorrow, but I'm sure there will be.' A beat. 'We've interviewed all the neighbours – no witnesses. We've started collecting CCTV from the area, but the closest cameras are over five miles away.'

Holly took a second.

'This last kill worries me, because the killer has shifted targets and agendas. The time between kills has been three years until now. This was one week.'

'I've been wondering about the timeline, the three-year gap, and I think it's because the killer knows that after twenty-four months the murders get classed as a cold-case. It will go from having a team of forty officers plus extra CID to one or two officers with no overtime. He's very smart with a lot of self-control and he's got the patience of a—'

He stopped himself and Holly said:

'Saint?'

'I was going to say that.'

She nodded and added:

'Andy Brooks was never part of his original mission – he

couldn't have been. This was clearly an extreme response to the article Brooks wrote and the drawings he sold.'

'So what does that tell us?'

'That the killer can be indiscriminate and choose targets at random if he feels the impulse or gets angry. That's going to make it almost impossible to predict his next victim. What if he starts killing random people who are pissing him off?'

'Are we included in that list?'

'Our names were both mentioned in that newspaper story, he'll know who we are. The Animal didn't kill me when he could. I don't think I'll get as lucky with this one.'

'Then I'll arrange for someone to be outside your flat.'

'Thank you, but you don't need to that. We have security cameras everywhere and I will triple-lock my door and won't open it to strangers.'

'Or people you know.'

'Apart from you,' she smiled.

'Deal.'

He smiled back and she stared at him, slurped her beer and coughed a fine spray over the table. *God she was classy.* He laughed and she laughed back, and then they both drank their beer and Bishop got a call and—

'Hello?' he said. 'Yeah, I can hear you . . . hold on,' he shook his head, 'He did? . . . Okay, thank you. Where are we on the CCTV in Brighton? Keep looking.'

He hung up.

'Andy Brooks made two phone calls on the night he was murdered. One of them was to the police.'

'You're joking. What did he say?' she asked.

'Nothing. The call lasted seven seconds, then he hung up.'

'And the other?'

'Was to his ex-wife, Penny Wotherspoon. Apparently they remained close friends after the divorce. We're going to talk to her tomorrow morning. And the bloods came back from the knife we recovered from Dustin Eccles' house. A negative hit for all of the victims; it was Dustin's blood, he said he cut himself cooking last week.'

'He's a regular Masterchef.'

'He's a skinny wank-stain, that's what he is.'

Holly lost it and spat another mouthful of beer on the table.

'You bastard,' she said, laughing.

He got some napkins and handed them over.

'Clean yourself up. Can't take you anywhere, can I?' he smiled.

Holly couldn't stop laughing.

I'm in so much trouble, she thought. I think I really do love him.

Forty-three

Nothing had happened between them when they had gone
their separate ways after the night of beers.

She had been tipsy and had aimed for his mouth when they
initiated their talk tomorrow/goodnight kiss. She had got the
cheek, he had been surprised, or rather she thought he had
looked surprised, and then she had gone home to bed and
hugged her pillow as if her life depended on it.

Their relationship was moving so slowly – if you could even
call it a relationship. She knew she had feelings for Bishop but
hadn't quite worked out in her mind what they were. She had
first felt the pull on her heartstrings during the Sickert case
last year and hadn't pushed them aside. Deep down, she still
had insecurities in fostering relationships, something that had
plagued her since her parents had been killed, and the thought
of losing someone she loved all over again was more than she
could bear. Could she be loved? Could she let someone in?
There was something there and she would be a fool to ignore
it, but she wondered if he felt the same.

She was still in bed the next morning when her phone buzzed. It was Bishop – he was waiting downstairs.

Penny Wotherspoon's house was on Eton Road in Datchet.

It was detached with two cars in the gravel driveway. The front garden was large and Holly suspected the rear garden would be larger. They rang the bell and someone asked who it was, Bishop identified himself, and Penny opened the door.

The voice had been strong but the woman underneath the floral dress was willowy and fragile. Her face was puffy and red and her lips quivered when she spoke.

'Come in,' she said.

They followed her along the hallway and into the living room. The woman had a handkerchief clasped in her hands. She reached for a fresh one as she sat in a chair and Bishop and Holly took seats opposite.

'Thank you for seeing us, today, Mrs Wotherspoon,' Bishop said. 'I know how hard this must be. We know you spoke to Andy on Friday night at nine thirty. What was your last conversation about?'

'He'd left me a message earlier that day saying he'd sold those drawings to the newspapers and would I like to meet up, so I called him. I said yes, that would be nice, and we agreed to meet on Monday for lunch.'

'So you still got on quite well with each other?'

'Yeah. I mean when we were married, he was a difficult man sometimes – he thought the world owed him, and he drank too much – but underneath there was a good person. He was always generous with me. I know he still loved me, I loved him too, but not in that way any more. I didn't tell him that, maybe I should have.'

212

'When you spoke, did he seem anxious about anything?'

'The opposite. Full of life and . . . Like I said, we were supposed to be having lunch tomorrow.'

'So there was nothing you talked about, or picked up on while you were speaking that could have caused him concern?'

'No. Why?'

'He called the police three minutes after you spoke to him.'

'He did?'

She blew her nose.

'He sounded fine to me.'

'Did you hear anything in the background while you were talking to him, Mrs Wotherspoon? Any other voices or someone knocking on the door or ringing the bell?'

'No, nothing. He just said he had to go.'

'Did he say why?'

'He was watching some sort of re-enactment on TV,' she said. 'About the girl who was murdered in Brighton.'

Forty-four

'I wonder if Andy Brooks saw something on the re-enactment and that's why he called the police?' Holly said.

They were driving back towards the station.

'I've watched it twice,' said Bishop, 'so have all the team.'

'Something we missed, something that made no sense to us, but made him think twice and pick up the phone.' She took a second then: 'Have SOCO finished at his house?'

'Yes.'

'I want to go back there.'

There was a police car outside 22 Eastbourne Crescent and an officer stood by the door.

Bishop parked in the street and showed his warrant card. They ducked under the police tape and opened the front door. Inside, the hall floorboards were stained red and they walked with booties and gloves on.

Holly led the way, looking through the kitchen, the bedroom and the living room. She stopped by Andy Brooks' chair.

'Something made him pause the television and get up,'

Holly said. She looked out of the back window at the scattered rubbish and the trash can. 'But he was killed at the front door.'

'You want me to go outside and knock?' Bishop said.

'Yes.'

He opened the door, went outside and closed it. Holly walked back to the chair; she didn't sit but stared at the television. Andy Brooks – you've just made a lot of money selling those drawings to the newspapers and you've just spoken to your ex-wife and are looking forward to lunch with her on Monday, but you've also just called the police.

KNOCK-KNOCK-KNOCK.

She walked to the door.

'Can you hear me, Bishop?'

'Yes. Can you hear me?'

His voice was slightly muffled but—

'Yes, I can. I'm opening the door.'

She turned the latch and Bishop was in her face straight away – one step in the door and he already had his hand close to her stomach. Holly stepped back. The shock and attack would have been so quick, Andy wouldn't have stood a chance.

'He wasn't expecting something bad,' she said. 'The chain wasn't on the door and he just opened it wide. Why?'

'Someone he knew or a voice he recognised or trusted.'

'The one difference with the two new drawings Andy gave us is that one of the victims appears to be a child,' she said and took a moment. 'Maybe that's it? As warped as it may sound, maybe the killer wants us to know he would never hurt a child?'

'And Andy Brooks missed the point and paid the ultimate price?'

'Exactly. If that's his motivation, he's telling us so much

215

about himself with this kill. Our psychopath has a clear narrative and children do not appear in his vision.' She stopped, annoyed. 'But that doesn't explain why Andy Brooks had a piece of the drawing clutched in his hand.'

'The killer opened the door and gave it to him as a distraction, or maybe it was posted, with or without an envelope.'

'Maybe. But the drawing is his signature and he will have left it for us to find.' And she moved to where the body had lain and crouched down. 'When I first saw him, he had tape left around his eyes. I said the killer panicked, didn't I? That he didn't have time to remove it, but I was wrong, he didn't panic. I think he wants us to know he taped Andy's eyes open. He wanted Andy Brooks to see him for who he really was.'

She stood up. The hall mirror stared back at her.

'After the kill, the first thing he sees is his reflection. His reflection . . .' She was murmuring under her breath as if she were half asleep, but acutely aware that Bishop was still listening. 'I think he took his mask off in front of the mirror. I'm not a child-killer, that reflection said back to him. I know I'm not and I have just proved it by killing Andy Brooks. Mentally he's fighting with himself, Bishop. He's cracking slightly and this murder proves it. His passion for his truth is his strength, but it's also his weakness.'

She stared at the mirror. A vision of a bloody man with fierce eyes stared right back at her. The Animal. She blinked him away. Back to the other man – the shadow who killed without a trace.

'My God, he is so desperate for us to see him,' she said.

A quick glance around the hallway at the walls and the ceiling with its arterial spurts and the shoes neatly placed under the hallstand.

'There,' Holly said. 'The mirror. He's in the mirror.'

'What?' said Bishop.

'He's been watching us ever since we got here.'

She tiptoed over to the thin gilt frame and examined it.

'It's screwed into the wall.'

Bishop went outside and grabbed a Phillips-head screwdriver from his car. Holly held the mirror as he worked on the four corners.

Hands together, they lifted the mirror. It had barely moved when a sheet of paper fluttered down and landed on the hall table.

It was creased and bloody with one of the corners missing, but Holly could immediately see what it was: a stickman drawing entirely in orange of the grinning killer and Andy Brooks lying dead in the hall. But it was what was written on the top that took her breath away.

'Jesus Christ, you were right,' Bishop said.

In bright orange crayon were the words *I don't kill children.*

Forty-five

After eleven hours of watching soaps and awful reality shows, coffees, lasagne, monopoly and re-heated lasagne, Ryan Atkinson had been looking forward to the end of the day shift at St Albans fire station.

And then the station bell had rung. It was eight-thirty in the evening.

He heard the order: 'Let's hustle!' Bodies bumped against him as he semi-gripped the brass pole and let gravity do the rest. On the ground floor he went through the motions of grabbing his jacket, his helmet and slipping on his boots.

There was a roar from the engine and the electric whine as someone opened the bay doors. Cold air and rain blew inside and Ryan felt himself shiver. At fifty-seven he was the oldest crew manager on call that night, neatly tucked in on the left of the cab. Squeezed in next to him was Joey-the-face, a good-looking lad, twenty-one last birthday. Marian Danforth was driving, head bobbing in time with a song that was playing in her head alone.

'Cap'n said two trucks have already contained the fire,' Joey said as he adjusted his helmet strap. 'We're just mopping up again.'

'Most important job, Joey,' Ryan said as they rounded a corner at forty, tyres sounding like sirens as cars parted before them.

'Left in fifty,' Joey said.

They spun left.

'Two hundred metres. Then left again. Then right onto Spencer Street.'

They were heading up towards Market Place. My old hunting ground, thought Ryan, and the familiar street was streaked in a blur of house lights and smudged pedestrians.

'What's the address?' Ryan asked.

'Two-storey terraced house on Pudding Lane. Some old bakery.'

Ryan leaned on the dash, eyes wide and alert. Not just some old bakery, Ginger's Bakery – named because of a stray ginger cat that the owner had adopted a week before opening. He remembered Ginger's Bakery fondly from when he was a kid. Four doughnuts for a pound and flapjacks that tasted like a slice of oat-filled love.

'Sir?' Joey was smiling with excitement. 'We're here.'

The men and women piled out as the engine screeched to a stop, lurching in their heavy boots, hitting the pavement that was already drenched from rain and the now silent hoses. Ryan spotted fire crews from Napsbury and the Oaklands Estate and the inevitable crowd of locals who had gathered to watch beneath the safety of umbrellas.

Smoke rose lazily through the ruined building like the breath of a sleeping dragon. The roof of the bakery had gone, leaving a cradle of black timbers pointing towards the heavens, and the chimney had toppled.

The watch manager from Napsbury pulled away from his people and shook Ryan's hand.

'Electrical fire due to some renovation work,' he said. 'No casualties. The bakery was shut and the tenants in the flat directly above are on holiday. The two flats either side got out in time and made the call to us. Anyway, it's all yours,' he said and went back to his crew.

'Joey and Marian! Up front. Room to room,' Ryan said. 'Take the Halligan and pull the ceilings.'

Heavy boots waded through the slush of ash and Ryan was the last to walk through the remains of the window. The display cabinets had melted and the day's Chelsea buns and lardy cake were clumped together like roasted birds with sad sultana eyes. Behind the counter were the massive oven domes, and he wondered if these had been the same ones that had made his flapjacks.

In the restaurant were scattered Formica-topped tables and skeleton chairs, an archway led to the toilets and a spider-plant covered in ash looked like a silver sculpture. A part of the ceiling had sagged until it cracked, and burnt belongings had fallen through from the tenants above: a handbag, a photo frame, a pair of toasted shoes.

The ceilings were still smoking and there was danger of collapse, so Ryan barked another reminder for Joey and Marian to be careful as they went from room to room. Joey was carrying the Halligan, a thin stick about six feet long with a metal claw on the top, which he pushed into the plasterboard above, twisting and then ripping downwards until the ceilings collapsed.

'Clear!'

Marian was behind Joey, hand hooked onto his belt to give him a tug if she spotted something he didn't as Joey pushed the pole up again. He gave it a twist then a tug and a single length of wood came down and landed by Ryan's feet. He picked it up. It was about a foot long with running groove down its middle and a beautifully knobbled top like a Victorian cane.

'There's a lot of weight up here,' Joey said, struggling with the pole.

Another shove, a great shudder of dust and a ball suddenly dropped through a small split in the ceiling, bounced off Joey's helmet and rolled across the floor. Marian laughed.

'Not funny,' Joey said. 'Bloody Halligan's got stuck.'

'Give,' said Ryan, and he went over and took the pole. Marian stepped in behind him and Ryan felt her hands grip his belt. He shoved at the ceiling and immediately felt the pressure bearing down on his shoulders. He shifted a few feet back and pulled again.

'Sir?'

Joey was calling to him.

'Hold on, Joey.'

'Sir, you need to stop!'

Ryan looked over. Joey was streaming sweat, his sooty face shining from the lights outside. He had picked up the ball and was holding it in both hands as if it were alive. Only he wasn't holding a ball. It was a skull.

There was a victim here. Maybe one of the tenants hadn't gone away on holiday? No, that made no sense, there was no charring on the bone, no heat fractures, residual flesh or fat. It was caked in dust with empty sockets, which meant it must be old. It was an old building, medieval perhaps?

'What do I do?' Joey said.

'Put it down slowly,' Ryan told him.

Then the whole ceiling seemed to shift above him as if in the throes of an earthquake. Ryan tried to wrench the Halligan free but its claw had twisted into place and he had no choice but to pull it down.

There was an almighty crash as the plasterboard buckled and split.

And suddenly it was raining bones.

Forty-six

Monday morning and the incident board had been updated with a photo of Andy Brooks and the final autopsy report was in: the bite on his lip was probably self-inflicted during the struggle, toxicology stated he had both chloroform and GHB in his system, less than the other victims, and it appeared to have been inhaled as traces were discovered on his face as well as in his lungs. He had been stabbed seven times in the stomach, each was a deep cut, but none of them fatal. He had been castrated before he had been stabbed in the eyes, approximately ten times in each one. The blade marks left on the orbital sockets were consistent with the other murders.

The stickman drawing Holly and Bishop found had been put together with the corner taken from Andy Brook's dead hand and there was no doubt it was from the same piece of paper. The crayon colour had been analysed and it was burnt orange, consistent with the orange used on the other three stickmen drawings, but it was the message the killer had left that Holly kept coming back to: *I don't kill children.*

Why?

The stick-drawings are childlike. Have you lost children? Did they die? Do you work with children? Was there a divorce that left you separated from your children?

Whatever it was, the killer felt justified in his anger. Righteous even.

In one sense everything was tying up neatly, but that was part of the problem: there were no new physical clues from the Andy Brooks slaying. The killer had been rushed, but he had still been incredibly careful. The calls from the Brighton re-enactment had ground to a halt and she watched the television show again to see if there was anything she had missed. Holly was on her second repeat when Bishop put the final nail in the coffin as he announced:

'They've got CCTV of Samantha Eccles in Brighton getting drunk until five in the morning on the night of Vee's murder, using her husband's iPhone, so we can take Dustin's statement as genuine,' he said. 'His name comes off the board.' He scrunched up Dustin's mugshot and threw it in the bin.

'Good shot,' she said.

'Thank you.'

She was thinking about lunch when she received a call from Moira Drake – her victim liaison officer.

'Are you at home, Holly?' the woman said.

'No, I'm working.'

'I think it's important we talk.'

'What's wrong?'

Holly wondered if perhaps The Animal had died, and Moira wanted to break the news to her before the media broadcast it, but when she asked the question –

'No, he's not dead. Shall we meet at your flat?'

'I can be back in forty minutes.'

She gave Moira her address and told Bishop where she was going.

The traffic was light and she had been home for half an hour when the intercom buzzed.

Moira was all brusque and super-suited, and Holly offered her a drink when the woman entered her flat – which was declined – and they both sat on the sofa. If Moira noticed the incident board above the fireplace, she didn't mention it.

The woman said:

'I wanted to tell you in person rather than hear it from somebody else or see it on the news. Sebastian Carstairs has issued an apology and the Parole Board have made their decision.'

'What?'

'He has written a letter to every single family member who lost a loved one. This is for you.'

Moira reached into her handbag and took out a white envelope.

Holly stood up and pulled away.

'I don't even want to touch it. An apology?'

'You're the fourth family member I have spoken to today and I have two more visits to make. Two of them read the letter, the other two handed it straight back to me. I can't tell you how to deal with this – I'm just the messenger and I'm sorry.'

'This is bullshit. Why is he apologising? He's had over twenty-five years to apologise. What's changed now?'

'I don't know. Each letter is different.'

'Have you read it?'

'Yes. We have to.'

'But he doesn't know who I am, does he?'

'No. You were witness number fourteen. Do you have someone to talk to, to help you come to terms with this? A professional, I mean.'

'I've been through my fair share of shrinks, thank you, Moira.' And she had. Some she had fired, some had fired her.

'Perhaps now you can have closure.'

'I don't want closure—'

'Holly—'

'He'll be dead soon, that's his closure. Don't you get it? This is his last laugh, the final stab of his knife and the twist to kill every single one of us.' She took a breath. 'You said the board have made their decision?'

'They are staging the press conference on the courtroom steps in twenty minutes.'

'A press conference? We weren't supposed to hear for another week.'

'Meetings were held behind closed doors and because of the obvious publicity they wanted complete anonymity about their discussions.' Moira lowered her eyes. 'There are situations that must be adapted to, and every now and then there are cases that appear as if they should go one way but then inexplicably go the other.'

'Please don't tell me—'

'They're letting him out. I'm sorry, Holly.'

'Jesus. How? Why?'

'Officials have said they have a very stalwart plan in place that will manage him on release. He will be under intensive supervision for the rest of his life, which won't be long, and his licence conditions will include curfew, exclusion zones and other restrictions to prevent contact with any of the victims' families.'

Holly wanted to know who his psychologist was. Who was the shrink who had said The Animal no longer posed a threat to society? Perhaps he didn't? Bedridden with drugs from chemo. Morphine to help ease the pain. Perhaps Moira was right and he would be dead soon, but it still didn't feel right. Her parents hadn't been given parole.

'He will be GPS tagged and made to continue psychological therapy and counselling. Initially there was talk of a transfer to a hospice placement, but Sebastian stated that he did not want to be released to the hospice facility, but to an address provided by his family.'

'His family?'

'Yes. He has a sister. Her name is Cassandra—'

'I know her name. You think I don't know everything about him? About his sister, about his mother and father? I have thought more about him and his family than I have thought about my own over the past twenty years and that is the saddest thing in the world. Do you know what it feels like to be heartbroken, Moira?' She didn't wait for a reply. 'Sometimes it's a sharp pain but more often than not, it's just a dull ache that refuses to leave.'

'I'm so sorry, Holly, I really am and I know I can't put this right.'

'No one can. And yet here we are.'

'There was an update released this morning in regard to his condition and that was why he has been released so quickly.'

'What update?'

'Sebastian decided to stop treatment two weeks ago. He doesn't have long left, Holly. The doctors think a few weeks at most.'

'Really? I've heard of quite a few murderers who have been

released on compassionate grounds who have gone on to live long and very unproductive lives. I don't see why this should be any different.'

'It's more palliative care than anything else. He will never be allowed out by himself, Holly. Never.'

'Can we appeal?'

'The Parole Board's decision is solely focused on whether Sebastian represents a significant risk to the public after release. He doesn't. He can barely walk.'

'Have you seen him?'

'No. You want to appeal, do it. It would take months and he will be dead by then. By law the Parole Board will have to publish the full details of their findings and the reasons for their decision, but according to the phone call I received this morning he is already being prepared for his release from Broadmoor.'

'They knew he was going to be released all along.'

'I don't think so, Holly.'

'Things don't work this fast, I know they don't. Someone, somewhere had a plan. They had agreed to this and we, the victims, were the only ones that didn't know.' A pause and then she said:

'The letter – give it to me.'

Moira held it up and Holly snatched it from her.

'I will read his shitty letter but tell Sebastian Carstairs I want something in return.'

'What?'

'My mother's necklace that he stole.'

The Old Bailey was mayhem.

Hundreds had gathered. Placard-waving, angry men,

women and teenagers. All crying out for the same thing: Justice for the survivors. A banner had been unfurled listing all of The Animal's victims. She saw her parents' names at the bottom – the final two casualties – and had to turn away. It was suddenly very real again. There was a police presence but they all stood to one side, arms folded, not sure where to look. They understood the frustration and anger themselves. The sixth victim had been a police constable from Esher in Surrey named Rory Anglesey. Only thirty-five years old with three children. He had responded to a report of a break-in at a warehouse. There had been no break-in. The Animal had made the call himself and the constable had walked into a trap. Holly wondered if Rory's children and wife were here. One of the officers on duty was comforting a woman. Perhaps that was her.

The media were having a field day. Capturing sad faces, happy to share someone's grief with a million strangers. After a while Holly felt like an outsider watching a play she didn't understand. She didn't chant or shout, she merely stood at the side and watched. Managed to avoid being filmed or photographed and her anger subsided to sadness as she saw men and women in their fifties and sixties crying and holding up photos of their loved ones whose lives had been taken.

Forty-seven

When Holly got home from The Old Bailey the rooms in her flat were full of shadows that seemed to move.

She eventually picked up the letter from The Animal which was still in its envelope on the coffee table and she was immediately nine years old again. All the years between had slipped away and she was back in the unhappy place that had been her life.

He can't hurt me any more, she said to herself and her words echoed sadly against the walls, the fireplace, the photos of her dead parents. She hesitated, shaken by an awful doubt.

Then she read it:

I have wanted to write this for many years now
knowing that in reality I would probably
never get to see you in person but it was important
otherwise I might not have the opportunity to
write what needed to be said.
What I did in the past is horrific and shameful.
How you ever managed to cope, to live and to

emerge from the hideous crimes I committed
required such strength of character and an
energy that I cannot begin to fathom.
You are the person I think
of every day when I try my best to
understand how I did what I did. Believe me, I
lie awake at night and ask for forgiveness.
I pray for my redemption knowing how
very hard it must be for you to live and
enjoy your life after bearing witness to what I have done.
Justice is blind I know.
Everybody I have ever known
says the same thing – find peace within.
Some say I should not be forgiven and
I can understand why. Most days I
cannot forgive myself, but I die in hope.
Amen.
Or perhaps there is life after death?
Redemption for the most twisted
souls that exist not just on this plane but in
hell itself. The incendiary heat
or sulphurous flames I do not fear. Living
under Milton's clouds within his epic poem Paradise
Lost casts no doubt as to my final resting place.
Divine is he who has no fear and
I know what will await me. But what awaits you?
Cherubs?
Angels? Or a Hades type of
limbo inhabited by the demon
Lucifer himself?
You are not as blameless

or innocent as you might want to think.
Uncovering the truth about oneself is never pleasant.
Have you heard of the Furies
of Greek Mythology? Three sisters
Living with vengeance in their hearts,
Listening to the voices in their heads until they scream
You would do well to hear their ancient cry as
I would shed a tear for their fate rather than my own.
As my final night draws near.
May the seconds spread for hours
and my hours for days and may they
last until
I take my final breath which
very soon will be upon me.
Eventually, whether we are a man, woman or child, we
all die, but it is
not how, but what we will be remembered for that counts.
Did I live out my dreams
while taking others?
Always. I chose the path of most destruction,
lying, cheating, poisonous, sinister.
Killing those who walked with
innocent blood in their veins.
Nothing was ever wrong in my head though.
God forgave me as I
took life after life. Forgive me please I ask of you, for in
God's eyes
am I not your brother too? Simply a lost soul? I will
leave you and this world with nothing but
love.
Sebastian Carstairs x

It had been handwritten and signed at the bottom of the page in black.

She lay it on the table then picked it up and folded it away in its envelope. Took the edges as if to tear it in half but stopped as if all her energy had suddenly slipped into the floor.

Goddamn you, Sebastian Carstairs.

She had so much anger she needed to get it out, she needed to punch something. She changed into her workout gear and went to the gym.

Forty-eight

'They're dislocated.'

'What?'

'Your fingers. Look at them.'

Holly did. The fingers in her right hand looked like baby breadsticks that were somehow twice as long as her other fingers and floppy. Then the pain kicked in.

'Ooh,' she said.

'Yeah,' he said. *He* was an Australian called Anthony Kleeman. World Champion heavyweight stick-fighter, and Holly's kick-boxing and sparring partner. He was six foot four, two hundred and fifty pounds and whenever he spoke there was a slight smile on his lips and now was no exception. It was her own fault. She had been hitting the heavy bag but thinking about The Animal and how much she wanted to hurt him. After twenty minutes she had been sweating as if she was swimming – a quick jab-jab-cross and then her right hand skimmed off the bag, knuckles first, and there had been a series of unhealthy pops.

'Bugger, that hurts,' she said. 'What do I do?'

'Need to go to the hospital probably and have an X-ray, unless you want me to pop them back in?'

Said so casually, as if he were asking, Would you like a smoothie?

'You can do that?'

'It will hurt.'

'It hurts now.'

'Take off your wraps and give me your hand.'

She unwound the ten-foot red wraps, balled them and dropped them on the floor. Her arm from the elbow down felt as if it didn't belong to her and she winced when he grabbed her middle finger.

'Look away,' he said.

'I think I'll watch,' and she ground her teeth.

Twist.

POP.

MOTHERFUCKER!

Then the immediate pain was gone. A dull ache. Like being whacked on the shin or having your finger dislocated and put back . . .

'Next one?'

'Go on then.'

She held it out. He was actually smiling when he grabbed her ring finger. For some reason it made her smile too.

'Glad you find this funny,' she said.

'Sorry.'

'Do it.'

Twist.

POP.

MOTHERFUCKER HATE YOU SHIT-FACE BASTARD!

He let go of her hand and she whipped it away. Held it above her head then shoved it between her thighs.

'Christ, that was worse!'

'Little fingers going to be the cranky one,' he said.' The joints are really small.'

'Get it over and done with.'

He grabbed her little finger, twisted and pushed and it popped back into place.

WHAT A WANKER!

It was the sort of pain when you just wanted to lash out – so she did with her other fist and caught him on the shoulder. It was like hitting a brick. He smiled and winked at her.

'Smoothie on the house? I think you've earned it.'

By the time Holly got home her whole arm was starting to ache.

She got a bag of ice out of the freezer, shoved her hand in the bowl and took a couple of painkillers. She knew she had to be careful because Anthony had told her that dislocated knuckles were like Pringles – once they pop, they won't stop.

After five minutes the pain wasn't going so she opened a bottle of red wine. She ended up using her knees, her mouth and her elbows to uncork it. She downed the first glass and was halfway through the second when Bishop called.

'I saw the news. I've been trying to get hold of you,' he said.

'It's shit. It makes no sense.'

'I know, I'm sorry. This is so wrong.'

'A psychopath's one job in prison is to convince the Parole Board and his lead therapist that he is no longer a threat to society. Well, guess what? He succeeded.' She wanted to vent and swear, but she couldn't. 'I'm trying to look on the bright side,' she said, 'but I can't for the life of me see what that is.'

'Can you appeal?'

'Along with about a hundred other people, but I can't see it being successful. I don't trust him or them any more.'

'Do you want me to come over later?'

'No, tonight I will be really shit company.'

'Okay. But I'm here to listen when you need me.'

'I know, thank you,' but she could feel herself hardening against the world and against everything again. Things had been going so well. The rollercoaster, the sliding doors of life, whatever you wanted to call it. 'Keep me up to date,' she said.

'I will.'

She didn't say anything for a while and neither did he, so she hung up before she realised what she had done. She wanted to call him back, but her mood was foul and she downed the rest of the bottle of red wine, which didn't help.

She stuck her hand back in the ice and enjoyed the pain. It took her mind away for a while and then it suddenly felt as though the floor had come up and hit her, she was so tired.

Forty-nine

Bishop stared at the skeleton on the autopsy table.

It was stained a very pale yellow but seemed complete.

'When did they find this?' he said.

'Late last night. There was a fire in a bakery in St Albans and it took the fire crew by surprise when it landed on them. All very exciting,' Angela Swan said. 'They thought it must be medieval, so they called in the local anthropologist who took one look at it and said rubbish, because our bony friend has a very nice twenty-first-century filling.'

'And why am I here?'

'The anthropologist is used to battlefield injuries and has been following the murder cases in the newspaper. She noticed the unusual marks around the orbital cavities. Have a close look at the skull.'

It was soulless and the eye sockets haunting, both of them fractured, with crazy-paving lines that reached up to the forehead and down the bridge of the nose and into the upper jaw. Bishop squinted closer – the sockets also had dozens of nicks and incisions circling the bone.

He was trying to mentally catalogue what he was seeing when Angela spoke:

'The injuries are consistent with the previous three victims.'

He looked up at her, shocked—

'You mean to say this is another one?'

'I find it hard to believe it's a different killer.'

'Another victim?'

'It's just too similar and it *feels* right – please don't quote me on that. There are approximately sixty stab wounds in all to the eyes; there may have been more, but some might be repeater cuts where the blade found the same groove as we have seen on the other victims.'

'What else do we know about him, or is it her?'

'He was male, aged between twenty-five and thirty-five and he met a violent death. It could be ground zero, Bishop, or as we say – victim number one.'

'What's the yellowish glaze on the bones?' he said.

'Staining from hydrofluoric acid. Whoever killed him stripped his skin with acid before he was put underneath the floorboards. Inconsistent with the other victims and you *can* quote me on that. An usual MO these days; the process requires the use of a bathtub or a metal drum of some kind, and modern enamel bathtubs tend to dissolve if the solution is strong enough. Hydrofluoric acid is a weak acid in itself, but is very corrosive and extremely toxic. It dissolves in liquid to form various solutions which are colourless and visibly indistinguishable from water.'

'So you could be stepping into a bath and have no idea?'

'Something like that.'

'Would it make a smell? Putting a body in acid.'

'Yes, the chemical reaction of HF coming into contact with

human flesh and bone would result in an odour akin to dead or dissolving flesh in extreme heat.'

Bishop knew that smell from the streets of Afghanistan to the streets of London. Flesh smelt very differently after it had lain in the hot sun for a few days. Different when the flies had made an appearance too.

'Where can you buy hydrofluoric acid?' he said.

'On eBay.'

'Seriously?'

'The laws haven't tightened up that much – not even after all the acid attacks in London.'

One attack in particular last year jarred Bishop's memory. A woman named Janine Gordon had been targeted after she had left a homeless shelter where she worked. She was the wife of Sam Gordon, a part-time employee of the MIT, a profiler who was working on a double-murder case. After the attack he took compassionate leave to care for his wife, which was why Bishop had first contacted Holly and she had assisted on the Sickert case.

'Very little chance of an ID, I'm afraid,' Angela said. 'We can get DNA from the bones and we can X-ray his teeth, but if he's not on the system we're stuck. Missing persons might be an idea, but as for how far you need to go back, I don't know,' Angela said. 'The only other thing we can do is to attempt to reconstruct his face.'

'How do we do that?'

'We contact Stephanie and Edward Edwards, they're anthropologists from Oxford who do facial reconstruction for a living. They've helped on a few missing persons cases for me. Do you recall the body of the Polish prostitute we found in the dumpster near Putney about five years ago?'

'Yeah, I remember her.'

She had been a sex worker. Straight off the boat and trafficked around the system until someone had got pissed off with her and cut her throat. She had been hidden in a dumpster behind an industrial estate for the best part of five weeks before she was found. The rats had taken most of her flesh off, first targeting her throat, eyes and her face. The only part of her that hadn't been chewed on was her feet because she was still wearing her Dr Martens boots. Bishop had a pair of Dr Martens and to this day every time he laced them up he thought about her.

They had never caught her killer and the girl had never been identified, even though the reconstruction had been quite remarkable. A petite blonde with a nice smile, high cheekbones and a straight nose. The only thing they weren't sure about was her eye colour, so they had gone with blue.

'Bishop?' Angela jarred him from his thoughts.

'Yes?'

'Do you want me to contact Stephanie and Edward and ask them to go ahead with the facial reconstruction?'

'Make it a priority.'

Fifty

Holly had spent most of the afternoon nursing her right hand.

She'd slept sporadically and then taken a second dose of pain pills before trying to drive to the station, but her hand was too swollen and painful. It was all she could do to drive once around the block and re-park. She should have put it in a sling but instead bandaged her hand and hid it deep in her jacket pocket as she walked to the Underground station.

The tube was busy and so was Hammersmith, and once inside Bishop's office she showed him the bruising on her hand.

'You're getting the week off to a good start, aren't you?' he said.

She smiled for the first time as he brought her a coffee and showed her photos of the skeleton.

'The fact that it was hidden shows how his MO has changed,' she said. 'And if we stick to the theory that each victim is three years apart and this is our first victim, then our John Doe would have been killed in St Albans in 2010, yes?'

'That's right.'

'What's the history of the property?'

'Back in 2008, all three flats were owned by the bakery below. They wanted planning permission to turn them into an upstairs café, but the council refused. The flats stayed empty until 2011, when they were bought by an investor called Alfred Reagan who renovated them.'

'And he didn't touch the floors?'

'Just sanded them down.'

'So the body was already there.'

'We've checked Mr Reagan and all of his renters and they come back as clean.'

Janet Acton knocked on the door and entered.

'Toxicology just came through on the skeleton – no GHB or chloroform present, but that isn't surprising after all these years.'

Bishop rubbed his temples.

'We already have facial reconstruction taking place, but that won't be ready for at least twenty-four hours. In the meantime, we need to check missing persons from 2009 to 2011.'

'There will be a lot of people on the database,' said Janet.

'Well let's get a finite list that we can begin to eliminate tomorrow. Male, aged between twenty-five and thirty-five and five feet ten tall. We have DNA samples from the victim's bones, so we can track and trace those families who left DNA for mispers. Families that didn't should be encouraged to do so.' He took a moment. 'I think that's it,' he said.

'I'm on it,' Janet said and then, 'Walker's here. You want me to send him in?'

Walker sat next to Holly in one of the chairs. He had a coffee but wasn't drinking it.

'I mean, the guy was a fucking dick, but Jesus, I wouldn't

wish that on anybody,' he said as he put down the photos of the Andy Brooks autopsy, and picked up the ones of the skeleton. 'And where was this found?'

'St Albans,' Bishop said.

'Hertfordshire. I don't remember having anybody on the suspect list come from there.'

'We didn't and we don't.'

'What are you doing, checking missing persons?'

'And facial reconstruction.'

Walker shook his head.

'I'm not a fan,' he said. 'I know they're getting better and better at it, but they all end up looking like Richard the Third.' He let the photo drop on the table. 'You look how I feel,' he said to Bishop. 'Are you sleeping here yet?'

'Sometimes,' he smiled.

'My office was downstairs, Holly. None of this glass and metal shit. Decent bricks and a decent sofa. I used to bring the coffee machine onto my desk so when I'd wake up I'd have that first sip lying down. No traffic, no travel expenses. I began to like it too much.' He frowned. 'The skeleton has got to be the first vic, right?'

'Possibly,' Holly said, 'which is why he hid it.'

'We had a victim down a well once. Never identified her. A kid who'd been strangled. Tough call,' he said. 'This whole thing just gets messier and messier.'

He stood up and they shook hands.

'Thanks for letting me come in, Bill. I just wish I could help, but I'll see you guys for dinner on Friday night, right?'

'Looking forward to it,' Holly said, but in truth she had forgotten and from the look on Bishop's face so had he.

Fifty-one

Holly took the call from Moira Drake at eight o'clock the next morning.

Sebastian Carstairs, The Animal, never made it to parole and was officially pronounced dead at 11.37 p.m. last night. Any final words? Nothing. He passed away in his prison bed, with no witnesses and no priest to give him his final prayers.

His body had been removed from Broadmoor and transported straight to an autopsy suite where he had been diagnosed as having died from complications of pneumonia. The pathologist concluded the cancer that riddled his body would have killed him within days anyway, most likely from renal failure. There would be no official funeral as such. The authorities were trying to keep it quiet. They didn't want any more protests in the street.

Holly thanked her and hung up. She had wrapped her hand in a bandage, but it was still aching so she took some aspirin. She switched her phone to Airplane mode and lay on the sofa, wrapped in a blanket, and closed her eyes. Her body was exhausted but her mind wouldn't stop working.

After all the commotion and angst over the last few days

Sebastian Carstairs hadn't even made it out of the prison. He had died where he had been living from the day he had been convicted.

Part of her felt this was just a cruel trick being played on her. None of the other victims' families, just her. She wanted to be sure that he was well and truly gone and she wanted to see him buried or go up in smoke.

She called up Bishop and told him what had happened, then she said:

'I want to know where the funeral is.'

Bishop said he would help and by early afternoon he called her back and gave her the details.

'It's happening today, Holly.'

'Christ.'

'It's been fast-tracked. Anything to stop it turning into a media circus. Do you want me to come with you?'

'No thank you.'

This was something she had to do herself.

Holly had had a hard time deciding on what to wear, but had gone with black. She had taken a taxi to Lambeth Crematorium in south London, her hand still too painful to drive, and now stood at the back of the crematorium with a photo of her parents in her left hand.

It was a small room with brick walls and frosted windows on either side. There were no photos, no flowers, just a bamboo casket, a priest who was conducting the ceremony, two policemen standing to one side acting as witnesses and a woman. She was tall, but heavy, wearing a dark brown trouser suit, black jacket and black hat, and she watched the proceedings from the front pew.

The priest said very little. Holly was sure he knew who was in the coffin but his face stayed expressionless as he read Mark 8:31, the Resurrection of Christ:

"'He then began to teach them that the Son of Man must suffer many things and be rejected by the elders, the chief priests and the teachers of the law, and that he must be killed and after three days rise again.'"

His left hand discreetly pressed a button at the side of the table and blue velvet curtains parted at the back of the platform. A few seconds later and the bamboo casket started to slide noiselessly into the furnace.

"'I said to myself – God will bring into judgement both the righteous and the wicked, for there will be a time for every activity, a time to judge every deed.'"

The priest gave the woman a slight nod, but she didn't move and remained silent.

A chilled hush seemed to fall across the room.

This was it then. The final chapter in a sordid and murderous history reduced to what? A quiet farewell by an audience of five. The priest was just doing his job, the police were there as witnesses, and the woman? His sister? The only surviving member of his family? And Holly? Why was she here?

This was it. Sebastian Carstairs – The Animal – was finally dead and Holly felt a surge of emptiness all of a sudden. He was being burned in a small oven less than fifty metres away and she wanted to laugh, but couldn't. It was a strange mix of emotions – a fight she had been involved in for over twenty-five years had suddenly ended and she felt emptier than she ever had in her life. Not for the first time she wondered if she had made a mistake in coming here.

The blue velvet curtains closed. Nobody moved and she left

the room as silently as she had entered. Outside, other people were queuing in line for the next ceremony. A busy day at the crematorium, their loved ones boxed and sent to heaven at 1900 degrees. She was walking through the gardens by the fountain when she sensed someone following her and turned instinctively. It was the woman from the cremation. She wore square-heeled shoes that skidded on the gravel as she stopped.

'Are you Cassandra?' Holly said.

The woman kept her hat on and pulled at her veil to make sure her face stayed covered, but Holly could see she had blonde hair that had turned grey a decade too soon.

'Who are you?' the woman said. 'Why did you come to the service?'

Because that bastard brother of yours killed my parents and I wanted to come here to make sure he was dead. I wanted to gloat, to laugh and to dance. But instead I didn't, and I kept my mouth shut and stayed silent for you, whoever you are. That's who I am.

'I'm sorry,' Holly said. 'I'm sorry for your loss.'

'Did you know my brother?' the woman said almost fiercely, and through the veil Holly could see she was frowning, her lips tight.

Holly shook her head, her mouth suddenly dry.

'No.'

The woman stared but didn't say another word, then she turned on her square heels and walked quickly away.

248

Fifty-two

Wetherington Hospital on Cromwell Road, Central London, was a Georgian building transformed from flats in the 1960s to the psychiatric facility that now housed up to eighty patients.

The taxi dropped Holly off and she went through security and headed for the main detainment centre. Her brother was kept in Block B and she walked towards the end of the east corridor. She was nervous being here. Lee never wanted to talk about The Animal, but she had to tell him the truth. He had a right to know, just like all the other victims.

He had a rapist living to his left and a suicidal schizophrenic on his right. Both were quiet in their rooms as she swiped her security pass card at her brother's door. A gentle click, the door light went green and she pushed it open.

The cell was fourteen by fourteen feet square with a table, two chairs and a toilet, a sink and bed in the far-left corner. She sat on the chair by the table. Lee was lying on the bed. He was peeling a tangerine with his fingers, lowering the waxy skin to the floor in one long strand. The smell reminded her of Christmas.

'Long time no see,' he said.

'How are you, Lee?'

'I get dizzy on the new meds. I mustn't stand up too fast, I fell over last week.'

'Did you hurt yourself?'

'My pride and my elbow.'

He showed her. There was a scab on the bone. Then he sat up and plopped an orange segment in his mouth.

'What have you done to your hand?' he said.

'What?'

'Your hand – you've got a bandage on it – what did you do?'

'I punched something.'

'Animal, vegetable or mineral?'

Holly came straight out with it:

'Sebastian Carstairs is dead.'

Lee watched her for a while then wiped his trousers. He had finished his tangerine and his hands were sticky.

'He had cancer. I went to the cremation,' she said.

'I don't believe it.'

'It's finally over, Lee.'

He was quite content to stare at her, and she searched his face for any signs of hurt. It was expressionless today. Even his eyes.

'Jesus, Lee, have you taken in what I've just told you?'

'I have, but I choose to ignore it. He'll never be truly dead.'

'That's an unhealthy way to look at things.'

'Don't tell me what's UNHEALTHY!'

He moved so fast she suddenly felt herself lean back in the chair, his hands inches from her face. They were red and shaking and after a while he let them fall to his waist, then turned to face the camera.

250

'She's my sister! I would never hurt her!' But his voice sounded flat. 'Don't tell me what's unhealthy, Holly! Stuck in here is unhealthy. Three meals a day is unhealthy. Voices in my fucking head every day is unhealthy. Waiting for you to appear is unhealthy! I'm a lost soul, Holly.'

'I wanted to let you know.'

She stood up.

'Don't go. Don't leave me!' he said quickly. 'Please.'

'You always ask me that. I'm not going to leave you, Lee,' she said. 'I'm saying The Animal is dead, that's all.'

'This isn't some sick joke? My meds make me hear things. I hallucinate – are you really here?'

'I'm here, Lee,' and she reached out and touched his arm.

'He's actually gone?'

'He is gone, Lee. But we're still here. We'll always be here for each other.'

She sensed a smile but it never appeared. Her brother could be so brilliant, with his dark eyes that lit up when he laughed.

'There was a woman at the funeral,' Holly said. 'I think it was his sister.'

'I didn't know he had a sister.'

'Her name is Cassandra, I spoke to her.'

'What did you say?'

'I said I'm sorry.'

'Sorry?'

'Yes. I said I'm sorry for your loss.'

'Why? Why the fuck would you say that?'

'Because *she* wasn't *him*, Lee.'

'He killed Mum and Dad!' Blue eyes blinking fast beneath his thin red hair. 'He murdered them and I saw it! In the kitchen – hiding in the cupboard as he cut Dad's head off and

251

then Mum ...' he turned away and covered his eyes. 'I still speak to them,' he whispered. 'I still speak to Mum and Dad, and sometimes they speak back to me.'

His imagination? Voices? She wondered if he had told his therapist this.

'What do they say?' she asked.

'A lot of it doesn't make sense. Their mouths are moving, but I only hear one word, over and over again.'

'What word?'

'Kaleidoscope.'

'Kaleidoscope? I don't know what that means.'

'Like the toy we used to have when we were kids,' he said. 'Look through the eyepiece, twist one end and you suddenly saw rainbow colours. These beautiful moving patterns.'

Coloured beads and mirrors, if Holly remembered correctly.

'They never say anything else,' Lee said. 'And if I try to touch them, they always disappear.'

'I don't have dreams like that.'

'They're not dreams, Holly. I really see Mum and Dad.'

He closed his eyes and squeezed them tight.

'*Doubt thou the stars are fire. Doubt that the sun doth move. Doubt truth to be a liar,*' he said and waited for her to finish it.

'*But never doubt I love,*' she said.

He moved quietly over and hugged her from behind.

'I've got you,' he whispered into her ear, like her father used to: 'I've got you.'

He put his arms around her and held her like a child. She felt him rocking her and hoped he would never let go.

Fifty-three

Holly walked home.

She needed the fresh air, but when she arrived outside her flat she didn't go inside.

Instead, she followed the London lights and buzz of conversation.

There is no such thing as a lost soul, Lee. Everyone makes it home eventually.

She shed a tear thinking about him and looked into alleys and doorways as she passed that were somehow unfamiliar tonight. People were gathering and there were barks of laughter and she saw a loose knit of people around a corner and headed in that direction. She found herself at the Bedford pub and took a seat in a corner. A waitress approached and asked what she wanted to drink.

'Whisky. Double please.'

She necked it in one.

'And again.'

And did the same with the second. She wondered when Lee would be able to process what she had told him. She wanted to see more of him, but it wasn't healthy for her, and she thought of her parents and wondered why she couldn't speak to them in her dreams.

The waitress was with her again.

'Can I have a red wine this time please, that would be lovely of you . . .'

'House?'

'I live in a flat, but thanks for asking,' Holly said and laughed really loudly. After two mouthfuls of wine she felt sick and went back to whisky. People seemed suddenly blurry against the bar. Holly couldn't remember it getting so late or perhaps the drink was going to her head.

A man sitting thirty feet away on a bench opposite kept looking at her. She held up her hand to give him the finger but the bandage was too tight and she couldn't separate her fingers so it must have looked like some backward royal wave. He smiled and proceeded to place pork scratchings in his mouth every few minutes. He was a sucker, not a cruncher, and Holly wondered if anyone had ever told him that.

She ordered more whisky, drifted in and out of a stupor and suddenly woke when she realised people had sat down next to her. The place had filled with an early evening crowd – briefcases on the floor and work ties pulled aside like pageant sashes.

Holly had four messages on her phone about The Animal. Three were from Bishop and one was from Sophie Savage, a girl from her foster home, whom she had kept in contact with over the years. If you need to talk – I'm here, Sophie said. She called Bishop and left a message. It annoyed her that he didn't pick up. Where are you when I need you? She felt unliked and unloved and minutes later realised she had fallen asleep with her head slanted down towards her left arm and suddenly she had had enough.

She got up and pushed her way to the exit and fresh air and walked home so fast she was sweating when she got inside her flat and took a cold shower. She was sick in the toilet and took aspirin with ice-cold water. Put on some thin cotton PJ bottoms and a T-shirt just before she made it to the sofa and woke up forty-five minutes later when Bishop buzzed from the ground floor. He came in, all shoulders and chest, and she couldn't remember the last time she had washed her hair.

He was silent for a while. Staring at her.

'You've got big arms,' she said, and thought she was being particularly amusing.

He half-smiled.

'How much have you had?'

'Don't know.'

She gave him an exaggerated wink as if it was their little secret, and suddenly her right hand was aching again and she pulled the bandage off, but it somehow got tangled up with her legs so Bishop helped her unwrap it and dropped it on the carpet and it looked like a dead snake. She listened to him rooting around in the kitchen cupboards. He came back armed with a pint glass of cold water.

'Drink.'

She took a sip. Put the glass down.

'Drink,' he said.

'Uh. God. You're so annoying.'

She drank the whole pint in one. Saw him through bleary eyes and slammed it down like a shot glass.

'God, I feel sick now.'

He took the glass, filled it up and put it back in front of her.

'I can't do that again.'

'Just sip it now.'

She did and he sat next to her.

'How was the funeral?'

'Shit.'

'It's the end of the chapter,' he said. 'The beginning of a new one.'

'That is such a lame cliché.'

'I'm full of them today.'

'Like those funny acronyms you and Walker come out with.'

'Christ, you really are drunk.'

She wanted to say – *but do you still love me?* – and laughed but could feel the tears ready. She turned her head back to him and tried to straighten her shoulders.

'All my life, Bishop, I've thought about getting revenge on that bastard,' she said. 'Killing him. Watching him die. Watching him beg for mercy, even though I knew he never would have. He didn't understand life and death, to him it was the same thing. When he was alive, I felt as though I had a purpose. I felt as though I was doing something that mattered—'

'You are.'

'No. Hold on, Bishop, let me finish. But now he's gone, now he's dead, I don't know. I don't think I need to do this any more. The killing. The people. The insanity. I don't think I want it in my life any more. Do you understand?'

'I do.'

Of course he did. He always understood her. He always knew what to say.

'So what do I do now?' she said.

'You carry on, Holly.'

'Carry on with my life? It's almost like I have nothing to prove.'

'You just have to prove it to someone else, that's all.'

'Who?'

'Yourself. You can stop doing it for him, for your parents, because you don't need to any more. Do it for you, you're the only one that matters now.'

She lay back on the sofa and started to cry. Felt the blanket being tucked around her and his hands holding her. She took deep breaths and suddenly felt very, very warm. Minutes passed but it could have been hours. Then she felt him kiss her on the forehead.

'Where do we go from here?' he said, and Holly had no idea if he was talking about the case any more. She let herself fall into her imagination and when she heard the door shut, she knew he was gone.

Fifty-four

Stephanie and Edward Edwards liked to consider themselves forensic artists.

They always warned police that the method could never be 100 per cent accurate, and the end result was never an exact image, it was simply a projection based on what the skull told them, but everything they saw, from the eyebrows, the jawline, the bridge of the nose, was reconstructed based on the facts of the bone shape that they had been presented with.

The unidentified skull had been scanned by the MRI at the Radcliffe Hospital in Oxford less than twenty-four hours ago and the results emailed to them at the School of Anthropology and Museum Ethnography at 51/53 Banbury Road. The information was then downloaded into the latest imaging software for the purpose of skull-image superimposition. Studies had shown there existed a strict individual identity and exclusiveness in relation between the human face and its skull, and by early Wednesday morning they were both very happy with the results.

One last check to make sure all of the information was in

the proper format for recovery and then they pressed send on their computer.

Sergeant Ince was the recipient of the email in the incident room at Hammersmith police station.

He opened it up, having no comprehension of the numbers or graphs that accompanied the file but the photographic-like image he understood immediately. He emailed the findings over to DI Janet Acton with the words:

'Ma'am, we've had something come in!'

Janet opened the file and stared at the man's face that had been digitally recreated. She sent a copy to everyone on the task force and one to the missing persons team who sat three desks away. She said:

'Sandra – we've got a very nice image of our Richard the Third. Fingers crossed.'

Sergeant Sandra Lowlands downloaded the file image into her Mac.

The missing persons folder she had created for the skeleton found under the floor in St Albans had over three thousand two hundred names of males who had gone missing in the UK during time period 2009–2011 within the age bracket of twenty-five to thirty-five who had never been found or accounted for. She pressed enter to begin the search and pushed out of her chair. She needed another coffee and now would be a good—

Her computer pinged. She looked in disbelief at the two images side by side on screen and the green word 'MATCH' that kept flashing and said:

'Bloody hell, that was quick.'

She sat and pondered. The photograph on the left of her screen was of a thirty-year-old man that had been sent to the police mispers division by his parents nine years ago and the 3-D image on the right from Oxford anthropology was almost identical. The software had picked up on measurements and statistics no human eye could see and had locked in at 92 per cent accuracy. That was pretty conclusive. She printed off the family details, stood up and glanced around the incident room.

'Where's Bishop?'

Fifty-five

'Are you sober?'

It was Bishop on the phone and it was 7.33 a.m.

'Probably not,' said Holly.

'I'll be there in ten minutes.' ·

'What? No – I need to—'

'We've got an ID on our skeleton,' he said. 'His name was John Reynolds.'

A cold shower woke her up.

Bishop drove.

Holly had drunk coffee with paracetamol but it hadn't helped. Her hand still ached and her head was spinning. She was normally more of a hot chocolate than a whisky drinker, and now she remembered why. Hilly banks of bright green trees and yellow cornfields flashed by either side. It looked psychedelic and she was trying not to be sick.

'Are you going to puke?' he said.

'No. Can you slow down on the corners?'

'I'm only doing forty.'

'Pull over,' she said.

He did and she puked in a blackberry bush. She immediately felt better and took her seat with a smile.

'Onwards, Miss Daisy,' she said and closed her eyes. 'Now, tell me about John Reynolds.'

'He was thirty years old when he went missing from central London on the twenty-sixth of May, 2010. He lived in a two-bedroom flat in Knightsbridge and on the night he disappeared he had been with a group of friends at the Wellington Club. They had all said their goodbyes in high spirits, a little drunk perhaps,' she felt him glance over at her, 'and they all agreed to meet for a civilised brunch the next day at The Wolseley on Piccadilly.'

'Needless to say, he didn't turn up?'

'He never even made it back to his flat.'

'How do we know that?'

'He had an alarm system and motion detectors that weren't de-activated that night. Concern was raised the next day by one of his friends when John failed to materialise for their brunch. He wasn't answering his phone or texts and by two o'clock they called his family. By six o'clock that evening, there was genuine concern and the police became involved. His phone records were examined and his phone had been turned off a mile from his home the previous evening. That was the last location they had for him. Phone records revealed no new numbers, no new contacts. It's the same MO as all the others. Everyone at his work was interviewed and his family started a Facebook appeal, but no witnesses ever came forward.'

'He didn't have a criminal record or anything?'

'Apparently, he liked a bit of cocaine, and there was speculation for a few weeks that it was some drugs deal that went wrong, but I think we can eliminate that now. The police followed the CCTV, which captured him going from the Wellington Club, but lost him in a taxi somewhere around High Street Kensington. The taxi driver was talked to at the time and swears blind he dropped his passenger off on Newark Street, east London.

'What's on Newark Street?'

'Residential houses and a few businesses, but somehow he ended up as a skeleton in St Albans.'

The pain pills were finally kicking in and Holly opened her eyes as Bishop turned off the main road and headed towards Nuthampstead. The psychedelic fields were replaced by knotted trees and thatched cottages.

'Did he have a partner?' she said.

'Not at the time, he liked his women but was in between relationships.'

There was quiet for a while, each of them working through different thoughts, then Bishop pulled over and turned off the engine as they parked near an old stone farmhouse with fields at the rear. Holly took in the barns, the stables and tractor in the rutted drive. It reminded her of her childhood home.

'Do they know why we're here?'

'Yes,' said Bishop.

Fifty-six

The farmhouse was early construction with flag-stone floors and timbers that crossed the walls and ceilings.

They all hovered in the hall for a few minutes while Bishop made the introductions, then the family invited them into the living room. Coffee and tea was brought out by Chloe, their daughter, and the silence for the first several seconds was what one might expect when a family whose only son had disappeared nine years ago were suddenly told that he had finally been found, but was dead.

'What do we do now, DI Bishop?'

It was Patricia Reynolds, the mother, who had spoken. Holly thought she was in her sixties, her face marred with worry. She stood next to her husband, a tall and thin man; he was younger by five years perhaps, and Chloe, who stood to one side, would have been in her late thirties.

'We need a DNA sample from any one of you to confirm that it's your son,' Bishop said. 'A swab from inside the cheek.'

'I'll do it,' said Chloe.

'Thank you.'

'How certain are you that it is John?' the father said.

'Very certain,' said Bishop.

The mother looked up from her armchair. She was still holding the 3-D image Bishop had presented the family with.

'Is there a small chance that my son may still be alive?' she said.

'I don't think so,' Bishop said. 'I'm very sorry.'

'How did John die, DI Bishop? Do we know that?'

'The exact cause of death is as yet uncertain,' Bishop said. 'We may never know.'

'But you found his skull?'

'His skeleton.'

Chloe gasped and her hand shot to her mouth.

'Not the skeleton in St Albans? Please don't tell me that is my brother.'

'It is, I'm afraid.'

'What skeleton?' the mother said. 'Where in St Albans?'

Voices cut into each other but it was Chloe who came out on top.

'There was a fire at a bakery in St Albans on Sunday night and the firefighters found a skeleton in the ashes, it was all over the news.'

'I thought that was medieval?'

'No,' said Bishop.

'And that's where my son has been for ten years? Hidden in some flat above a bakery in St Albans . . .' She finally broke down and her husband and daughter went to her side. 'How could that have happened? How could he even—' The grief was suddenly swept away by realisation. 'He was murdered, wasn't he?'

'It would appear so, Mrs Reynolds,' Bishop said. 'I'm very sorry.'

Holly could sense him juggling the words.

'This is a horribly indelicate question,' he said, 'but do you have any idea who might have wanted your son dead?'

'Of course not,' Chloe said.

'Mr Reynolds?'

'What? No.' The father spoke quickly and turned away in distaste.

'He had no enemies,' the mother said. Even as her face went white, she found the strength from somewhere: 'He was a lovely boy. Such a lovely boy.'

As Bishop was taking a statement from the parents, Holly found herself staring at the collection of family photographs on the tops of various pieces of Georgian furniture. John Reynolds had been an attractive young man – *GQ* type with dark hair and blue eyes. There were photos of him with beautiful women sitting in an Aston Martin and a brand-new Porsche. Chloe was in a shiny BMW Range Rover. The family had money and Holly felt that familiar bite. She had never experienced financial privilege at any point in her life: the foster home she had been brought up in, the second-hand clothes she had been made to wear to school, the one-present-at-Christmas rule.

Another photo of John and he couldn't have been more than twelve, a nervous smile in a starched school uniform with white shirt, green tie, green blazer and black shoes.

'He was precocious but fun,' Chloe had sidled over and picked up the picture. 'It is him, isn't it? He's dead?'

'It is,' said Holly. 'I'm so sorry for your loss.'

'We've been expecting it for years. But not Mother, she still burns a candle.'

'He was a good-looking boy.' Holly stared at the photo.

'He was. We all thought he would become prime minister one day, he was so sure of everything.'

'Do you live here, Chloe?'

'No, I'm based in south London. I run an interior design company near Sloane Square, and came straight away when dad gave me the call this morning. I don't think I've ever driven so fast.'

Chloe put the photo down, but something about it was bothering Holly. Not the photo itself, but the familiarity of John.

'How old was he here?' she said.

'Ten, eleven?'

'Do you have any more photos of him?'

'Lots in the attic, but there are probably still some in the dining room.'

Holly followed her through the corridor and into a large room with claret walls and dark brown furniture. The photos were in frames on the mantelpiece and Holly's heart began to race. John at school playing rugby, football and water polo. John on a horse, John wearing a chef's hat in the kitchen, John with his arms around a girl with red hair.

Holly suddenly went very still.

It was the same photo found in Vee's bedroom, but this looked like the original. Her thoughts spinning, she held her eyes on the photo, but eventually pulled them away and said:

'This photo. John's with a girl—'

'Ah, yes,' Chloe smiled wistfully. 'The star-crossed lovers. They were cast together in a school play, *Romeo and Juliet*, and dated for a while, but it was never meant to be.'

'Why not?'

'John went to Chesterton All-Boys' School in Petworth a

few miles down the road and we all went to Harringay Girls'
School. There was a fire at the girls' school, a terrible accident,
and the school had to close. It was just awful for everyone.
Our family came to live up here, John moved on with his life,
we all did.'

'And the girl?'

'Verity? I don't know what happened to her.'

'That was the girl's name? Verity?'

'Yes,' Chloe said. 'Verity Ellis Baxter.'

Fifty-seven

'Verity Ellis Baxter,' Bishop said, 'is the name of the sex worker from Brighton.'

They were back at the station and Holly watched as Bishop addressed the team from beside the incident board.

'Verity went to a school in Petworth called Harringay Girls' School, along with John Reynolds' sister, Chloe, who we have just spoken to and who positively identified her. The Reynolds family had the original of the photograph that we found in Verity's bedroom, showing her with their son,' he said. 'Chloe didn't know her that well, she was a year below Verity at school, but what she remembers of the pair was that they were both smitten with each other. So now we have a connection between what we believe is the first victim – John Reynolds – and Verity Ellis Baxter. They dated each other when they were at school and now they are both dead.'

'How did they meet?' Janet asked.

'Holly?' Bishop turned to her.

'Chloe informed us that John went to another local school in Petworth called Chesterton Boys' School,' she said, 'and on

269

sports day in 1994 John went to watch his sister play lacrosse and was introduced to Verity after the match. Verity was the class prefect and handed out the trophy, and according to Chloe their romance blossomed from there. Verity was fourteen, he was fifteen at the time.'

Back to Bishop:

'I know we've been looking at John Reynolds' missing person's report that was filed nine years ago,' he said, 'but now we need to go right back to when John was at school and when he and Verity were dating. Contact his old school friends and find out about him. I want his school reports, I want interviews with his old teachers, the headmaster, his best friends – anything you can find. His parents said he didn't have any enemies, but he was murdered so there will be someone.'

He paused and motioned to the photos of Verity:

'So how the hell did this young girl go from a very prestigious private school to working on the streets? Sergeant Kenny, remind us when was she first spotted in London?'

He riffled through his notes—

'Our informant, Grace, first remembers seeing Vee in 1998.'

'She would have been seventeen at the time, so it's the years before that that are vital to this investigation. We need to do for Verity what we are doing for John. His sister told us there was a bad fire at Verity's school that forced it to close, so we need to contact the teachers' unions and the education services and ask where all the teachers went and get the attendance records of all the pupils who went to Harringay during the 1990s until it was closed. Who were Verity's old school friends? Where are they now, and most importantly, did any of them keep in touch? By the end of the day I want a statement of some kind from every pupil and teacher at that school who knew Verity.'

People started to move. The sound of papers shuffling, the occasional clearing of a throat as phone numbers were dialled.

'Janet, do you have the address for Verity's parents?'

'Rose and Ernest Baxter live at Rydacre Manor off Gove Street, which is in the village of Petworth about ten minutes from the old school.'

'Did her parents ever report her missing?' Holly asked.

'No record of anything like that.'

'We'll see the parents first,' Bishop said. 'Contact them and let them know we'll be with them in approximately' – he checked the wall clock – 'ninety minutes. Wear kid gloves when you talk to them – they may not be aware of what their daughter was doing for a living or that she is even dead.'

He turned to Holly.

'We're leaving now.'

She nodded. She already had her jacket on.

As soon as they were in the corridor:

'The fire at the girls' school,' Holly said. 'I think we should look into it, find out if it was an accident.'

'You think it may have been started deliberately?'

'I don't think we can discount anything in this case.'

'I'll get hold of Pete Burns in the forensics department to look at the report, he specialises in fire analysis. How's your hand?'

'It was fine until you just asked me,' she said.

Fifty-eight

Rydacre Manor was Georgian, and made from pale yellow Cotswold stone with deep sash windows and fluted columns by the dark wood door with stone lions either side.

Bishop parked on the gravel drive and the two of them got out and walked the stone steps. There was a heavy iron knocker on the door. Bishop rapped it and the noise echoed.

A minute passed until the door clicked and opened and Verity Ellis Baxter's father stood there. He was a grey man, in his sixties, slightly built with receding hair. It was early afternoon, but he was well-dressed in a suit and Holly wondered if he had worn it for their benefit.

'Mr Baxter?' Bishop said.

'Yes.'

'DI Bishop and Holly Wakefield.'

'Yes, the station called me, I've been expecting you. Perhaps you should come in and we could have a cup of tea?'

'Thank you, that would be very nice.'

He held open the door and led them inside past the stairs

and the timber and white plaster walls towards the back of the house.

'Was the traffic bad on the way down from London?' he said.

'It wasn't too uncomfortable,' Bishop replied.

Holly wondered how forthcoming Mr Baxter would be. His casualness at conversation was unnerving.

The kitchen was old with oak furniture and wooden cabinets.

'We have builders' tea or Earl Grey,' Ernest said.

'Earl Grey would be nice, thank you,' Holly said.

'Builders' for me,' said Bishop.

Ernest put the kettle on and got three chintz mugs from a cupboard, dropped a teabag in each and lay a spoon by the side of the cups. 'Sugar?'

'No thank you.'

He checked his watch, pulled a fourth mug out and put it down. Placed another teabag inside and stared at the kettle as it hissed.

'You know why we're here, don't you, Mr Baxter?' Bishop said.

'Yes, they told me over the phone that Verity was dead.'

'That's right.'

'Murdered.'

'Yes. I'm very sorry about your loss. Has Mrs Baxter been informed?'

'Not yet, no.'

'We believe Verity's murder is connected to a series of other killings, so any help you can give us will be greatly appreciated. We know she went to Harringay Girls' School, but after that we're still trying to piece together her life.'

'I haven't known my daughter for over twenty years,' he said quietly, and turned the kettle off before it boiled.

'Milk?'

'Thank you,' Holly said as he passed over a mug first to her and then to Bishop. Ernest carried the two other mugs on a tray and backed up to a door that swung open as he leaned against it.

'It swings fast, so be careful.'

They followed him along a wood-panelled corridor into the living room. The curtains were drawn, with a single arrow of light where one curtain had failed to pull tight. Oil paintings hung within gold frames on the grey walls – landscapes and ships in high seas. The heat was stifling, the radiators on full blast.

There was a woman in an armchair positioned in front of a small television. Holly hadn't noticed her at first, she was so still. She was as grey-skinned as her husband and flinched when he turned the overhead lights on.

'It's all right, love,' he said. 'We have guests.'

Despite the heat she was wearing a thick woollen cardigan and had a tartan blanket over her knees. The sound on the television was muted, but the woman sat and watched.

'We don't get many visitors,' he said, 'and you will have to forgive me for not formally introducing my wife. This is Rose. There you go, my love.' He put the tea in her hands and she closed her fingers around the mug automatically. 'It's just the right temperature,' he said. She didn't acknowledge, but took a sip and he dabbed at her lips with a tissue from his pocket.

'Rose had a stroke two years ago,' he said. 'The doctors didn't think she would make it, but somehow she did. A nurse comes in twice a week, the rest is up to me.'

'That must be hard,' Bishop said.

'In one way it's easy. We have a routine that we are both very used to.'

Holly and Bishop took seats on the sofa. Ernest sat opposite and watched them. His eyes were rheumy and unfocused.

'I don't know how I can help you,' he said flatly. 'I don't think we truly knew who Verity became in the end. But the woman who died in Brighton wasn't the girl who was raised in this house.'

'When was the last time you saw Verity, Mr Baxter?' Holly said.

'Three months ago.'

'That recently?'

'She didn't knock on the door if that's what you mean, but I knew she was in the village.'

'How did you know?'

'This has been our family home through seven generations, Miss Wakefield. We know everyone here and everyone knows us, from the Morleys in Crest House to Tracy and Stephen who run the antiques shop on the corner. These are family friendships that have run through the centuries. Verity would come to Petworth once every six months or so. She would never come here, but she would wander around the village and sometimes watch the house. Perhaps she thought she was being clandestine, but everybody knew she was here and after she left people would always come and tell me.'

'She would watch the house?' Holly said.

'That's right.'

'Well, if she didn't come to see you, do you know why she came?' Holly said.

He paused.

'Will it help catch her killer if I tell you?'

275

'Possibly.'

He shrugged.

'She came to see if her daughter was here.'

Fifty-nine

'We adopted Juliet when she was just under a year old,' Ernest Baxter said. His voice was so low it was barely a whisper.

'What did you tell her about Verity?'

'As little as we could. She had questions when she grew older, what child wouldn't, but we made a decision and we stuck to it. We told Juliet her mother was a drug user and didn't live in a safe place, which is why she gave her up. We tried to make it sound noble to begin with, but as Juliet grew older she asked to see photos and I relented and showed her some from Harringay School. I couldn't help myself, but I felt that telling Juliet the whole truth would be an injustice and hurtful. She had been through enough.'

'And where is Juliet now?' Bishop asked.

'She moved away from here when she was twenty. She lives in another part of England and is training to be a teacher for a local primary school, she loves children and is very happy. She is engaged to someone – and before you ask, I will not divulge her address. We have protected her from everything as much as we could and we intend to carry on doing so.'

'Does she know what happened to her mother?'

'She does, I informed her just before you came.'

'How did she take the news?'

'She is neither angry nor in denial. To her, perhaps to us as well, it was expected in one way or another. If you live life on the edge, at some point you will always fall off.'

'Tell me about Verity,' Holly said. 'Tell me about her when she was young.'

'She was gregarious, excitable, a dreamer who loved the ballet and acting. She loved the school as well.'

'Harringay.'

'That's right.

'And there was a fire there?'

'The fire?' He paused. 'Oh, yes, the fire changed everything. The sort of tragedy the school could never recover from. It was a devastating event in the theatre that happened at the end of summer term production of *Twelfth Night*. Verity was part of the cast and we were so close to losing her. The other three girls died—'

'Three girls died?'

Holly glanced at Bishop. Their eyes met and he nodded slowly.

'Go on, Mr Baxter,' he said.

'They were all close friends of Verity's and for months after she suffered from what they call "survivor's guilt". She couldn't sleep, she had nightmares, flashbacks. We took her to London to see a therapist, but it didn't help. They gave her sleeping pills, drugs, she started cutting, starving herself, and became more isolated. We thought she was suicidal . . . I can't . . . even after all these years I find it hard to talk about this, I'm sorry.'

'We understand,' Holly said. 'Take your time.'

'The school closed after the fire and while the pupils were moved on to different schools in other towns and cities, Verity refused to continue her education. She kept going back to the remains of the theatre and reliving that night again and again. She became addicted to the sleeping pills, and then she would disappear to London for days at a time, then weeks and we could do nothing. She started to look different and act differently when she came home and by then she had got into other drugs and the wrong crowd and once, when she came back, she brought someone with her. A man whom we didn't know.'

'Did she ever tell you his name?'

'No, and if he mentioned it, I don't remember.'

'Can you describe him?' Bishop said.

'He was tall, strong looking, I thought possibly military, there was a confidence about his movements, although I don't think I ever heard him speak. We realised he and Verity were in a relationship of some kind, despite him being much older than her, and then six months later she told us she was pregnant and we both thought he was probably the father. We asked her to come home. She was going to have a baby and we wanted her to be safe and to take care of her, but she didn't want to come back. She began to ignore our phone calls, then she changed her phone number and we had no way of communicating with her. We didn't hear anything and it broke my wife's heart,' he glanced over at her. 'Rose wanted to report Verity missing and we thought about hiring a private detective, someone who could find her, we were both so worried about our daughter and the baby. And then Verity sent us a message.'

'Do you still have it?'

He went to the old wooden bureau and pulled out a postcard.

'There was no return address,' he said, 'and only a single phone number written on the back in pen. She had signed it Vee, which was her nickname. We called the number and found out it was Carestrom, the adoption agency, and realised what she had done, so we explained who we were, that Vee was our daughter, and that we would very much love to have our granddaughter in our house. But it takes months, sometimes years to get qualified and cleared, so Juliet slipped through our fingers as it were. We were, however, on their books and six months later we were informed her foster mother had suddenly passed and we thought it only natural we should have a chance at taking care of our own granddaughter. This was all hers anyway,' he gestured with his arms: 'the house, the land, the title, so why not bring her up within her real home? There were no complications with the adoption and Juliet fitted in here quite beautifully. It was almost as if we had Verity back again,' he paused and the words sounded strained, 'as if we had been given a second chance. We didn't see or hear from Verity for about ten years, and part of us presumed she was dead, but then the rumours began: a woman who looked a little like Verity had been seen around the village – it was the red hair that gave her away. We dismissed the talk as idle chatter, but when the same woman came back a few months later and again and again we thought it must be true. One of the locals took a photo and when he showed it to me, I knew it was her.'

'But she never approached you?'

'Not until four years ago when she suddenly appeared and knocked on the front door. I barely recognised her. I found it hard to look in her eyes, and I wanted to take hold of her and make her come inside, Rose was making lunch and Juliet was in the garden having tea, and I asked if she wanted to see her daughter. I could see the indecision in her eyes, but she said "not yet – but soon". She said something had changed in her life and she had a plan and was going to make things better.'

'A plan?'

'Her exact words. She said she needed help and asked for money.'

'And did you give her some?'

He looked away and shook his head.

'She asked for ten thousand pounds. I told her I didn't have that sort of cash in the house, but I could get it for her and she agreed to come back one week later. Rose and I fretted all week and when the day came we were ready and waiting. We both promised each other we would stay calm, but when Verity knocked on the door it was more than Rose could bear. She started sobbing and tried to grab Verity, but our daughter would have none of it, she literally pulled the bag of money from my hand and ran.' He faltered and pushed a hand through his hair. 'And that was the last time we saw her.'

Bishop asked him a few more questions, but Holly finished her tea in silence. There was such sadness in this house and when she looked up next, Ernest had a photo of Verity in his shaking hands.

'So many things I should have told her,' he said.

Rose made a noise and Holly looked over. The woman was staring at them.

'What do you need, dear?' Ernest wiped his eyes and stood up. 'What do you need?'

Rose angled her head and her gaze went to the postcard.

281

Her arms were taut and she snapped her fingers. Ernest handed his wife the postcard and the old woman put it on her lap.

She stared at it for a while then her eyes drifted back to the television.

Ernest Baxter saw them off at the front door and stood on the steps as Bishop pulled away.

'So Verity pays her pimp, Stefan Spenski, off with money from her father and then she moves to Brighton. Why?'

'It's closer to here,' Holly said. 'She had a plan, Bishop.'

'Which was what?'

She stared back at the mansion – the oak door with the stone lions.

'I think she did want to come back, Bishop. Something had changed in her life and that's why she was getting sober and cleaning herself up. She finally wanted to come home.'

Sixty

Harringay Girls' School looked more like a cathedral than a place of education.

It was a massive medieval building, three storeys high, facing north with stone towers, brick and flint parapets. Bishop parked on the large gravel driveway by old yew trees next to half a dozen other vehicles.

Holly exited the car and as they headed to the front door, it opened and a dozen children scampered onto the gravel carrying balloons and chattering excitedly. Their parents trailed behind and loaded them into SUVs and people-carriers. One woman remained in the doorway; she was in her forties and wearing a summer dress with her hair in a neat bun.

'Miss Eckhart?' Bishop showed his warrant card.

'Yes,' the woman said, 'I took the call from your police station, but it's my mother you need to talk to, she has been the custodian since the school closed. Which entrance did you use?'

'The one off Church Road,' Bishop said.

'You wouldn't have seen the damage from there. The fire was on the east side of the property. I'll take you around.'

She led them along a gravel path to the side of the building, through an archway, and suddenly the contrast to the rest of the building was stark. The centuries-old stone was still stained black, the wooden beams and steel rebar stuck out of the masonry like dead arteries.

'The theatre used to extend all the way to the trees, but the remains of it were excavated and the area landscaped,' she said.

'Were you here when it happened?'

'No, but my mother was a teacher and saw the whole thing.'

They passed empty classrooms behind dark windows and crossed through to a small interior garden full of ferns and lilacs. In the middle was a square stone resting on a plinth.

'This is the memorial for the three children who were killed. I'll leave you here for a moment and collect my mother.'

Miss Eckhart exited and Holly took the area in.

'It's a beautiful here,' she said as she approached the plinth. There were photos of the three girls under a strip of plastic and their names were carved underneath: *Crystal Cummings – Derby St Claire – Olivia Pond.*

A quote from Shakespeare:

Good night, good night! Parting is such sweet sorrow. That I shall say goodnight till it be tomorrow.

'There's not a day goes by that I don't think of them.'

The voice came from behind and Holly turned.

'I'm Mrs Eckhart,' the woman said. 'Custodian of the school.' She was in her sixties, prim and proper with clear blue eyes. Bishop introduced them and Mrs Eckhart said: 'I hear you want to know about the fire?'

They retreated to another part of the garden and sat on stone benches. The sun was hot, but there was a slight breeze.

284

'It was June the twenty-fifth 1995 and it was supposed to be the highlight of the summer, the school's theatrical play to mark the end of term. There were five girls in the cast, all playing several roles, and we took our seats in the audience and waited for the show to begin. A few minutes later the understudy, Meredith Kane, hurried out from the side of the stage and ran over to the headmaster in the front row. Words were exchanged. Mr Kerridge turned to us and said – "Excuse me, let me see what's going on."

'He disappeared behind the curtain and came back within seconds and told us there was a fire in the dressing rooms and we needed to evacuate immediately. The parents were ushered to the doors, but myself and some of the other teachers headed backstage. It was so much worse than we thought. Four of the girls were trapped inside the dressing room. We could hear them screaming and Mr Kerridge, the headmaster, was trying to open the door, but it was jammed and there was smoke coming underneath.'

'Didn't you have the key?'

'One of the other girls had already tried to unlock the door, but the key had broken off and was stuck in the keyhole. We all tried to push, but it was no good. Mr Roberts, the maths teacher, took a fire extinguisher and tried to smash it down but he broke his hand. It was ...' she shook her head and took a moment.

'We kept yelling at the girls inside to try to stay calm and we told them the fire brigade was on its way – but all of a sudden we could smell something acrid and the girls' screams quieted. The silence was all the more upsetting because we knew what it meant. The fire crews arrived a few minutes later and we were led out to the grounds where all we could see was a massive cloud of black smoke coming from an upper window and we realised the fire had spread to the second floor. Next thing I remember was a loud bang and the whole building went up. There was an oil-heating system in the basement and the flames had found it. There was nothing else the firefighters could do and the three girls died.'

'But Verity survived?'

'It was a miracle. She somehow managed to crawl through the air conditioning unit to the vent that opened by the back of the school before the explosion. One of the firefighters found her and gave her CPR. I went to visit her in hospital two days later. She couldn't remember much or didn't want to.'

'And how did the fire start?'

'Some say the girls were smoking cigarettes in the dressing room and they dropped a match on one of the scripts in the bin and things escalated from there, but the firefighters found out there were chemicals inside the room that shouldn't have been there.'

'What chemicals?'

'From the science lab – they had been put in there as cleaning products by mistake.'

Mrs Eckhart pulled an old photo from an envelope and passed it over. Six girls dressed in the Harringay uniform – a combination of bright reds and blues: red socks, red shirts and a navy blue skirt, tie and blazer.

'The uniforms,' Holly said softly.

'Yes, the girls were known as the Crimson Sunbirds, it was our school logo,' Mrs Stephens said.

The girl second from the right caught Holly's eye.

'That's Verity, isn't it?'

'Yes. She was the class prefect and wore her Crimson

Sunbird badge with pride. And next to her are Crystal, Derby and Olivia.'

'And these two girls on the far left? Who are they?'

One of them was petite with short dark hair, the other was a large girl with long blonde hair and a big smile.

'The one with the dark hair is Charlotte Cole, she was the stage manager for the show and was in the wings at the time, and the blonde girl was the understudy, Meredith Kane.' There was a slight faltering in the woman's voice when she said: 'After the fire, the school started the summer holidays, and during that period the board of governors met and funding was pulled and the decision to close the school was made official in July 1995. After that I lost contact with so many pupils and I don't know what happened to them.'

Holly held the photo tightly in her hand, her silent mind churning. They said their goodbyes and were walking across the gravel to the car when she finally spoke:

'Four out of those six girls are dead, Bishop,' she said. 'We need to find Charlotte Cole and Meredith Kane. I'm wondering if they could be next on the list.'

Sixty-one

Holly and Bishop went straight back to the incident room.

Around them the task force worked at a frantic pace – pieces of paper were pulled from printers before the ink was even dry and quickly studied as officers asked and answered questions in overlapping conversations.

Bishop pulled Thompson aside.

'Where are we on statements from pupils at the school who knew Verity?'

'It's slow going,' the DI said. 'When Harringay closed, the pupils and their families scattered across the UK. As they got older some of them emigrated, some lost their last names due to marriage, but the biggest problem we're having is a lot of the girls removed Harringay School from their CVs because of the stigma attached to the fire.'

'Understandable – where's Janet?'

'Janet?' Thompson turned and shouted.

The woman was hunched over a printer and arrived carrying a sheaf of papers.

'What have you found out about Verity?' Bishop said.

'A few things,' and Janet reeled off her notes: 'According to the teachers we have managed to track down she was very likeable,' Janet said. 'She was a straight-A student, good at art, loved her drama and was class prefect from the age of eleven to fifteen. Until the fire, she was one of the pupils voted most likely to succeed.'

'Do we have any more photos of her?'

'Yes, hold on.' Janet grabbed the clicker and images of Verity appeared on the white screens. 'She would have been fourteen here, fifteen here.'

Holly watched the montage of photos as they flashed by. Verity in the school restaurant, Verity at assembly collecting her Crimson Sunbird prefect badge, Verity at the head of the class holding a book and smiling.

'They were emailed over by a friend from her English class.'

'Who?'

'Diane Faulds. She had nothing but good things to say about Verity. She remembered her having a bit of a wild side, an artistic nature, but nothing outrageous, she was conscientious and very smart.'

'But she didn't keep in contact with Verity?'

'No, and we can't find anybody that did. They appeared to have all made an effort, but Verity seemed to shut everybody out.'

'What about her relationship with John Reynolds?'

'Everybody knew about it – the two of them were often spotted walking home together after school. Some say they were sexually active, but then he moved away and it ended.'

'So what do we have so far? She was a great pupil who was well-liked and had no enemies?' Bishop sighed. 'What about after she left school?'

'Juvenile arrest records – we found one charge against her in 1995 for shoplifting in Petworth which was later dropped. Two charges of possession of a class B drug, the first was in October 1995 which was for amphetamines, and the second was December the same year, for cannabis and codeine. Both charges were dropped. We can't find any evidence of an address outside of Petworth. No evidence of her claiming any government benefits, no income support, no jobseeker's allowance, no utility bills, no TV licence, no voter registration, it's like she vanished off the grid until she reappeared in London known as Vee.'

Bishop nodded – Holly could see he was getting frustrated.

'Everything points back to this school and we need to find out why,' he added quickly. 'All the teachers who worked at Harringay School need to be checked out and that includes the part-timers or substitute teachers who may only have taught there for one day. Pull criminal records on every single one; include the cleaners, caterers, gardeners and the groundsmen as well. What did we find out about John Reynolds?'

'All his old school friends were interviewed when he disappeared in 2010,' Thompson said. 'We've gone through the statements again and contacted as many of the friends as we could. To summarise: much like Verity, he seemed to be well-liked and a good student.'

'No enemies?'

'None that we can tell.'

Bishop pulled the photo of the girls from the school drama class and passed it over to Janet.

'The two girls on the left – their names are Charlotte Cole and Meredith Kane – they were in the same drama class as Verity. Have you come across them yet in the search?'

Janet studied the photo.

'Yes, they're on our list.'

'Well make these two our priority – everything you can find.'

Janet hurried away. Ambrose approached:

'Sir, Pete Burns from fire forensics is on his way up.'

'Tell him to come straight to my office.'

Sixty-two

'Adipoyl chloride hexane solution and lead tetroxide were the two main chemicals found in the fire debris in the dressing room at Harringay School.'

Pete Burns was sharply dressed and to the point. He read from the fire report on his lap.

'Both are highly toxic and highly flammable and can be fatal if swallowed or if they enter the airways. You would normally expect to find PAHs after a blaze, they're by-products of building materials commonly used in construction, but the other two chemicals shouldn't have been there.'

'So what were they doing at the school?' Bishop said.

'They're used in chemistry classes all over the world and by themselves they are innocuous and safe, but put them at the centre of a fire and you have all sorts of problems. According to the report, the chemicals had been delivered to the school three years previously, but a month before the fire there was a stock-count and they got lost in the shuffle and somehow ended up in the dressing room. The three girls that died,' he opened a report, 'all suffered from internal chemical burns through the epiglottis and the lungs, which caused blood poisoning and massive organ failure – I mean they were basically breathing in acid. I don't need to go into all the details, but the exposure would have been lethal in just a few minutes.'

He put the report on Bishop's desk.

'I'm not sure what you need from me,' he said. 'The Chichester Fire Service did a thorough job of investigating and I would agree with their findings that the results of how the fire started were inconclusive. There were no precursors found, no accelerants in either the fieldwork or laboratory analysis.'

'Where did it start?'

'In one of the lockers. There was a metal ashtray inside with the remains of cigarette butts, and copies of the scripts and the chemicals. Obviously I didn't see the scene myself, but the fire chief made a note that when he talked to some of the other pupils there were rumours the theatre girls smoked in there.'

'Did Verity give an account of what she remembered? She was the girl that escaped.'

'Verity Ellis Baxter?' he skimmed the report. 'She said the girls sometimes smoked in there but not before a show.' He closed the file. 'It's hard to prove either way. The room they were in was soundproofed, and essentially made of wood and plasterboard. One careless cigarette in a bin without thinking about it and it's highly probable that's how it all began.'

'Thanks, Pete,' Bishop said.

The two men shook hands.

'Keep the file and if you need anything else, let me know,' Pete said as he left.

There was a silence for a while as Holly took the report and flipped through the pages. She thought it was still possible the fire was started deliberately. All you would have to do is light the paper, close the locker and leave the room – the fire and chemicals would do the rest. She looked up as the door opened and Janet entered.

'Bishop – the two girls who were at the theatre – Charlotte Cole and Meredith Kane—'

'You found them?'

'Charlotte was born in Farnborough then moved to Petworth for the school and finished at Guildford. We have an address for her and a different one for her ex-husband. They got divorced in 2013.'

'What about Meredith?'

'She committed suicide in Victoria Park boating lake in east London in November 2017.'

'She's dead?' Bishop said.

Holly and Bishop shared a look and she could see he was thinking the same thing. 'It was definitely suicide?' Holly asked.

'According to the Office of National Statistics she took an overdose and drowned. Here's the report.'

Holly skimmed the pages. Five of the girls were dead now, but then she saw something in the report.

'It says here police divers spent three days searching for Meredith in Victoria Park, but they never found her body.'

'Doesn't mean she's not down there,' Janet said. 'Five women have disappeared in that lake over the past ten years and only three bodies have ever been found.' To Bishop: 'You want me to call up Charlotte Cole and let her know you're coming?' Janet said.

Bishop hesitated for the briefest moment.

'Yes,' he said. 'But I want to talk to her ex-husband first.'

Sixty-three

Simon Winston was red-faced and harassed when he opened the front door of his terraced house in Whitechapel. He was wrapping a tie around his neck, the white collar still upright. Bishop showed him his warrant card and Simon stopped with the tie and screwed his face up.

'I hear you want to talk about my ex-wife?' he said.

'That's correct.'

'I haven't seen her for years and have no wish to. I'm a single dad, I got custody of our kids and she gets them once a week. We exchange at a neutral place – McDonald's on Croft Street. I drop them off – she buys them lunch and they go to the park or the mall and then I pick them up two hours later. The kids are old enough to sit by themselves for a few minutes so we don't have to see each other.'

'No love lost there then?'

'Not for me and not for the kids.'

'How did you guys meet?' Holly asked.

'Seriously?' he tugged at his tie. 'A dating app.'

'Did she ever talk about her old school?'

'What old school?'

'Harringay in Petworth.'

He stopped and took a second.

'I don't remember, to be honest. Why? What about her school?'

'Just making enquiries,' Bishop said. 'This may be a bizarre question, Mr Winston, but did Charlotte ever mention anyone – someone who didn't like her from when she was younger? Someone she was afraid of?'

'Afraid of?' His eyes flickered over to Holly and back to Bishop. 'Are you serious? Is she in danger? I mean we don't get on, but she's my kids' mum, you know?'

'Where did you go to school, Mr Winston?'

'Wexham School in Slough,' he said. 'Went straight into a trade after that. I'm a carpenter.'

'You use power tools and all that sort of thing?'

'I wouldn't be much of a carpenter if I didn't.' He smiled for the first time.

Holly said: 'Did she ever mention a Meredith Kane to you? She was an old friend from the school in Petworth.'

'Meredith?' he said and looked at her as if she had said something particularly stupid. 'Of course she did. That was who Charlotte left me for, they were having an affair.'

'They were? I'm sorry, we didn't know,' Holly said.

'You and me both. She kept Meredith a secret from me and I had no idea she was seeing someone else, especially a woman. I suggested therapy to try and save the marriage, but Charlotte was adamant she didn't want any of that, so it was a bit of a bombshell. I came home one day and she was gone and there was a note and that was it. She said she'd had enough, she wasn't interested in me, wasn't interested in the

296

kids. The week before we had talked about booking a holiday with each other to the Amalfi Coast. It was like a switch, I didn't get it, I still don't.'

'Did you ever meet Meredith?' Bishop asked.

'A couple of years after the divorce Charlotte tried to introduce me but it didn't go well. I was just angry in those days and I kept saying, "What, is she going to be a dad to the kids? Do you two want custody?" But she didn't put up a fight. You hear of it happening all the time, but you don't think it will ever happen to you, do you?'

'Did you know that Meredith was dead?'

'Yeah, I read about it in the papers. Suicide.'

'So when was the last time you actually spoke to Charlotte?' Holly again.

'Maybe a year ago. We text each other now and that's it. The less communication, the better.' He finished his tie and folded down his collar. 'Look, I have to go, I'm dropping the kids off at Granny's for the night and I'm meeting a client and I don't want to be late.'

'That's fine,' Bishop said. 'We really appreciate your time.'

Sixty-four

Charlotte Cole looked like her school photo but twenty-five-years older.

The hair was still short and dark, her face a little rounder, but her eyes were the same.

'Are you DI Bishop?' she said.

'Yes,' Bishop said and showed his warrant card.

'I don't understand why you wouldn't tell me what this was about on the phone.'

'It's rather delicate,' Bishop said. 'Can we come in?'

The three-bedroom Victorian house was open plan downstairs and they were led towards the living room and an L-shaped sofa. Charlotte offered them a drink, but they declined. Holly watched her as Bishop started talking and the woman seemed to relax as they sat opposite each other. He told her they had visited her ex-husband and she nodded as if she already knew, but her whole body went tense when he mentioned the case they were working on and the fire at Harringay School.

'I don't understand,' she said. 'That fire was when we were children, it was over twenty years ago, how is it even remotely connected?'

'Have you had any random phone calls or hang-ups or seen anyone in your neighbourhood you don't recognise?'

'No, no one.'

'Do you remember John Reynolds from Chesterton Boys' School?'

'Yes.'

'He's been a victim as well.'

She went suddenly pale and stood up.

'You're scaring me.'

'I'm sorry, I don't mean to, but five out of the six girls who were involved in the school play are dead, Charlotte, and until we get this case sorted out we'll be putting an unmarked police car in front of your house for your safety.'

'But Meredith wasn't murdered – she committed suicide.'

'We know.'

'Well then, that doesn't count, does it? Three girls were killed in the fire, which was an accident, Verity was a prostitute, so she lived that sort of life, perhaps it was even suspected she might die in a horrible way, and Meredith took her own life – so they're not all connected, are they?'

'Please sit down, Mrs Cole,' Bishop said.

So she did and Holly leaned forward.

'Tell us about Meredith. We know you knew each other at school. Were you best friends?'

'Yes, we just got on straight away. We had a lot in common, music, television shows, and she could be funny. I felt sorry for her as well.'

'Why?'

'She was a large girl – some of the others picked on her, but I didn't.'

'Some of the other girls at the theatre?'

'No, we were all like a family there – none of us were particularly sporty, so we turned to the arts.'

'And the night of the fire you were the theatre stage manager?'

'I was backstage, in the wings on the left side. I was in charge of the lights and the actor cues – I would tell everybody to get ready, hurry them up and raise the curtain.'

'So you saw the girls that night?'

'We'd been rehearsing for two weeks and did a dress-run that afternoon. Everything was going well and we were having a good time. We were given the afternoon off and came back at four o'clock for another rehearsal – the show was supposed to start at seven o'clock. Meredith watched with me from the side of the stage.'

'And she was the understudy?'

'Yes. It's the hardest job – I mean she knew everybody's lines in case someone was sick or couldn't be at rehearsals and when she wasn't on stage she helped me and helped the girls with their costume changes.'

'Before the show began,' Bishop said. 'Was there anyone else backstage?'

'All the time. Not pupils, they weren't allowed, but the headmaster came by and a few of the other teachers.'

'Do you remember who?'

'Mrs Simmons, the music teacher, she was our director and was conducting the orchestra so we worked a lot with each other, and Mr Roberts the maths teacher was there quite a bit.'

'Was he involved in the show?' Holly said.

'Not directly, but he liked amateur dramatics, I think he was part of a company somewhere, he'd always come around and offer advice and watch us rehearse.'

'And he was there before the show that night?'

'Yes, he watched the dress rehearsal as well.'

'What was he like?'

Charlotte shrugged.

'He was okay. He was a bit of a stiff, you know? A maths teacher who wanted to be cool, but wasn't.'

'And the night of the fire, Meredith first spotted that something was wrong, didn't she?'

'Yes. She came to me at the side of the stage and said the key was stuck in the dressing room door and the girls couldn't get out. I went backstage with her and saw she was right and then I heard one of the girls start shouting and we could smell smoke. Meredith went to get the headmaster from the audience and I went to get Mrs Simmons and then . . . when we got back there was white smoke everywhere and the door was metal and it was hot and Mr Roberts said he would help rescue them and tried to break the door down with the fire extinguisher but he broke his hand. He started shouting and then everything went horribly wrong . . .' She stopped talking as her voice faltered.

'After the school closed, I think we all felt a little lost, our lives had been shattered. My parents moved closer to London so I finished school in Guildford and Meredith and I went our separate ways. We spoke a few times on the phone but our friendship fizzled out, and then in 2012 we happened to bump into each other in a bar in London. I didn't recognise her at first, but we started talking and there was something nostalgic about it. She seemed more confident now and our catch-up was intense, to say the least.'

'Did you talk about the fire?'

'It was inevitable. We both went through it and we both had – they call it PTSD now, don't they? You don't forget something like that, it's with you forever. But that night when we reconnected, something else clicked between us, a bond. She seemed unhappy with her life and I'd just had my second baby and was suffering from postnatal depression. I wasn't in a good place and my husband was working all the time, and Meredith was . . . she just seemed to understand me. At school I was there for her and now she was there for me. I needed someone to talk to, does that make sense?'

'It does,' Holly said. 'And the two of you started a relationship?'

'Almost immediately. I know it's a horrible thing to say, but I just wanted to be with her. There were times when I didn't miss my kids, I didn't miss my husband, it was all about her and she made me feel good. It was like starting over. I tried not to leave my husband, but in the end the pull was too strong, it was almost inevitable. She was damaged, he kept telling me, damaged goods, and nothing good will come of it.'

'Were you both living here?' Holly said.

'Originally we rented over in Ilford, she knew a flat was coming up and took me there. She said she loved it, so I said yes. We stayed there until we moved here. We were happy, and I tried to make her happy, but she could still get very depressed sometimes.'

'About the fire?'

'I think she had other issues as well.'

'Did you know if she ever saw anyone about it, a professional?'

302

'She saw a shrink, I don't know who. She talked to me a bit, but she never really opened up.'

'Did she ever tell you she felt suicidal?'

'Our relationship had started so well, but there were times when she just couldn't pull herself out of it, and when you love someone and can't help them, it obliterates you inside and you feel worthless. She started to put on weight again, we argued and over the months the depression spread to me. One night we got really drunk and she talked about what a relief it would be to be gone. Her parents were both dead and she said she had nothing to live for – not even me. She asked if I loved her – I said yes and then she said we should do it together. Kill ourselves in a suicide pact.'

'And you went along with it?'

'I was enraptured with her. I don't know – looking back it was stupid, but she convinced me it was for the best and in the end I believed her. Meredith got the drugs and we went to the boating lake in Victoria Park. We hired a boat and sat down for a picnic and she made it fun, like a party and we had wine and sandwiches and pills. We were going to go out in the boat, but then she told me to take the pills first, so I did. I thought she was going to take hers as well, but she just held me. Stroked my hair, said don't worry, it's going to be over soon. I remember falling asleep with her holding me and stroking my hair. Next thing, I woke up and there was an ambulance crew shoving a tube down my throat and shouting. I remember asking where Meredith was and nobody knew who she was, they thought it was just me, but they found the boat later that night with her clothes folded neatly inside and an empty bottle of the pills. They had scuba divers and everything, but they never found her body. They made an appeal in the press, I told them she had a history of depression and we had made a pact, but they never found her. I went back to the lake a week later to say goodbye. Two months after that I knew she was gone forever.'

'Do you have a photo of Meredith?' Bishop said.

Charlotte got up and went around the sofa. She picked up a frame that had been placed face down on the mantelpiece and brought it over.

'It's the only one I have. I thought we might be talking about her so I didn't want her watching. Does that make sense?' And she passed the photo to Holly. 'That was taken three months before Meredith took her own life.'

The photo was of Charlotte and Meredith at a sports bar. There were football supporters everywhere in blue and white and most were watching the match on the TV on the wall. Meredith and Charlotte were both smiling and holding cock-tails. Meredith was still large with long fair hair, but the smile was broader.

'You wouldn't know, looking at that, would you? She looked so happy that night.'

Charlotte took the photo back and put it on the coffee table and flicked a strand of hair behind her ear.

'Is it really necessary to have a car outside? I mean, I don't ... I live on my own but ...' she said.

'You'll be safe,' said Bishop. 'We really appreciate your time, Charlotte, sorry to have troubled you, you've been very helpful.'

Bishop started the car and Holly became quiet as she tried to piece together the jigsaw that was forming in her head. Her hand was hurting again and she needed more pills so for once decided to let her thoughts go and just watch the streets blur by as the car picked up speed.

Sixty-five

It was nearly eleven o'clock by the time Bishop dropped Holly at home.

He had picked her up at 7.45 that morning when she had been hungover; now she still felt hungover and realised it was lack of food. She raided the fridge and found a bar of chocolate in the icebox. She chopped it up with a knife and sat on the sofa and ate chunk after frozen chunk, her mind buzzing, losing herself in her incident board above the fireplace:

Let's start at the beginning:

Harringay School and the fire.

Was it an accident – one of the girls dropped a cigarette in the locker by mistake?

Or was it deliberate? Someone started a fire, closed the locker door and let the flames and chemicals do the rest?

If so – who started it?

The dressing room door in the theatre had been jammed. The key broken off in the lock.

Easy to do. Put the key inside and hit it sideways with something heavy.

The fire extinguisher would be perfect.

Mr Roberts the maths teacher had tried to save the girls by smashing the door down with the fire extinguisher. He said something – what did he say to Mrs Simmons the music teacher?

'I'll rescue them . . .'

Who was this teacher who loved watching the girls rehearse? How did Charlotte describe him?

'A bit of a stiff. A maths teacher who wanted to be cool, but wasn't.'

Maybe he started the fire? Maybe he suffered from Hero Syndrome and lit the match, creating a situation that he thought he could resolve? Validating his own self-worth in front of the whole school? He wants to be seen as brave by the others – accepted by the girls and they'll all call him a hero.

It's possible. He was hanging around the theatre all the time.

So he sets the fire – a slow burn inside the locker until he knows the girls are inside the dressing room getting ready for the show, then he breaks off the key in the lock, walks away and takes his seat in the audience. But his plan goes horribly wrong. When he goes backstage to save the day, he breaks his hand trying to smash open the door and he has no idea the poisonous chemicals have been left in there by mistake. All of a sudden it's murder. Three girls are dead and it's murder.

He moves school when it closes and keeps a low profile. He got away with it, but if it was him why wait twenty years to kill Verity? Because she escaped?

Perhaps Verity knew it was him? How? She saw him light the fire? Then why wouldn't she have told the police at the time?

And what is his connection to Mike Thomas and Stephen

Freer? A gallery owner and a doctor? There isn't one at the moment.

Was it another teacher at the school? Was one of them having an affair with one of the pupils? But the other found out and were going to tell. The teacher would have gone to prison – life over – that's a good motivation for murder.

Holly went through the list of teachers at the school, but none had any black marks or discrepancies against their names.

John Reynolds – killed in 2010.

Was he at the school on the night of the fire? She checked her notes – no – he was away on holiday with the family – a skiing trip in Aspen. Cross him off the list.

She took a break. Maybe the fire was just an accident and had nothing to do with the murders today and then she remembered something Bishop had told her once:

'Two's a coincidence – three's a crime.'

And what about Charlotte?

She is the only girl out of the theatre group who is still alive and seemed genuinely scared when we spoke to her today. She also appears to be in denial about the murders, making excuses for them. The three girls were an accident, Verity was a prostitute and Meredith committed suicide – so in Charlotte's eyes none of them are connected.

But they are connected, Charlotte, they have to be . . . !

And Meredith.

You left after Harringay closed. Where did you go? Were you scared you were on the killer's list? Is that why you disappeared? And then the suicide a year and a half ago.

The depression took its toll on Verity and you seem to have been a victim too, but maybe it's more than that. You came back into Charlotte's life, but then you got scared again? Maybe you knew who the killer was at the school and he found you and you had to get away and the only way was to fake your own death?

Meredith's body was never found. Did she freeze to death under the water or did she somehow get to shore and disappear? Was she really dead or was she hiding again? Frightened to come out in the open or tell people what she knew.

Holly got up and started pacing; she was close to something but didn't know what.

Then the phone rang and everything changed.

Sixty-six

She was expecting the call to be from Bishop, but:

'Holly?'

A female voice she didn't recognise.

'It's Alison here.'

'Alison?'

A pause – Mike Thomas's ex-wife – the second victim from 2016.

'Of course, I'm sorry.'

'You gave me your number when we saw each other and asked if I ever wanted to talk.'

'I did, yes.'

'Is it too late – shall I call you tomorrow?'

'No, it's fine, what can I do for you?'

'When we spoke before I wasn't entirely truthful with you.'

'Oh?'

'You asked if Mike had been having an affair when I was going through my chemo and I said no. I lied.'

Holly took a second.

'He was having an affair?'

'I didn't want people to know what he had been doing to me, how I was being treated. I felt like a fool and didn't want it to get into the newspapers, so I never said anything and I kept it a secret. I suspected he'd been seeing her for some time – he'd stay late at the gallery until the early hours – "What were you doing there?" I'd ask. "Checking the inventory," he'd say – which was rubbish. He would smell of her when he came home.'

'Perfume?'

'No – just her.'

'Do you have any idea who she was?'

'I tried to play detective once and told him I was leaving for a couple of hours to go shopping and I sat outside in the car and watched the house, but no one ever came. I asked him about it after I started having my chemo. He denied it with silence, and that's when I knew the marriage was over. I decided to go to my parents the next weekend because I needed their help if I was going to get a divorce. When I came back, I found him dead. But I knew she had been in my house again.'

'How?'

'She had used the shower at some point. There was a hair left on the soap. A long blonde hair.'

'And it wasn't yours?'

'My hair had fallen out by then, Holly, and it wasn't Mike's. It was hers.'

'I don't suppose you kept it, did you?'

'No, of course not, I threw it away.'

Holly was thinking. The silence grew.

'I'm sorry to have bothered you with this, Holly, but I had to get it off my chest. I've told no one else apart from my parents – not even my husband. Maybe this woman – maybe this woman saw something?'

'Maybe. Thank you, Alison.'

Holly hung up and stared at the phone, replaying the conversation she had just had, her mind ticking smoothly.

So Mike, victim three, had been having an affair. A horrible thing to do when your wife is having chemo, but the woman he was with could be another key and they needed to find her. A press release? Social media? If the woman was married herself, she probably wouldn't come forward, but she was vital to the investigation because Alison was right, she could have seen something.

Holly stopped – *she could have seen something.*

She played the words in her head again and again and a sudden dread filled her.

Not something. She could have seen *everything.*

And an idea began to grow and the thought was so outrageous it almost made her sick, but it was that feeling she got when she was on the edge of something and she let her instincts guide her. She started riffling through her pages of notes in the living room because there was something she desperately needed to find. Something she had seen.

Where had she put it?

And her hands went over to the incident board and she started ripping photos and statements down, glaring at them, then discarding them on the floor. No clues in the search for the killer in nine years, no real leads or suspects, and Holly was beginning to see why.

She felt herself pulled to the coffee table and skimmed through Walker's notes, hoping it was there, then she went through the case files from Stephen Freer and Mike Thomas.

Pages and pages of black-and-white autopsy notes, victim statements, thrown across the room.

And then she saw it – peeking out from under a pile of photos. And her fingers trembled as she slowly pulled the piece of paper towards her.

It was a stickman drawing, the one she had done herself last week. She gripped it tight and held it up to the light and immediately saw the three lines she had rubbed out when she had made a mistake drawing the dress that had left an impression in the page.

And she could still hear the conversation she had had when she had been with Bishop in his office looking at the drawing that had been left at Verity's murder scene.

'Did you see this, Bishop?'

'What?'

'The killer drew Verity on the left to begin with – you can see the outline of the dress where he rubbed it out.'

'He made a mistake or changed his mind. The other two drawings both have the victim on the right.'

'Yes, but I wonder why that's so important to him?'

'No, Bishop,' Holly said quietly. 'That's not important to him. The killer wasn't drawing Verity on the left. He was drawing himself.'

And she felt a sick apprehension in her stomach.

'Dear God,' she whispered, and her body went cold as she crumpled the paper in her hands. 'You are a woman.'

Sixty-seven

Bishop hated two things in life.

One was being shot at and the other was being woken up when he was asleep. He didn't sleep well at the best of times so when it came, he held onto it like the Holy Grail, but now someone was knocking on his door.

He was fully awake in one second and out of bed and at the front door in three. Whoever it was had better have an amazing excuse or be the woman who—

'Holly?'

As he stood in his boxers and T-shirt.

'Can we talk?' she said, and pushed past him into the living room.

'Put some coffee on,' he mumbled. 'You know where it is, right?'

She didn't answer but he could hear cupboards opening and the kettle being filled to the brim as he went back in the bedroom and pulled on a pair of tracksuit bottoms.

'It's five o'clock in the morning,' he said as he made it to the living room and flopped onto the sofa. She sniffed the milk from the fridge.

'This couldn't wait.'

He watched her make the coffee. She brought it over to him in his favourite mug and perched on the edge of the sofa like a baby bird.

'Go on then,' he said.

He saw a sudden shift in her eyes, then she said:

'It's been six years since Stephen Freer was killed and all of our leads fall at the first hurdle and every suspect has a waterproof alibi. I believe there is a reason for this. I spoke to Alison last night. Her husband, Mike Thomas, was having an affair.'

'He was?'

'Alison thinks she was in the house the weekend her husband was murdered.'

'Can she prove that?'

'She found a blonde hair in the shower.'

'Why didn't she ever mention this?'

'She was embarrassed and didn't think it was a part of the case.'

'Well, it's important we find this woman.'

'Very important. Do you remember the triangle dress that Verity was wearing in her stickman figure picture?'

'Yes.'

She opened an envelope and removed the stickman drawing found at her crime scene.

'Is that the original from my office?'

'That's why I was late – I had to go there first and pick it up.'

He let it go as she lay it on the coffee table.

'And remember the killer drew a triangle dress on the other figure, then rubbed it out?'

'I remember. We thought he was drawing Verity.'

Bishop took the drawing and held it up to the light. He lowered it and wondered where exactly this was going.

'So we know there was a woman over at Mike's house on the weekend he was murdered, and we have a drawing left at Verity's crime scene that initially had both figures wearing a dress.'

And then it dawned on him what she was saying.

'Are you serious? Oh, shit,' he said. 'You think it's a woman?'

She paced in front of him like an angry kid with too much energy and then stopped and stared at him with her big brown eyes.

'I can give you a list of thirty female serial killers throughout history—'

'—I know you can – it's a neat party trick but—'

He felt the hair at the nape of his neck tingle. Holly was still speaking but he wasn't listening. His mind was churning over the possibilities. The mistakes, the answers, the implausibility of what she was saying, but the nagging feeling that she could also be right.

'Hold on a second,' he said. 'What you've just been saying – repeat it again. Slowly.'

'There are fundamental differences between men and women who kill, and the clues have been right in front of us – I just can't believe I didn't see it. Men are hunters by nature, they'll find random strangers to kill; women rarely kill strangers, they're gatherers by nature, and about eighty to ninety per cent of them will have a relationship with their victims. There were no signs of forced entry at any of the victims' houses because they all let her in. They trusted her, Bishop! This woman has stayed at large for nearly a decade with at least six kills to her name, which means she is smarter than any of us. I still haven't worked out exactly who she is or why she does it, but I do know my instincts are screaming at me, and I have this idea, an image of this woman infiltrating all of these lives and destroying them one by one.'

'But why? Why is she doing this?'

'I don't know yet, but it started when she was young, when she was at Harringay School, and her first act was the fire.'

'You think she was a pupil there?'

'Yes, I do. It won't be one of the teachers,' she said. 'They'll be too old now. And this girl, she wanted those other girls at the theatre dead, she missed Verity but tracked her down later, then John—'

'—John was first—'

'—Right. And she has stayed hidden so bloody well, we just haven't connected the dots – and I should have. I was sidetracked by the information from the old investigations. I should have come at this with fresh eyes. Walker's notes, the old case files, everything we had pointed to a man, but it's a woman, and she is so angry and so psychotically violent that she's beyond anything I have ever seen or read about. My God, she'll be off the scale on the PCL-R.'

'The what?'

'The PCL-R. It's a chart we use as psychologists to measure psychopathy. A questionnaire of perceived personality traits and recorded behaviours. Nearly every serial killer in captivity has been asked to take the test. Some love it, they want to prove they're as insane as they think they are. Aileen Wuornos scored thirty-four out of forty.'

'Who?'

'A female serial killer in America. She ended up killing

317

seven men, but they were all shot, they weren't cut up like these ones, this is something else. Our killer will be up there with Aileen. She'll probably score higher, to be honest.'

She was stumbling over her words, they were coming out so fast, but Bishop was keeping up.

'Do you believe me?' she said.

'Yes, I do.'

Her eyes were shining.

'And you know what's the worst thing about this?' she said. 'I am so mad at myself for not seeing it sooner. I was distracted with the parole hearing and The Animal and I lost sight of what was right in front of me on this case and I shouldn't have – that was ... I don't do that – I'm better than that. Maybe Andy Brooks didn't have to die?' And her voice grew softer. 'If I'd been better, I could have saved him – I could have saved ...'

He watched her with a certain amount of sympathy and wondered if she was talking about her parents and had a chilling realisation that she might be, so went and stood in front of her – it was the only way he could stop her pacing.

'Enough,' he said. It had come out like a growl and he coughed to clear his throat. 'Take a deep breath.'

He put his hands gently on her shoulders. Her skin was hot. She took a breath and shook her head at the same time, because she was still in that place, and he knew he couldn't talk her out of it, not yet, but all of her points were valid.

'So it has to be one of the girls.' He paused. 'Well, there's only one left who was involved with the theatre and had the opportunity, and that's Charlotte Cole.'

'Maybe not,' Holly said. 'How difficult is it to fake your own suicide?'

He took a second and ran a hand over his eyes.

'You have to be patient and committed, and when you assume a new identity you have to maintain that lifestyle perfectly.'

'But it's not impossible?'

'By no means.'

'So maybe Meredith just rowed to the other side of the lake and walked away?'

'Jesus Christ – I can see it now, it's just a question of whether the two women were working together or not.' He grabbed his phone and dialled. Janet sounded groggy when she answered and a dog barked in the background.

'Bishop?' she said.

'Dredge Victoria Park lake – I want a team out there immediately and then get to the station. I need everything you have on Charlotte Cole and Meredith Kane.'

Sixty-eight

The water at Victoria Park boating lake was mirror-black.

Holly stood on the pontoon where dozens of blue and white rowing boats and pedalos looked like ghosts in the early morning mist.

It was 6 a.m., and she watched the dive teams take their boats out, put on their wetsuits and scuba gear and disappear under the black. They were a hundred metres away, but she could hear the muted splashes.

Bishop came and stood by her side.

'We've got two more dive teams coming in an hour. If Meredith committed suicide and she's down there, they'll bring her up. If she walked away—'

'Sir?' It was Ambrose, approaching them with a man in his fifties, tanned and lean. 'This is Graham Sykes, the hire-boat manager. He was working the day Meredith disappeared.'

'Thanks for coming out,' Bishop said.

'Anything I can do to help.'

'Do you remember that incident?' Bishop said.

'Yep, the two women hired a rowing boat, pulled it into the

bank about a quarter of a mile from here, sat down on the grass and had a picnic.'

'Was it busy that day?'

'It was too late in the year and it was too cold. I asked them if they were going to go swimming and they said no. I told them not to because it was about ten degrees in the water. Most people don't realise how cold that is, it will cramp your muscles up and you can't swim, it doesn't matter how strong a swimmer you are, you won't survive. They seemed like nice ladies, but by four o'clock it was getting dark and they hadn't brought the boat back, so I went to find them. One girl was asleep on the grass and the other girl wasn't there and neither was the boat. I tried to wake the girl, but she didn't respond and I knew she had taken drugs, people do that all the time around here. There was also a note on the blanket under an empty bottle of wine. I couldn't stop myself reading it, it just said – *We all have our own journeys – I'm sorry.* I called the ambulance and the police because I told them another girl was missing.

'When the police arrived I went out in the dory with a few of the officers and found the boat thirty minutes later floating near a sluice gate by the eastern end of the lake. The anchor was down and the oars were missing. I thought the girl would be lying at the bottom of the boat, that she would have taken the drugs and fallen asleep like her friend, but she wasn't there. Her clothes were folded neatly on the seat and there was an empty bottle of pills as well as a suicide note that said the same thing. If she had gone into the water naked with drugs in her system, she wouldn't have stood a chance. She would have gone down in seconds.'

There was a splash from the mist as another diver went in.

'You reckon they'll find her?' Neither Holly nor Bishop answered. 'Last time they thought she might be caught up in the sluice gate.'

'The woman who went missing – her name was Meredith Kane,' Holly said. 'And the other was Charlotte Cole.'

'I remember the other one, a sweet thing. She came back about a week after she got out of the hospital. I saw her sitting on the grass staring across the water. She brought flowers and threw them out there. I thought they were friends. It said in the press they were lovers.'

'Did you speak to Charlotte when she came back?'

'No. She wouldn't have recognised me and I didn't want to intrude. I remember her sitting and watching the flowers float away until it got dark. I never saw her again.'

The mist had cleared by eight o'clock.

The three dive teams had worked non-stop, but so far nothing. Holly and Bishop crunched in silence on the gravel as they walked back to where they had parked the car.

'If Meredith Kane is alive,' Holly said. 'How the hell do we find her?'

Bishop shook his head. 'I don't know.'

Holly thought the same thing and said a silent prayer as they drove to the station.

Sixty-nine

There was a new energy at the police station and an incident board had been erected with photos of Charlotte and Meredith at the top.

'Come on,' Bishop said to Holly. 'Let's see what Janet has got for us,' and she followed him to the desk in the middle of the room.

Janet didn't take her eyes off her computer screen but knew they were there:

'Charlotte Cole went from Harringay School to Christ's Hospital School in Guildford,' Janet said, 'which is where she finished her education. After her A levels she was employed at an accountancy firm in Bow, east London where she has been ever since. Two children. Divorced. No police record, not even a parking ticket in the last five years, she's clean. However, we did get a copy of the toxicology report on her suicide attempt at the lake. She never took enough drugs to kill herself, nowhere near enough.'

'Well, maybe she already knew that,' said Bishop.

'So it wasn't a suicide pact?'

'Only Meredith stuck to the deal. At least, that's what she made everyone think at the time. Do we still have a car outside Charlotte's house?'

'Yes.' She switched reports: 'She went shopping at Tesco's this morning and came back an hour ago.'

'Get the officer on the radio.'

She did and passed it over.

'This is DI Bishop.'

'Sergeant Ince here, sir.'

'Has anyone left or entered the house apart from Charlotte Cole?' Bishop said.

'No, sir, not through the front door anyway.'

'Good. There's been a development in the case. Charlotte Cole has now become a suspect, along with another woman called Meredith Kane, who may have faked her own suicide last year. I want you to knock on the door and inform Ms Cole that the enquiry is taking a different direction and you will be leaving your post as of now.'

'Leaving?'

'That's right, I want her to think we've lost interest. Then drive one street away, park and wait.' He turned to Janet: 'How soon can we get a surveillance team out there?'

'Within the hour.'

'Do it.'

Back to the radio:

'Sergeant Ince, did you hear that?'

'Yes, sir.'

'Sit tight and don't leave until the surveillance team are in place.'

He hung up the radio as:

'Holly, Bishop – we have something!'

The call came from Thompson and they quickly made their way to his desk.

'After Harringay we have no record of Meredith Kane at all,' he said,' but we've found out she was born in Ockley, Surrey on the eleventh of November 1981, which would make her thirty-eight now. Her father was Robert, her mother Melanie, both parents deceased – the father in 2009 and the mother in 2013. And here's the kicker,' he said and licked his lips. 'Mike Thomas, the second victim, was born in Ockley, Surrey, in the same year.'

'You're joking?' Bishop said. 'They knew each other?'

'More than that, they went to the same infant school, St Jerome's Parish. We have their report cards and photos of them together as kids.'

'That's the link,' Holly said and felt goosebumps on her arms.

'Then Meredith left Ockley when she was ten years old and the family moved to Petworth.'

'Why?'

'The father got a job there – he was a carpenter.'

'With an electric saw, I bet,' Bishop said then shouted across the room: 'Ambrose! Any news from Victoria Park?'

'Nothing yet.'

Holly went to the new incident board and, like numbers on a clock face, drew black lines from Meredith to each of the victims.

'Stephen Freer is the only one not connected to Meredith,' she said. 'He was a doctor. Did he ever work in Ockley or Petworth?'

'No, and we've checked all of his patients and there's no mention of either Charlotte or Meredith,' Thompson said.

'What about their medical history? Who was their doctor when they were at school?'

'They were both registered with the same one in the village – a Dr Kate Plantin.'

'Is she still practising?'

'Yes.'

'Contact her and get all of their details sent over.'

'Stephen Freer is the odd one out,' Holly said, 'and the only one not in the same age bracket as the others, which makes me think he was chosen because he was a doctor. So why would either Meredith or Charlotte go to a different doctor?'

'Privacy? They're in a village, everybody knows everybody's business.'

'Right, so if I wanted a different doctor – what would I do? Google one, right? Who's here from IT?' Holly said.

Bishop scanned the room.

'Sergeant Hachette, over here!' Holly recognised the sergeant from the Pickford case.

'Our doctor, Stephen Freer, is it possible to see who searched for his name on the internet back in 2012 or 2013?'

'It's going to be a challenge,' he said. 'If we can find out the old IP address of his website, we can possibly see who looked him up. He was a doctor, so I imagine there will be hundreds of hits on him, but if the killer found him that way and then cleared their search history or used a remote viewing platform to find him, we don't really stand a chance. But we can have a crack at it.'

'Go back to May 2012 and see what you find.'

'Bishop?' Janet called across the room. 'The officer knocked on Charlotte's door. All the lights are off and there was no response.'

'Did he see her leave?'

'No, and he went around to the rear of the property and the back gate was closed.'

326

'Shit. Start canvassing the area and get a warrant to search her house. Put her car number plate through ANPR and see if she's making a run for it. If she is, tell the officers to approach with caution and detain immediately. Send a car over to her ex-husband's as well. I doubt if she's gone there, but desperate people do desperate things.' A beat, 'Where are we on her social media?'

'She's pretty inactive but she does have a memorial page set up for Meredith on Facebook.'

'Can you get to it?'

Janet scrolled through the timeline and clicked on it. A new page opened with a burning candle on the left and the words:

IN MEMORY OF MEREDITH KANE
   Today I lost my best friend and my love. We all have our journeys.

Underneath was the same photo Holly and Bishop had seen at Charlotte's house. *Both of them standing at the bar, drinks in hand, handbags hanging off the backs of their chairs.*

'Can we print that photo please and give everyone copies,' Bishop said.

'Bishop . . .' Holly looked at him, 'I'm thinking of faking my death, what's the first thing I do when I come back?'

'You need money,' he said. 'Most likely stashed away in cash. Get some fake ID and you would have to change your name and your job.'

'But we don't even know what Meredith did,' Janet said.

'She must have been working while she was living with Charlotte.'

Ambrose approached:

'There were forty-seven Meredith Kanes registered with the Inland Revenue over the past decade. Seventeen of them were based in London.'

'What did they do?'

'Everything from a circus performer to a chartered accountant.'

'Charlotte works as an accountant in Bow. Maybe they worked together?'

'Are there any other photos of her on social media?' Holly said. 'Other than the one on the memorial page?'

'Nothing,' Janet said, 'this is all we have to go on.'

'Can you enlarge it?'

'Hold on.'

Janet took a screenshot and copied it into Photos.

'What are you looking for?'

'I don't know, it just seems strange Charlotte only had that one photo.' Holly hunched closer to the screen. Her eyes were stinging they were so tired.

'What's that hanging off Meredith's handbag,' Thompson said. He had sweat trickling down his face and he blinked to clear his vision. 'It looks like a tag or a pass or something.'

'A membership card?' Thompson said.

Janet enlarged it. They all leaned closer into the screen.

'The last letters look like *s-t*. Possibly *u-s-t*. It's hard to tell,' said Thompson.

Holly grabbed her handbag and pulled out her own Wetherington Hospital security pass.

'It's NHS *Trust*. Meredith Kane was a nurse. Ambrose?'

'I remember a nurse.' He flicked through the pages of the IRS report. 'Meredith Kane – here she is,' he suddenly shook his head. 'It says here she's still filing her taxes.'

'That can't be right,' Bishop said.

'She filed her taxes in February this year.'

'Let me see that,' Bishop took it, read it and passed it on to Holly.

'Well it can't be her,' she said. 'It must be a mistake.'

'What hospital is she registered at?'

'West Middlesex.'

'Janet – contact the hospital – get a staff rota and find out what's going on.'

She made the call and got put through to the hospital administration.

'This is DI Janet Acton at Hammersmith police station – I have a quick question regarding one of your staff who would have left West Middlesex hospital employment about a year and a half ago. We'd just like you to confirm that she did in fact leave. Her name was Meredith Kane.'

Janet listened, frowned, took a pen and started writing. When she finished she thanked them and hung up.

'According to staff records, Meredith Kane still works there.'

'Well that can't be right, there's got to be some mistake.'

'She a nurse in paediatrics.'

Paediatrics – Holly thought – *I don't kill children.*

'And,' Janet said, 'she started the afternoon shift today.'

There was a stunned silence that ate up the seconds.

Holly's head was spinning.

Who the hell are we dealing with here?

Seventy

West Middlesex hospital was on Twickenham Road in Isleworth, west London.

Bishop drove and Holly was next to him in the passenger seat. Janet and Thompson were in the rear. There were three more cars from the station following them.

They pulled up to the front of the hospital entrance and parked. Two specialist firearms officers trailed behind Holly as they entered the building and walked to reception.

'DI Bishop,' he said as he showed his warrant card to the reception staff. 'Do you have a Meredith Kane working here today?'

'Which department would she be in?'

'Paediatrics,' Holly said.

The woman put the name into her computer.

'She'll be upstairs on the third floor. What's going on?'

'Nothing to worry about. Fastest way up there?'

'The lifts to your left, then follow the signs to the Starlight Ward and ask for the matron for Paediatrics at the Children's Services reception.'

'Thank you.'

The receptionist picked up the phone, but Bishop said:

'Please don't tell her we're coming.'

'I'll need to let Matron know.'

They walked three hundred metres to the elevators. Bishop pressed the call button. There were three lifts stuck at different levels. They waited for five seconds . . . ten seconds . . .

'We'll take the stairs,' he said.

They had to ask three people where they were and followed the coloured lines on the floor, getting looks from nurses and patients at the guns bouncing in their harnesses and the slap of heavy boots on polished floors. Another fifty feet and they found stairwell number three. Bishop led with his bad knee from a hit-and-run years ago, but as they arrived at the first landing Holly saw him pick up the pace, and by the time they got to the third floor they were all running. At the top of the stairs, Bishop pushed open the door and they emptied onto a corridor.

A second of confusion, more coloured stripes on the floor and then a sign to the Starlight Ward. A left, a right and another long walk and the walls began to be decorated with kid's drawings and they reminded Holly of the stickmen. Up ahead was the reception with three nurses on duty all waiting. They looked horrified at the armed officers. One of them spoke:

'I'm the matron for paediatrics, how can we help you?'

'Apologies for the intrusion, my name is DI Bishop and I'd like to talk to Meredith Kane.'

Her eyes flickered right and Bishop started in that direction. The woman was fast and not used to her authority being ignored.

'You can't just barge in! There are children in there, you'll scare them!'

Bishop reined the team back.

'How many children?' he said.

'There are eight with her now, it's story time. What is this about?'

'I can't tell you, I'm afraid, but we have full authority to arrest Meredith immediately.'

'On what charges? You obviously don't know her and you won't need a gun, she's a gentle soul, trust me.'

Holly watched him as he made a split-second decision.

'Everybody else hold back,' Bishop said. 'Holly, come with me.'

'I'll lead the way,' said the ward nurse.

She walked down the hall, stopped at a door, cleared her throat and opened it. The first thing Holly saw was a handful of children sitting cross-legged on the floor in a crescent shape, and at their entrance their faces all turned like sunflowers. Meredith was sitting in front of them, an open book in her hand. She was large, wearing a pleated skirt and a T-shirt and had long hair like her photo. When she saw Holly and Bishop, her reading juddered to a halt.

'Meredith Kane?' Bishop said.

'Yes.'

'Can we have a word, please?'

'Meredith,' said the matron, 'I will take care of the children for a while. Go with the officers and you can sort it out.'

Meredith stood shakily and passed the book over to the ward sister.

'Page forty-nine,' she said. 'Danny is about to drive into Hazell Wood.' She patted the nearest child on the head.

'Children, the ward sister is going to look after you for a while, I'll be back in a minute.'

Bishop led her out of the room and closed the door behind them.

'What's this about?' Meredith said.

'I think you know.'

Meredith seemed to sag and her hands fell to her sides as if they were broken.

'It started off as a hobby and then . . . I'm so sorry,' she said. 'Please don't arrest me here. I'm an idiot I know, but it was all Eric's idea.'

'Who's Eric?'

'My boyfriend. I knew I shouldn't have listened to him.'

Holly watched her carefully.

'What was his idea, Meredith?' she said.

'The pot in the greenhouse. That's why you're here, right?'

'We're not here about pot, Meredith,' Bishop said, 'we're here about the murders.'

'Murders?'

'We're arresting you on suspicion of killing six people.'

'What?'

And then the fear hit and tears came. Her hand went to her mouth and as if she were made of paper she suddenly folded up and collapsed onto the floor. Holly stared at her. This wasn't what she had expected.

'I didn't do anything – I have no idea what you're talking about, why would I murder anyone?'

Holly pulled Bishop aside.

'This doesn't feel right.'

'Charlotte had a photo of her in her own house. It has to be her.'

'Give me a second.'

She knelt by the woman.

'Meredith, can you hear me? Meredith, if you don't look at me it makes me think you're not listening and I really need you to listen to me. My name is Holly.'

Meredith had stopped crying but her chest rose and fell with every breath.

'I don't know what you're doing to me,' she said.

Holly showed her the photo of her and Charlotte from the sports bar.

'Meredith, this is you, isn't it?'

'Yes, that's my local pub.'

'And the woman who is with you?'

'I've no idea.'

'You don't remember the photo being taken?'

She paused.

'Vaguely. I was there with Eric watching the football and she came over and asked to take a photo with me.'

'And when was this?'

'Last year – November, I think. She said she was on holiday and wanted to show her friends. I thought it was a bit weird, but then I did it and went back to the game. I never saw her again.' A pause. 'Who is she?'

'Her name is Charlotte Cole,' Holly said. 'Did you go to school with her?'

Meredith shook her head, thinking hard.

'I don't remember her.'

'What about the fire? Do you want to talk about the fire?'

'What fire?'

'The fire at the school.'

'I didn't know there was one. Is everybody all right?'

334

Holly felt something tugging at her stomach.

'Did you go to Harringay School in Sussex from the age of eleven to fifteen?'

'No, I went to Brighton Hill School in Basingstoke.'

'You never went to Harringay Girls' School?'

'I've never even heard of it.'

Holly shook her head at Bishop. He pulled away and she followed him.

'It's not her.'

'It has to be.'

'Yes, her name is Meredith Kane, but she's not *the* Meredith Kane we're looking for who went to Harringay School. Charlotte used this woman's picture on Facebook as a fake.'

'Then what the hell are we doing here?'

'We've been played, Bishop,' Holly said. 'Charlotte Cole is buying time.'

Seventy-one

There were no lights on in Charlotte Cole's house and it looked empty.

Holly was tucked behind Bishop and a specialist firearms unit on the front path. The door was less than three feet away. Bishop told her to put one hand on his shoulder.

'Follow me in and stay close,' he whispered.

Her mouth was dry, she couldn't talk, so she squeezed his shoulder to let him know she understood.

'Echo One, you have control,' Bishop said.

The firearms team gave multiple shouts of 'Police!' A battering ram was used and the front door was taken off its hinges on the first blow. The team crashed through in two-two formation, guns sweeping side to side. Holly felt Bishop lurch forward and she kept her hand on his shoulder as she hunched in close and followed him into the darkness.

The hallway led to the open-plan living room, which looked bigger at night. Bishop had told Holly they would do the initial sweep in darkness, the team would be using flashlights and infra-red sights on their rifles.

The guns and lights swivelled around Holly as if they were dancing. The flashes bounced off the sliding-glass windows in the living room, the white sofa, the cold fireplace. How long that initial search downstairs lasted it was hard to say, probably seconds, but there were shouts of 'CLEAR!' and then she heard footsteps on the stairs. One firearms officer stayed by the door.

Silence and then a shout:

'DI Bishop, upstairs!'

There were five rooms, all with their doors open.

Holly followed Bishop to the furthest bedroom. It had a massive bed and a white duvet, white carpet, a dresser and a walk-in cupboard. There was no ceiling light, but a standing lamp with a frilly red shade in the far corner.

Charlotte's body was hunched over itself in the middle of the bed. She was on her knees with her torso flopped forward, one arm outstretched, the other tucked into her belly. Her head was buried face down in a pillow. She was wearing a bright pink dressing gown that along with all the blood on the sheets made her skin look very white.

Holly snapped on latex gloves and ran her torch over the shape. Something flashed in the beam of light.

'Bishop, it's hard to see because of her positioning, but there's something sticking out of her stomach.'

They found themselves on opposite sides of the bed and realised they were staring at each other over the body.

'It's a knife,' he said. 'A big one.' Holly could feel his impatience, it radiated off him like heat. He went into the en-suite bathroom and a few seconds later: 'In here.'

She found him by the vanity mirror, holding up an empty

337

bottle of sleeping pills. There was a sheet of folded pink paper on the washstand.

'What does it say?'

'I just don't care. You will never find Meredith's body. I didn't put her in the lake.'

He looked at her, stunned.

'It's as close to a confession as we'll ever get,' he said, and they both took a moment until Thompson's voice broke the silence:

'Bishop?'

He was standing by the bedroom door.

'We found something else,' he said.

Thompson led them past an office and a bathroom, until he stopped at the end of the corridor.

'It looks like a spare bedroom. There's a blanket box by the far wall, we found it like that,' he said. 'They're inside.'

He stayed by the door and lowered his eyes as Holly passed.

The room was smaller than the others, ten feet by ten, with mattresses on bunk beds in one corner, a chest of drawers and the blanket box made of dark oak. There was a broken padlock – the key discarded on the floor and the lid had already been flipped open.

Holly looked inside.

Placed on a clean white sheet and spaced equally apart from each other were five large glass pharmacy jars about ten inches high with cork stoppers. One was empty but the others were full of cloudy liquid, and each jar had a greenish-brown object floating inside, trailing feathery skin like fishtails.

Holly could smell the formaldehyde and knelt, eyes inches from the jars. Like something from a horror film she half-expected the lumps inside to suddenly move and thrash against the glass.

Thompson said:

'We think they might be the men's ... you know ... Her ... um—'

'—Her trophies,' Holly said. 'Yes, I would agree with that.'

Seventy-two

'Can we clear a way, please?' Angela Swan pulled up her mask.

The photographer moved aside and the pathologist circled the body on the bed as it if were a dangerous animal. She shone her torch under the torso of the crumpled figure as her fingers worked over the stiffened joints.

Holly stood in the bedroom doorway with Bishop and she watched the slow process of the forensic team with a certain daze.

Angela said: 'She smells of chloroform. Traces of burns around her mouth and nostrils where she may have inhaled or drunk directly from the bottle, have we located the bottle yet?'

'No,' from Bishop.

'The knife in the stomach is large,' she said. 'A hunting knife of sorts.'

'Is it *the* knife?'

'Possibly, it's big enough, but I won't know until I can get her back to the lab. Blood loss is consistent with a cut to the abdominal aorta, which would have resulted in a very fast rate of exsanguination. She would have been unconscious in minutes and, judging by the angle of the blade, I would say substantial damage to the internal organs with perforation of the intestines. What do we think happened here, Bishop?'

'There are pills in the bathroom and a suicide note.'

'Does the victim have a history of suicide attempts?'

'One we know about.'

'Then I would agree. She made herself up first as well.'

'What do you mean?'

'Put make-up on. She wanted to look pretty when she went.'

Holly saw Bishop shake his head.

'She's got two kids,' he said.

'Not any more.'

'You going to be okay for a minute?' he said to Holly. 'I need to talk to her ex-husband.'

'Sure.'

She watched him leave, then went to the window and pulled the curtain to one side. There were lights and press vans outside. The crowd was big but strangely quiet: a well-behaved group of mourners who would no doubt start flapping like landed fish when the body was brought out.

'Are the ghouls still gathering?' Angela said.

'Increasing in numbers,' and she let the curtain fall back into place.

Seventy-three

'It's psychotic and brilliant at the same time,' Holly said.

She and Bishop were in his office.

'Charlotte tracked down another Meredith Kane who lived in London who was tall and had blonde hair and could pass as her old school friend after twenty-five years and manufactured the fake Facebook account last year in case we ever came to investigate,' she said. 'That whole elaborate scheme was simply to cover her tracks.'

'You said she was clever.'

'It's bordering on genius.'

The phone rang.

It was Angela. He listened for a minute, hung up and smiled.

He gave the thumbs up through his office window and the incident room erupted in a cheer. Someone opened a champagne bottle and the cork hit someone in the face and there were howls of laughter.

Holly felt the relief flush through her body. Everything in this case, this absurd jigsaw, had finally come together.

Almost.

'What is it?' Bishop said. He was getting good at sensing her thoughts.

'There were five jars at the property – but only four had trophies inside.'

'Then there's a very lucky man out there. Someone she didn't get to and now we'll never know who.'

Ambrose knocked and opened the door—

'The CPS are closing the case and there's news from Victoria Park. They've just pulled out the remains of a body caught in the east sluice gate. There's not much left of it but it's female and the height is similar to Meredith Kane. They're taking dental impressions to see if they can get a match.'

'Thank you, Sergeant,' Bishop said. 'Don't drink too much champagne tonight!'

Ambrose smiled as he left and Holly felt Bishop's eyes on her. 'Talking of champagne,' he said. 'Are you ready for tonight?'

Holly got up and stretched.

'What's happening tonight?'

'Date night at Walker's.'

'Oh, shit. I'd forgotten.'

She needed a shower and wanted to wash her hair and—

'I'm not exactly dressed.'

'Neither am I,' he said and looked at her, hesitant.

'I have to admit to something,' he said, and if Holly hadn't known him any better it looked like he was squirming. 'I've been seeing someone,' he said.

Holly thought she'd misheard and tried not to show her disappointment.

'Oh, I had no idea. That's nice. Are you . . . I mean – ' stumbling like a child – 'Sorry, do you want to take *her* tonight?'

'What?'

343

'To the meal with Walker.'

'No, God no! I mean I've been seeing a therapist about Sarah. I wanted to let you know I'm getting help.'

'Oh.'

'I have my last session tonight. I don't want to miss it, so I'll meet you over there. Is that okay?'

'Of course. That's amazing, well done.'

'Yeah, never too old to admit that I'm messed up.'

'Messed up is good,' she said.

They shared a moment. Tonight could be the night, and she felt herself smile.

'I'll take wine,' she said.

'I'll take flowers.'

'I'm looking forward to this.'

'So am I.' Then he added, 'Unless Walker's doing the cooking and then it will be a fucking disaster.'

Seventy-four

Holly stopped at a mini-mart and got a bottle of red wine and a bottle of white then drove to Walker's house.

She sat in the drive for a moment, tempted to wait for Bishop so they could go in together but then she took the bandage off her right hand and got out of the car.

Skyler opened the door and gave her a big smile and a hug.

'Where's Bishop?'

'He'll be along shortly – he's having to tie things up at the office.'

'Thank you, Holly,' Skyler said as she took the wine and led her into the kitchen. 'Eddie's been downstairs in his dungeon all night. Between you and me – I would love it if he would finally get rid of all that stuff. I know he won't, but we can all dream.'

'How's he been?'

'Quiet. I think he's reliving the case and he's a little sad. Even though he was retired, this was still keeping him going, you know? Hopefully I can keep him occupied and take his mind off things. Go down, I'll let him know you're here.' She shouted at the basement door: 'Eddie – Holly has arrived!'

No reply, but Holly followed the stairs down past the first security door, which had been left open, through the first room with the sofa, the wide-screen TV and stereo sound system and into Walker's office. The man was sitting in his chair at his desk, the *Cape Fear* poster behind him. He was reading from an open file and took off his glasses when he saw Holly. A faint smile.

'Congratulations, Holly.'

'Thank you. It was a—'

'—Joint effort, I know. I used to say that all the time too.' A deep breath. 'There are things Bill kept to himself, obviously, but I still don't understand everything. What convinced you it was a woman? I mean I've been going through things again and . . .'

Holly told him about the stick figure drawing with the dress and how Alison came forward with the hair she had found and the thoughts of an affair and he looked at her incredulously.

'I would never have even gone there. And her name was Charlotte Cole?'

'She was from Farnborough originally, but it all began at a school called Harringay in Petworth. Why, we don't know yet, but hopefully we'll find out.'

'And the other one?'

'Meredith. We think she was murdered as well. Divers have found a body in Victoria Park boating lake and are running dental checks now.'

'And this Charlotte left a confession?'

'As good as.'

Walker folded his arms. Unfolded them. Face tinged with uncertainty.

346

'What do you look for, Holly?'

'What do you mean?'

'Bishop said you could get inside their heads. I was sceptical, but is that how you did it? Do you think like them?'

'Sometimes I have to,' she said quietly.

'It's hard, isn't it?'

'It is.'

She could hear the clang of a metal spoon on a saucepan upstairs. There was an occasional murmur of conversation, but it was like listening to a radio from another room, and she wondered if Bishop had arrived.

Walker suddenly moved fast and tidied up his papers and smiled.

'Come on, Skyler's already opened some wine.'

'I went to school in Malmö, Sweden until I was eighteen then studied architecture and came over here at twenty-one,' Skyler said.

She was at the stove stirring the meatballs and pasta. The smell was divine.

'I was married once, but no children. How about you, Holly? Are you married, divorced?'

'Single.'

'Really? What about Bishop? Walker says he is a good catch.'

'I'm working on it,' Holly said and took a mouthful of wine.

'Maybe we can speed things up,' Skyler smiled. 'Shall I tell Holly my joke, Walker?'

'No, it's crap. Top up, Holly?'

'Thank you.'

'Where's the whisky gone, love?'

'The dining room.'

347

Walker went searching.

'I told him a joke, Holly, but I don't think he appreciated it.'

'Go on.'

'Why are hairstylists the best psychopaths?' she said. A pause and then: 'Because they want everybody to dye.'

Holly couldn't help laughing and ran her fingers through her hair which made her wince.

'Ow.'

'What's wrong?'

'It's nothing, I hurt my hand the other day.'

Her phone rang. It was Janet. Holly excused herself and passed Walker, who was holding two big glasses of whisky.

'Janet, hi, what's going on?'

'Is Bishop with you, I can't reach him?'

'No, he's going to be here in twenty minutes or so. Are you guys drunk yet?'

'The opposite. I hate to kill the mood, but we've got a bit of a cluster-fuck going on over here and I think we're only just touching the surface.'

'What do you mean?'

'The skeleton the divers found is not Meredith Kane. The dental match is for a Fiona Stracken, who disappeared at the lake four years ago. We've sent another three dive teams out there and they're going to be there all night, but it's not her.'

'Shit.'

'We also got a response from Meredith's doctor in Petworth, who sent through her medical history. Nothing of note to begin with and then by the time she had been at Harringay for three years she was prescribed the morning-after pill five times over a period of eleven months. She would have been

fourteen at the time. So we can see she was sexually active –
the question is, with who?'

'John Reynolds, I would have thought,' said Holly. 'We
already knew he slept with Verity, so maybe he was sleeping
with both of them?'

'Right,' Janet said. 'And then in March 1995 Meredith
was prescribed antibiotics for pelvic inflammatory disease by
her doctor.'

'Do you know how she got it?'

'She had an abortion.'

'At fourteen?'

'The operation wasn't performed in Petworth though, they
didn't have the facilities, so she was referred to another clinic.
A clinic in London – and with that clinic came another doctor.'

'Stephen Freer,' Holly heard herself say.

'Yes.'

'But why wasn't her name on his patient list?'

'She was under fifteen and had no ID so she used a
pseudonym.'

So that was the connection. The final black line on the
diagram. Holly sat down. She was feeling fuzzy and wished
she hadn't drunk so much wine. Pelvic inflammatory disease could spread to the reproductive organs and she had a
sudden thought.

'Were there any complications with the procedure?' she said.

There was a pause and Janet said:

'How did you know? According to her records, Meredith's
fallopian tubes were damaged and scarred. She became
infertile.'

Holly gazed at the carpet, lost in thought. After a long
moment she gave a little shake of the head.

'Thank you, Janet. That all makes sense now.'

'Holly?'

'I need to go, I don't feel too good.'

She put the phone on the coffee table and looked up just as Walker came in.

Seventy-five

'Everything okay?' Walker said and offered her another glass of wine.

'Good.' She took the wine but didn't drink. 'Where's the bathroom?'

'Just there.'

She went inside and closed the door. Put the lid down on the toilet and sat.

'Infertile,' she said softly. 'The childlike stickman drawings, the castration. Meredith wanted children and she blames the men. John for getting her pregnant, Stephen for damaging her during the abortion, Mike ... why Mike?' She couldn't think straight. 'The body in the lake is not Meredith, which means she's sure to still be alive and you can't discount anyone and she'll be closer than we think. Closer to who? To me? To Bishop? To Walker? ...' and suddenly an idea struck her and she got the shivers and felt sick and was hot and sweating and she stood up and splashed cold water on her face. She dried her hands with a towel and stared at her pale face in the mirror. She put the thought to the back of her mind – it was outrageous – but it suddenly came back stronger than before and now she couldn't shake it. The initial shock had passed and she was thinking now, putting things together.

Oh my God . . . and there was no way she could prove it. Or could she?

She reached into the medicine cabinet above the sink, found a bottle of aspirin and stared at them curiously, and then she emptied the pills into the toilet, flushed and went back to the kitchen.

'You okay, Holly? You look a little hot,' Skyler said.

'I'm fine.' A beat. 'Actually, do you have any aspirin, my head's a bit woolly.'

'There should be some in the bathroom cabinet.'

'Thank you.'

Holly went back inside the bathroom, made a point to leave the door open and rummaged through the shelves. She pulled out the empty bottle then walked back into the room. To Skyler:

'Just this I'm afraid.'

Walker took the empty bottle and threw it in the bin.

'There's more aspirin in our bedroom in one of the bedside cabinets,' he said. 'Upstairs, second door on the left.'

'Thank you.'

Holly followed his directions and steadied herself on the landing. She was beginning to feel wobbly. Her movements were slowing down and she wiped a hand over her forehead and looked at her fingers. Damp with sweat.

Second door on the left.

She pushed the door open and leaned against the frame. The carpet was plum-coloured and Skyler's flight attendant uniform was draped on the right-hand side of the bed, freshly ironed and ready for her next flight. Holly went to her bedside cabinet and opened the drawer. It was packed with all manner of things from throat sweets to sleeping pills and a diary. She picked up the diary and flicked through it briefly. The writing was blurry, or was it her eyes? She pulled the drawer out, found the aspirin bottle, then she saw something else. A small shiny object that was somehow familiar. Holly thought it was a ring at first. She took it, but it fumbled between her fingers and she dropped it on the carpet. She bent down and picked it up which made her head swim. What was it? It looked so familiar and then she froze. It was a tiny badge with a safety pin at the back, and on its enamelled front was a red bird with black wings.

A Crimson Songbird with the word *prefect* printed in gold at the bottom.

Verity.

A noise from behind startled her.

'Holly, did you find it?' Skyler said. 'Did you find what you have been looking for?'

Holly tried to turn but it changed into a stumble. She held up the tiny badge.

'Do you mean this?'

And suddenly Skyler was too close.

She had a perfume bottle in her hands and Holly felt a fine spray catch her in the face. It was sweet and pungent. Chloroform. And she knew then the wine had been drugged with GHB and she tried to hold her breath as long as she could, but the back of her throat felt funny and she knew she was going to pass out, and the last thing she thought of before she hit the floor was Bishop.

Seventy-six

Bishop sat in a red chair at the back of a small square room.

Dr Madison Young sat a couple of feet to his left. She was tall with neatly cropped ginger hair, a mumsy blouse and skirt and clear glasses. The only thing separating them was a small rectangular table with an unlit candle, a metal figure of a dolphin and a box of tissues.

'The sunsets were beautiful back in Afghan,' he said. 'Sarah and I would watch them fade over the tanks together. It was always cold at night, but we kept each other warm when we could. One night we stayed out in the desert. Dug a hole and crept inside. She sneaked out a bottle of Scotch and I brought the *jalebi*, do you know what that is?'

'No.'

'It's a sweet made of flour dipped in sugar syrup. Sticky as hell on the fingers, especially when you're in a sand-pit,' he smiled. 'I didn't enjoy myself as much as I should have when I was with her.'

'Why do you think that was?'

'I'm always looking to the future. I don't want to think about the *now*. Why is that?'

'Being present is difficult for everyone. We get distracted by too many things. The bright lights. The promises we make ourselves.'

A silence.

'Are you still drinking, Bill?' she said.

'A little.'

'Are you off the drugs?'

'Yes, I am.'

'Do you sleep well?' she said.

He shook his head.

'Are you taking any pills to help?'

'I try not to.'

'But do you?'

'Sometimes.'

'How many hours sleep do you average per night?'

'Three. Maybe four?'

The room went quiet.

Bishop didn't like quiet. Quiet brought back flashes of gunfire, the surprise crack of an explosion, sand falling like hot rain.

'I still think about Sarah every day,' he said. 'The children we never had. I like the pain of the memories, but I feel as though I'm punishing myself too much now. I feel as though enough is enough.'

'Are you ready to move on?'

'My fiancée was killed by an IED. I thought I could keep her safe and I didn't.' He suddenly felt relief. 'I've met someone else. A woman and she has changed my life.'

'And this woman – does she have a name?'

'Holly.'

He shook his head and said quietly.

'When I'm with her, I'm not alone any more.'

Seventy-seven

When Holly woke up she was lying on her back.

Her head hurt and she felt very cold. The floor was concrete and there was a single bulb in the ceiling. The room was full of boxes and files and there were maps of London on the walls and autopsy photos and a desk and one chair, and against the far wall was the vintage *Cape Fear* poster and she realised she was back in Walker's office in the basement of his house. Skyler had carried her down the stairs. Something clanked when she moved her arm and she saw her right wrist was handcuffed to a metal pipe in the wall.

She felt in her pockets with her free hand for her phone but remembered she had left it on the coffee table in the living room. She had no idea how long she had been unconscious, but could still smell the pungent traces of chloroform in her nose. Where was Bishop? And Walker – and, more importantly, where was Skyler?

There was a series of beeping noises and the electric keypad by the door flashed green and the door clunked open. Skyler walked in and a cool breeze followed.

The two women stared at each other for some time.

'Do I call you Meredith or Skyler?' Holly said.

'Skyler. Meredith died in the lake.'

Holly strained her neck to look past the door and caught a glimpse of Walker on the sofa in the other room. His body was sagged unconscious and his hands and feet were tied.

'Walker!' Holly shouted.

'He can't hear you, Holly. I had to drug the whisky as well to be sure, but he's got enough of a cocktail in him to knock out an elephant. He won't ever wake up in time.' She flashed a smile. 'Shall we have some music? What kind of a girl are you, Holly? Cranberries? Mötley Crüe? I see some Floyd in there as well, but maybe not tonight.'

She left the room and Holly heard drawers opening and closing. She stared at Walker's comatose form in the other room and pulled on the handcuff. It jangled and hurt her hand. The music started and Holly immediately recognised the beats of 'Never Gonna Give You Up' by Rick Astley. It was loud and she knew why. It would drown out any screams.

Skyler came back in and walked over to a stack of boxes in the far corner and dragged the bottom one out. She tilted the top so Holly could see the label.

Skyler's secret box – no peeking!

'And he never did, because he is honest. How funny is that – everything right under his nose.'

She pulled off the packing tape and took out a hand-held electric saw and a large hunting knife. Holly felt an inner chill and realised her legs were shaking. She shifted them to make them stop, but wondered if Skyler had noticed. Then the woman took out a SOCO suit and brushed it off.

'Do you know when these suits were first introduced, Holly?'

Holly shook her head.

'The Met began using them in 1968 – Walker told me that. In Canada they're called bunny-suits. I think that's cute.'

She began to dress in the SOCO outfit.

'Nobody has ever got close, Holly. It took a woman. You should be proud of yourself,' she said.

'You're very good, Skyler. Constantly re-inventing yourself like this, it must be exhausting. You're leaving tonight, I presume?'

'I'm flying, yes, working a short haul, but I won't be coming back. You'll understand why.'

'Your face will be everywhere. How long do you think you can run for?'

'I won't be running, Holly. You weren't in the original plan, but I've adapted.'

'Like you did with Andy Brooks? We found your message behind the mirror.'

Meredith pulled the SOCO suit past her waist and pushed her arms into the sleeves.

'I wanted you to know I would never hurt a child; it was important to me.'

Holly watched her warily, trying to clear her head.

'And that's what this is all about, isn't it? You can't have children, can you?' she said. 'We found out about the abortion with Doctor Freer. The complications.'

Skyler's whole body tightened but her voice stayed calm and matter-of-fact.

'Did you know that a baby yearns for her mother's love as much as it yearns for her milk?' she said.

'I didn't know that. They took that away from you, didn't they?'

'After Stephen Freer mutilated my body, I couldn't go any-where without seeing a pram and a baby. The longing, my God, it's insane. Look into my eyes and think nice thoughts, he said to me in the hospital, Holly. He held my hand as he killed part of me and I watched those eyes until they filled my head. I used to dream of his eyes, Holly. I used to dream of death as he took my baby away.'

'Was John Reynolds the father?'

'John and I had been having sex for months behind Verity's back. He always came to me because I would do things she wouldn't. I was eight weeks pregnant with his child and I told him I was going to have it. When I told Verity her little heart broke and she cried and cried, but John chose her instead of me.'

'So you tried to kill Verity in the fire?'

'It wasn't my intention to kill her. I just wanted to damage her like I'd been damaged.'

'What do you mean?'

'The chemicals I put in the locker, the chloride hexane and the lead tetroxide, do you know what other side effects they cause?'

'No.'

'They damage fertility and unborn children. I wanted Verity to know how it felt to be childless for the rest of her life. But the fire had a mind of its own—'

'And three other girls died.'

'And I felt nothing.' Skyler's eyes and face were blank as if she had gone somewhere else. 'I always knew I was different,' she said, 'but the fire ... that was a quiet revelation for me. If you don't like your reflection – don't look in the mirror, but I liked what I saw.'

'And what was that, Skyler?'

'After the school closed, I went away, but I couldn't stop the feelings I had felt. I had gained back some control from the people who had taken it from me but I still blamed them all.'

'What did you want? Sympathy? Attention?'

'I wanted everything. Some victims die and some victims live. It took me a long time to realise I was one of the ones who lived. So I bided my time and fantasised a plan. I wanted to be physical, brutal. It was for my own healing, but I also realised it led the police to think I could only possibly be a man.

'John was first on my list and it didn't take me long to find him. Time is a wonderful healer, and people can forget the pain you caused them with a decade in between and a nice smile. I had lost over six stone by then, grown my hair, had collagen and Botox and started wearing coloured contact lenses. I rented a bedsit in St Albans, paid cash month to month and knew about the empty property above the bakery. I led him there, drugged him and killed him. I lay next to him as he bled to death. Have you ever watched someone die?'

'No.'

'Put it on your bucket list.'

'But why Mike Thomas? You went to school with him, didn't you? What did he do to you?'

'He bumped into me.'

Skyler laughed and her lips parted slightly as if at the beginning of a sigh.

'I looked so different when I walked into his art gallery. I had no idea it was his, but he recognised his childhood crush immediately. I didn't want anybody to know I was back or how much I'd changed. I'd already killed John and Stephen by then.'

'The three years in between kills was clever.'

'It made sense, and I had time on my hands. Verity was hard to track down, she disappeared almost as well as I did. I think deep down she always suspected me of starting the fire – of course she could never prove it – and she had read about my "suicide" and thought I was dead. The look on her face when I knocked on her door in Peacehaven was priceless.'

'And Charlotte?'

'The moment I slept with Charlotte I knew she was mine and she would do whatever I asked. Divorce your husband – she did. Forget about the kids – she did. Stick this photo of you and this woman on your mantelpiece and if anybody asks this was me. She was weak and easy to manipulate.'

'Then why leave her? Why fake the suicide? I mean it was clever, but—'

'Because I wanted Walker. I wanted to meet the man who had worked on my case. I followed him from the police station and watched where he went. *Accidentally* bumped into him in the supermarket and then again at a pub.'

'Which one?'

'The Duck, it's just around the corner. I couldn't help myself, Holly, he was the ultimate catch. It took a year to plan. A year of being miserable with Charlotte and pretending to be depressed. It was almost amusing how sorry she felt for me.'

'Because she loved you.'

'And she was my alibi at Victoria Park. I made sure I didn't give her enough pills to OD so she would survive and tell my story. She was the perfect witness. I had a wetsuit in my bag and a change of clothes and I swam to the shore from the boat and slipped away into the night.'

'And became Skyler.'

'I'd been Skyler for six months by then, working as a flight attendant, meeting new friends. I was still living with Charlotte but I was renting a flat about a mile from here at the same time. I made the move on Walker after two dates. He was an absolute gentleman, although he swears in his sleep, army stuff I think, but deep down he's a child really, I think most men are. Anyway, a month later I moved in with him. It was the perfect cover and I could read all about myself in his office and he had no idea.'

'And the set up for Charlotte?'

'I kept a copy of the keys to her house and crept in last night. After I killed her I almost got seen by that policeman outside. I had to go through the back gate three times to carry those jars upstairs in the dark and put them in her blanket box.'

'You almost got away with it.'

'I already have.' She zipped up the front of the suit and pulled up the hoodie. There was a deliberate sense of purpose about her movements, a horrible promise of things to come.

Holly needed to buy time. Would Skyler kill her now or would she take care of Walker first?

'The empty jar in the blanket box. Was that for Walker?'

'Yes, although I will just have to leave him here. I might mix him in with the meatballs.'

Skyler laughed without making a sound.

'You have about ten minutes, Holly,' she said. 'Say your prayers or your piece to whatever God you believe in.'

Skyler turned away.

'Wait!' Holly shouted after her. And she knew this was her last chance to try and get to her, to make her think. 'Charlotte? John? Have you ever really loved someone?' she said.

Skyler stopped. Her head bowed slightly and she came back in the room and knelt next to Holly's side. Her eyes had no shred of warmth and her lips tightened stubbornly.

'I don't *love*, Holly. That's the whole point. My mother told me when I was very young that I had been born with a broken heart. It took me many years before I understood what she meant.'

The woman reached out a hand and brushed her fingers against Holly's cheek.

'What's it like?' she said.

'What?'

'What's it like to *love*?'

'It's hard,' Holly said.

Skyler nodded as if she knew all along.

'Then maybe I'm better off this way.'

And she stood up and exited with the knife and the electric saw and slammed the door shut behind her. The key code flashed red and there was a heavy electronic thunk as the door was sealed.

Seventy-eight

When Skyler left the room there had been a sudden emptiness, as if a curtain had been drawn aside and Holly knew she would die.

She pulled at the handcuff until her skin bled raw. She tried to stay calm, but there was a ticking clock and she couldn't see its hands. She pulled at the pipe in the wall. It was bolted tight and impossible to shift. She couldn't break the handcuff and she couldn't break the pipe, and there was only one other piece in the equation: her hand. In that moment she saw with perfect clarity what had to be done. No matter how damaged she was, at least if she was free, she could fight.

She took a breath and the handcuff jangled as she raised her right hand as high as she could from the ground. Ten inches – it was more than enough. She needed to repeat what she had done at the gym – then by mistake; now by design. She screwed her eyes up. This was going to hurt.

And she punched the floor.

There was a single pop and a crack. Her forefinger dislocated again and the pain was like lightning and she bit her lip. The handcuff jangled as she raised her hand again. Do it quick – get it over and done with. She thought she might be sick, but couldn't stop now.

She punched the floor again.

Another pop.

As she kept her mouth shut and bit her lip harder and tasted blood.

She quickly tried to pull her hand free from the cuff. So close ... so close ... fuck ... one more and – she leaned to one side and dry-heaved. Everything was hazy now and she could smell bile.

On three.

One ...

Two ...

She surprised herself and slammed her hand down.

Pop – like someone opening a can of soda, and she pressed her bones down to nothing and ripped her hand through the handcuff with a silent shriek, and it was as she pulled herself away from the wall that she felt the scream crawling up her throat like a spider and she clamped her other hand against her mouth and bit her palm until it went away. And her eyes watered and she tasted blood and bile and the pain was a deep earthy fire.

The music thumped from the other room as she got to her feet and limped over to Walker's chair. She tipped it up and stamped on it. The thing splintered and two legs rolled free and she picked one up in her left hand and stood like a savage with a stick.

The music suddenly stopped.

Holly stopped with it, barely daring to breathe. She watched the keypad, expecting it to flash green and the door to open. She raised the stick ready and heard soft voices from next door. A man's voice. Groaning as if struggling to breathe.

'Walker? Bishop?'

She threw her shoulder against the wooden door. And then a buzzing noise began and with a shiver she knew it was the unmistakable sound of the electric saw.

'Walker!'

And the music started again. Rick Astley promising the world and the groans and the buzzing faded under the heavy beat.

Holly grabbed the remains of the chair and swung it in an arc, but it bounced off the door with a force that almost knocked her over.

'Walker!'

She didn't know the electric keypad combination, so the only way to open the door was to cut the power. And the only way to do that was to blow the fuses. She threw boxes of crime scene photos and witness statements across the room, dragged the table to the centre but couldn't find the fuse box and the only electric socket was the single bulb above her head. Her eyes watered as she stared up at the light. Then she made her decision and understood exactly what needed to be done.

She climbed onto the table, took off her jacket and cupped it over her left hand. She reached up and removed the light bulb and smashed it on the floor.

Instant darkness.

She felt along the ceiling to get her bearings and licked the forefinger on her left hand.

Then she stuck it in the empty socket.

Seventy-nine

'Oh for God's sake.'

Bishop sat in his car in Walker's driveway. He was on the phone to Janet Acton. She had just got hold of him and told him about the skeleton in the lake.

'What else?' he said. He had been in such a good mood.

'Angela's on line one. Do you want me to transfer?'

'Go on.'

The phone clicked.

'Bishop?'

'Yes.'

'It's the wrong knife.'

'What?'

'The microscopic defects in the blade are inconsistent with the marks left on the previous victims, and Charlotte Cole did not commit suicide. She was murdered. She had way too many drugs in her system to position herself like that on the bed and hold the knife and fall onto it. If she had attempted it, she would have collapsed onto the floor. The blood coagulation doesn't match with her being alive when she was stabbed and

I find it odd she was wearing a nightshirt and stabbed herself through the fabric.'

'Why is that odd?'

'Suicides have a certain style. You want to cut your wrists – you roll up your sleeves. You stab yourself in the neck – you pull down your T-shirt. You stab yourself in the stomach, which is a particularly unpleasant way to go, you pull up your shirt. You never stab through clothing. It's just—'

'What?'

'Irrational.'

'Isn't that the definition of suicide? Acting irrationally?'

'Suicides are not irrational,' Angela said. 'If anything, they are the complete opposite. A person with suicidal thoughts will have a plan. A well thought out plan, just like a very clever killer. They are, after all, murdering themselves, and they want to get it right. Your killer wanted us to think it's over, but it's not.'

He thought for a while and tapped his fingers on the steering wheel. He didn't have anything to say.

'How's your meal going?' Angela said.

'I've literally just got here, I'm late. I stopped and got some flowers.'

'Speak tomorrow then, DI Bishop.'

'Yes.'

He hung up. How the hell was he supposed to enjoy the evening now? But the anger ran out of him when he thought of Holly and he turned the engine off and checked his hair in the rear-view mirror. He grabbed the bunch of roses from the passenger seat and got out of the car.

It was as he was walking up the path to Walker's front door that he realised all the lights in the house were off. A power-cut. He looked around at the other homes, but they seemed unaffected.

He pressed the doorbell, but it didn't chime. Knocked on the door but no response. And then he saw a note taped to the window.

Oven not working – we've gone to the pub in the next village called the Rose and Crown – meet us there! Sky x

He sighed as he pulled out his phone and called Holly. After two rings it went to voicemail.

'Hey, it's me,' he said. 'Call me back, how far away are you? Maybe I could catch up with you and we could—'

The phone cut off. He walked a few steps back to the car and called her again. It rang and rang and for some reason he thought he could hear it buzzing somewhere. He went over and pressed his hands to the living room window and there it was – Holly's phone flashing on the coffee table.

He thought it strange that she would leave it there, but even stranger when he saw a shadow move against the far wall.

Eighty

Holly opened her eyes and thought she was blind.

Total blackness.

Then she remembered what had happened. She had been thrown off the table and had landed on the stacks of cardboard boxes on the far side of the room. There was no noise from beyond the door, no light, no music, no screams and no electric saw.

She had done what she needed to do.

She propped herself up on all fours and felt tentatively across the floor, hands sweeping from side to side, knocking into the table and more cardboard and paper files. Something rolled under her fingers. It was the chair leg and she gripped it tight in her left hand and felt her way to the door.

The keypad was dead. She raised the chair leg as she pushed down on the handle.

A gentle click.

She pushed the door open and a cold draught washed her arm.

A crisp, ruby light from an emergency exit sign above the

door in the other room. Water dripped from somewhere and heavy breathing rose and fell. Irregular and ominous.

'Walker?'

She moved towards the sofa. Her feet felt like lead and her eyes cut left and right. Skyler was nowhere to be seen. Would she have run? Got out of the house, or would she be coming back?

The big man was unconscious. His shirt was ripped and there were multiple stab wounds across his chest. One was deep and the dripping noise was coming from his blood as it spat at the concrete floor. She felt his forehead – cold and clammy. Felt his pulse – weak but still there.

'Walker . . .'

No reply.

She put down the chair leg and gently put her thumb inside the deepest cut. Pressure on the wound. Stop the bleeding. She felt the warm flesh as it tightened around her and his body shifted as he groaned.

'Sorry,' she whispered.

With her broken hand she tried to untie him, but her fingers were useless and the pain unbearable. She ripped off his shirt with her other hand and tore strips from the material, pulling it apart with her teeth. Twisting and balling a length and pushing it into the wound while she tried to wrap his chest and form a tourniquet. He was too heavy to move. A dead weight – *Don't think that, Holly, he's not going to die* – but shock was setting in and she needed to keep him warm. She found a blanket on the sofa and wrapped Walker up in it, glanced at the stairs and wondered if it was safe to go up.

And then a metallic clunk and the lights suddenly blinked back on. The fuse had been changed. Skyler was still in the house. And the music started and the electric saw buzzed angrily at her feet and Holly saw it and kicked the plug out of the wall and in the light realised how much blood Walker had lost. The floor was slippery with it.

His eyes were somehow open now, staring past her but not seeing. He groaned, but it was more than that. He was trying to say something and she leaned in.

'D ... B ...' he whispered.

'What?' she leaned in closer.

A bubble of blood fell from his mouth. Red as an apple.

'D ... B ... F ... K ...'

And then she remembered the funny acronyms.

D-B-F-K.

Duck – Big Fucking Knife.

And she quickly ducked to one side.

Eighty-one

The knife cut a happy smile on the back of Holly's neck.

It stung like a razor, but her adrenalin was so high she barely felt it. She rolled across the slippery floor and ended up on her feet. The chair leg was by the sofa – she had no weapon. Skyler took a step towards her and Holly saw the knife in her hand.

'You're full of surprises, Holly,' she said.

'I try my best.'

She needed to keep her distance, but it was a small room. Skyler edged forward slowly. She was being cautious – that was good – it gave Holly more time. Too soon she felt the wall against her back and grabbed a few of the DVDs off the shelf and threw them. One of them hit Skyler in the face and she looked shocked.

'You fucking bitch!'

Then the woman lunged and Holly leapt to one side and the knife slashed into her forearm. She scrambled away. Felt a hand grab her arm and suddenly she had skin and hair in her face. Spitting and gritting her teeth, she pushed and punched and Skyler fell to her knees and then over to the side as Holly kicked away, but a hand grabbed her ankle and the ground rushed up and hit her in the face. She struggled and somehow pulled free and was on the other side of the room, and when she got back to her feet she fumbled for the chair leg with her good hand. Clumsily but with the strength of panic.

The stairs were to her left. She could be there in two seconds and then up and out of this room and her phone was in the living room. Calculations in milliseconds but she couldn't leave Walker.

Skyler sensed her indecision and ran at Holly, but instead of pulling back, Holly took a step forward, closed the distance and swung the chair leg as hard as she could. There was a satisfying crack as it connected with Skyler's wrist. The woman screamed, the knife skittered under the sofa and then the woman dived at Holly.

Holly had never been hit so hard. She had no idea what part of Skyler had landed the blow on the side of her head. A fist, an elbow? She was back on the ground. Pressure on her throat. Scratches and a punch. Then they were somehow on their feet again.

Holly could see Walker watching her out of the corner of his eye. He was moving, trying to free himself, but the tourniquet had worked itself free and he was losing more blood.

Skyler charged again. Holly heard a scream and didn't know if it was her own. They both collapsed in a heap together. Struggling and punching. Indistinguishable from each other as if they were one animal. Skyler kept grabbing Holly's right hand and twisting. The pain was so much she almost blacked out.

Skyler was hissing, cat-like, smiling in her madness. Nails

scratching Holly's arms and reaching for her throat, pressing fingers in her eyes, then Holly twisted her hips and rolled them both over and was suddenly on top. She held Skyler's hair in what was left of her right hand and punched her in the face with the other. And again, and again until she heard something crunch and Skyler's body went limp. Holly collapsed on top of her, her vision cloudy, her body spent. The sudden sense of relief was overwhelming as she pushed herself up and looked over at Walker. He was still again and the blood was dripping. She shuffled slowly to his side and touched his face.

A noise behind.

She didn't have the energy any more. This was the end.

But when she turned, she didn't see Skyler on her feet, she saw Bishop running towards her with his meaty arms and she let him catch her as she fell.

He shouted up the stairs and two constables entered, faces white and gleaming. One of them reached for his radio and kept saying, 'Paramedics – we need paramedics!'

She must have passed out because the next thing she saw was a pen-light as it flashed across her eyes. She could feel gloved hands examining her body, until they came into contact with her dislocated fingers and she flinched and pulled away. A blanket was put over her shoulders and she felt arms holding her again and she knew it was Bishop.

And all she wanted to do was fall to the earth and take him with her.

Eighty-two

Holly spent the next two days at home.

The doctors reset the bones in her right hand and the cut on her forearm got eleven stitches and the one on her neck needed six. She was sent back to her flat in Balham with antibiotics and codeine.

Bishop came to visit.

He brought chicken noodle soup and a family-sized box of hot chocolate and he made her laugh, which was what she needed more than anything. Walker was out of intensive care. The knife wound in his chest had missed his heart by three centimetres. He was due to be discharged tomorrow.

At 10 a.m. on Sunday, 19 May, Holly had a breakfast of black coffee. She took more pain pills and put on a black dress and black shoes. She didn't have a black handbag, just a purse, so she took that. Bishop picked her up from her flat and they drove to the Sacred Heart Church in Petworth for Verity's funeral. The Met Police had sent a bouquet of lilies ahead and it was a beautiful service. Nearly all of the residents of the street in Peacehaven where Verity had lived turned up to pay their respects, as had Robbie Sweep, the AA sponsor, and some of the working girls. If Verity had been there to see them all, Holly was sure she would have wept.

Verity's mother didn't attend, but Ernest Baxter stood next to a young woman with striking red hair. It was Juliet, Verity's daughter. When the coffin was lowered, they held hands and by the time the vicar had finished the sermon, they were in each other's arms.

Holly and Bishop drove back through the countryside and stopped at the Black Horse Inn on the way to London, where they ate lunch outside in the sun on wooden benches with big cushions.

'You want a hot chocolate?' Bishop said.

'No, I'll wait until I get home, thank you.' Then she said: 'How's Walker?'

'The press are killing him: *Ex-Murder Squad Detective Living with a Serial Killer* doesn't look too good in print, but he's got a big set of shoulders and he's tough. He'll get through. He's moved in with his ex-wife for a while. She's taking care of him now.'

'Has Skyler talked about why she used the electric saw?' Holly said.

'Her father was a carpenter, remember? And he owned an electric saw. He showed her how to use it and let her play with it in his workshop when she was a kid. She was fascinated by the blade.'

'It also makes a great headline.'

'Yeah, there are no frills or soft edges with this one, are there? The box in Walker's office where she kept her murder kit – we found some interesting things in there. Timelines of the victims she killed, photos of other people – we don't know who they are. Our names were both inside.'

'Really?'

'She had planned the whole evening. GHB for starters and meatballs for dessert.' He smiled and it was infectious. 'Skyler had a midnight flight to Stockholm booked and would have no doubt disappeared again. She's in Drake Hall prison in Staffordshire and she'll stay there until the hearing, about three months from now. She pleaded not guilty to all the murders by reason of diminished responsibility. She also made a request: she wants you to be her therapist.'

'I can't, that's a conflict of interests.'

'After the trial.'

'The trial at which I will be a witness for the prosecution. I think she might change her mind when she hears the speech I have prepared.'

Bishop smiled: 'I just thought I would let you know; don't be too surprised if you receive a letter from her lawyers.'

Holly's phone beeped with a text. She read it and said to Bishop:

'Moira from victim liaison.' She paused as she took it in and explained: 'The day The Animal killed my mother, he stole her necklace. Moira spoke to his lawyers ... and they have it for me!' She smiled. 'Oh, my God, I can't believe it! The Animal must have told them where it was before he died!'

'That's wonderful news, Holly.'

'It was my mother's favourite necklace. It's beautiful.'

'Where are they holding it?'

'In an evidence bag with the Hampshire police and she's not sure how long it will take to clear it. Oh, God ...'

'Don't worry, I'll make some calls, see if I can speed up the process.'

'Thank you.'

She texted Moira back then wanted to change the subject.

'I forgot to ask,' she said, 'how was your final therapy session?'

'Good, thank you. Dr Madison Young was very impressed with my progress.'

'Dr Madison Young? She sounds hideous!' Holly smiled. 'Probably not even a real therapist. I bet she got her certificate online.'

'Actually, she was very good, and very complimentary about you.'

'Really? You spoke about me?'

'Your name may have been mentioned a few times.'

'How many?'

'Christ, you're demanding. At least once.'

'That's it? I talk about you all the time?'

'Who to? You haven't got any friends.'

'Walker's my friend. I saved his life.'

'I'm your friend too,' Bishop said.

'I know. Thank you.' They watched each other for a while and Holly couldn't resist. 'How's the knitting going?' she said.

'The what?'

'The knitting book at your house. I saw it.'

'Oh, I can explain – that was . . .'

'No need,' and she laughed and finished her ice cream.

Bishop drove and parked outside her flat in Balham, but before Holly got out of the car, she pulled a present from her handbag. It was wrapped in blue paper the same colour as his eyes.

'I know it's today and I know you don't celebrate your birthday,' she said, 'but you're stupid not to. Life just goes. You don't need to clap your hands and sing a stupid "birthday" song, but you should be able to spend time with someone you like. Other people rather than the ones from your past.'

She handed it over.

'Happy birthday, Bishop.'

He nodded reluctantly. She could hear him screaming inside. But he unwrapped it gently. It was a black metal Zippo lighter with a white enamel skull on one side and a red enamel heart on the other.

'It's a lighter,' he said, and laughed.

'You have to promise me from now on that it's the only lighter you will ever use.'

'I promise.' His eyes were cloudy. 'I thought you kept saying you think I should quit?'

'You should or you will die. But you just made me a promise to use it. Now every time you have a smoke, you'll think of me. And when that lighter runs out of fuel ... that's the last cigarette you'll ever smoke.'

She kissed him on the cheek. She wanted more, but not today.

Bishop watched her as she walked into her block of flats. Watched her until the door closed and he lost her shadow inside the window. He rubbed his eyes. He wasn't sure if he was just so damn tired, or maybe it was what she did to him.

She made broken look beautiful.

Eighty-three

When the security door opened to Lee's room, Holly's brother was already sitting at the table as if he had been expecting her.

'What's up, pussycat?' he said.

She sat opposite and let him examine her hand and the steri-strip on her arm.

'Are you deliberately trying to get yourself killed?' he said.

'It's been a tough few weeks.'

She reached into her pocket and placed a packet of Marlboro on the table.

'Thank you.'

He opened the packet and took one out. Flipped the cigarette backwards into his mouth and made the lighter appear from thin air.

'I would love to know what you get up to outside of these walls, Holly, but you never talk about it do you?'

'I can't.'

'The secrecy of working with the police?'

'No – if I wanted to tell you I would, but I just don't. When I come in here and see you, talk to you, it's the one time I can forget about what is out there and who I am. It's the one time I have that my mind does not go racing towards a problem I have to solve. You take that pressure away from me.'

'And that's a good thing.'

'A very good thing.'

She watched him for a while. There were times when he looked as if he knew every secret in the world. She said: 'My relationship with the police officer appears to be progressing. The glacier is moving.'

'All hail global warming.' He smiled. 'Tell me one thing about the case you just finished. Just one thing,' he said.

'It was very disturbing.'

Lee leaned back with one hand behind his head and blew a smoke ring.

'The best things in life always are.'

Eighty-four

A week passed and Holly felt herself getting back into her routine.

She still wore a bandage on her fingers and when the pain got too much, she took codeine and it held her. The door to her spare bedroom had stayed locked since the John Pickering case, but now she opened it and walked inside.

This was her murderabilia room. The place where she collected objects associated with murderers or their violent crimes. It held furniture and weapons, photos and police reports, dresses with blood stains and suits with exit wounds. She had been collecting for over a decade and for every case she worked on she was able to add something new.

She burned white sage and lit a candle, as was her ritual when she entered here after time away, kept her eyes closed and thought nothing but good thoughts.

The late eighteenth-century mahogany writing table where Holly kept all of her ephemera had belonged to an English killer and alleged witch called Mary Bateman. Mary had fed Rebecca Perigo a pudding laced with poison and had

been hanged in 1809 for her crime. The table had been purchased at a London auction and was small with a rectangular
moulded top on square tapering legs. It had two false drawers
over one real drawer which slid open smoothly. Inside were
a dozen scraps of paper Holly had purchased from all over
the world, mostly bought at auction but some obtained from
private hands.

One was a letter from Ethel Le Neve, the mistress of Dr
Crippen, pleading with the governor of Pentonville prison
to let her see her lover one more time before he was hanged;
there were three pages of a diary from Charles Warren, the
commissioner of the Metropolitan Police during the Ripper
years; another was a tenancy agreement from John Haigh,
the acid bath murderer, regarding his rent to be collected,
and now there was this: the letter from Sebastian Carstairs.

She removed it from its envelope and sat in a wicker chair.
She read the letter one more time, and when done, rested it
on its side. And it was as she was about to fold the letter up
that she saw something on the page. Sun-dazed and blinded
she picked it up curiously. Re-read it again. And again. And
each time she felt reality slipping further and further away.

When Bishop arrived she didn't bother with small talk, she
went straight for the jugular.

She picked up The Animal's letter and handed it over.

'Read it.'

'What is it?'

'He wrote it for me, it's his letter of apology, you'll understand what I mean.'

He sat down and read it. After he had finished he said:

'I don't see anything.'

385

'Read it again.' She held up a pen and paper for him to use. 'The first letter of each line, Bishop. It spells out a hidden message.'

I have wanted to write this for many years now
knowing that in reality I would probably
never get to see you in person but it was important
otherwise I might not have the opportunity to
write what needed to be said.
What I did in the past is horrific and shameful.
How you ever managed to cope, to live and to
emerge from the hideous crimes I committed
required such strength of character and an
energy that I cannot begin to fathom.
You are the person I think
of every day when I try my best to
understand how I did what I did. Believe me, I
lie awake at night and ask for forgiveness.
I pray for my redemption knowing how
very hard it must be for you to live and
enjoy your life after bearing witness to what I have done.
Justice is blind I know.
Everybody I have ever known
says the same thing – find peace within.
Some say I should not be forgiven and
I can understand why. Most days I
cannot forgive myself, but I die in hope.
Amen.
Or perhaps there is life after death?
Redemption for the most twisted
souls that exist not just on this plane but in

hell itself. The incendiary heat
or sulphurous flames I do not fear. Living
under Milton's clouds within his epic poem Paradise
Lost casts no doubt as to my final resting place.
Divine is he who has no fear and
I know what will await me. But what awaits you?
Cherubs?
Angels? Or a Hades type of
limbo inhabited by the demon
Lucifer himself?
You are not as blameless
or innocent as you might want to think.
Uncovering the truth about oneself is never pleasant.
Have you heard of The Furies
of Greek Mythology? Three sisters
living with vengeance in their hearts,
listening to the voices in their heads until they scream
You would do well to hear their ancient cry as
I would shed a tear for their fate rather than my own.
As my final night draws near.
May the seconds spread for hours
and my hours for days and may they
last until
I take my final breath which
very soon will be upon me.
Eventually, whether we are a man, woman or child, we
all die, but it is
not how, but what we will be remembered for that counts.
Did I live out my dreams
while taking others?
Always. I chose the path of most destruction,

lying, cheating, poisonous, sinister.
Killing those who walked with
innocent blood in their veins.
Nothing was ever wrong in my head though.
God forgave me as I
took life after life. Forgive me please I ask of you, for in
God's eyes
am I not your brother too? Simply a lost soul? I will
leave you and this world with nothing but
love.
Sebastian Carstairs x

I know where you live Jessica or should I call you Holly.
I am alive and walking tall

When Bishop finally understood, she heard the breath catch in his throat.

'Jesus Christ,' he said. 'It can't be true.'

'He's alive, Bishop. *Walking tall*, that's what the press used to say about him all the time.'

'How? He was cremated. You were there, you saw it.'

'I saw a box go behind a curtain.'

'The coroner confirmed it was him. The medical records. How the hell could he do that? How could someone engineer this?'

'I don't know, but I think he did and people need to be told.'

'Told what?

Bishop held up the letter.

'This isn't proof,' he said. 'This isn't anything but a letter written by a man who knows he is going to die.'

'We have to do something!'

'I can show the letter to the Home Office, the Parole Board, and see what they say. There will have to be an enquiry, an internal investigation. His sister was at the funeral, Cassandra, would you recognise her again?'

'She had a veil covering her face.'

'He was having chemo, for christsakes!'

He started pacing. Holly matched his stride.

'He's out there, Bishop. The Animal is free.'

'Holly—'

'You trust me don't you?'

'Yes.'

'Then trust me.'

'But if this is true – and I cannot believe it is, then this is the biggest escape since—'

'We have to catch him.'

'How?'

Holly stopped pacing. She already knew the answer. She looked at Bishop and he knew the answer too.

'I'll find him,' she said. 'I think that's what he wants anyway.'

Eighty-five

The next day Holly knelt by her parents' grave.

She touched the roses she had placed there last week. They were dead now and the petals were scattered on the warm earth.

'I love you forever,' she whispered.

In a way it felt as though everything had come full circle. She had stopped daydreaming of revenge against Sebastian Carstairs. She had put the darkness to rest and promised herself she would never think of him again. She had been free. But now he was back and there was a new dawn with a deadly sun.

She stayed there until she heard Bishop approach. There he was. Staring not at the grave but at her, as if he had just come home.

And she gasped when she saw he was holding her mother's necklace. It was more beautiful than she had remembered. A delicate silver chain with five blue and green enamel butterflies that hung like pearls. She reached out a tentative hand and when her fingers first touched the metal it felt cold and un-loved, but as he opened the clasp and fastened it around her neck, and she felt his warm hands skim across her hairline.

She turned to face him. He was staring at the necklace, but then his eyes came up to hers, and she wondered what he was thinking as he held out his hand. She took it and fell in beside him and they started the slow walk back to the car. They didn't talk.

They didn't need to.

Acknowledgements

I love writing. I always have and I always will, and I am so lucky that I get the opportunity to put my thoughts and characters onto paper and then someone is kind enough to make a book out of them. And then to top it all, people get to read what I have written and have been so generous with their words and responses. So thank you to my readers and my cheerleaders out there on social media and the real world, and thank you to the other writers I have met at the killer festivals up and down the country, who I have had drinks with and played football with, it's been an honour. And I have read all of your books over the decades with baited breath and you make me want to be a better writer.

I am so grateful to everyone who has helped me through the 2020 lockdown with Holly Wakefield's latest case. I must start with my mother first, who is always ready to listen to ideas and has forever championed my imagination.

My agent Luigi Bonomi at the LBA Literary Agency whose mellifluous voice calms me as I question my sanity, and to Alison and Hannah who I know are always there for me.

A massive thank you to Hannah Wann at Little, Brown who helped my limping corpse over the final hurdle. She has the patience of a saint and I apologise again for sending you endless tweaks . . .

Emma Beswetherick who always has my back and whose Zoom calls during lockdown were a welcome relief. She also encouraged me to delete the hamster (not literally) but the story is better for it. And the rest of the team at Little, Brown, Jo Wickham, Brionee Fenlon, Sean Garrehy and Kate Hibbert, who are tireless in their support with sales, marketing, publicity and some absolutely incredible cover designs.

Anne O'Brien, my copy editor, is simply a Jedi. She can spot the slightest mistake in the deepest sands of Tatooine and can sense a subtle shift of time-line within the noisiest of Mos Eisley cantinas.

Nicky Kennedy, Sam Edenborough, Jenny Robson, Katherine West and May Wall – my foreign rights magicians at ILA. Thank you for your continued support and encouragement.

And once again to all the readers out there – thank you. You are amazing.